Seventeen stories plot the present and the future like a mind-map diagram with a big "what if" at the center. Swinging from visceral reality to dreamlike fantasy with an occasional dose of humor, this collection tracks our existential moment as we teeter on the lip of the Anthropocene, trying to peer past the fog that obscures the abyss. From the imaginations of very different writers, these stories grapple with our world and our place in it. Sometimes up close and in detail, and sometimes at a strange remove, characters observe the world as they know it morph into something else. *Fire & Water* considers what might be beyond the fog, whether awful, surprising, or even delightful.

—Julia Stoops

Fire & Water is a stunning, necessary collection of stories that make the unimaginable realities of climate change feel absolutely visceral. Even the most fabulist stories here carry the shock of the real.

—Susan DeFreitas

In *Fire & Water: Stories from the Anthropocene*, Mary Fifield and Kristin Thiel have gathered seventeen stories that remind us climate change is an urgent, multifaceted global issue. The stories—which take place in North America, South America, Europe, and Australia—show us catastrophes ranging from flooding in England to a new Ice Age in Germany to fire decimation in California. Spanning realism, science fiction, and myth, they alternately terrify us with charred and frozen landscapes and delight us with animals able to seek their own solutions to the problems we humans create. These stories are entertaining, thought-provoking, and perfect for our time.

—Lucille Lang Day

Fire & Water

Stories from the Anthropocene

Fire & Water

Stories from the Anthropocene

EDITED BY

Mary Fifield

&

Kristin Thiel

INTRODUCTION BY NICOLE WALKER

www.blacklawrence.com

Executive Editor: Diane Goettel
Anthologies Editor: Abayomi Animashaun

Book and Cover Design: Zoe Norvell
Cover Art: "After Oil" by Wendell Shinn
 | ISBN: 978-1-62557-144-1

Published 2021 by Black Lawrence Press

Table of Contents

Acknowledgments

Many people were instrumental in helping make this anthology a reality. Our deep gratitude goes to friends and family for their unwavering support and encouragement. We sincerely thank Jenna Rose for her visual design and marketing wisdom. Without the fifteen authors included in this anthology, there would quite obviously be no book; we are thankful to have found kindred spirits in these writers whose stories answered our question before we posed it. Last but never least, we thank Abayomi Animashaun and Diane Goettel of Black Lawrence Press for championing this project and bringing it to readers around the world.

"Reef of Plagues," by JoeAnn Hart, was commissioned for "Reading the Currents. Stories from the 21st Century Sea," a project by the International Literature Festival Berlin 2017 in cooperation with the Science Year 2016*17 Seas and Oceans (an initiative by the Federal Ministry of Education and Research, Germany). It was presented at the 2017 festival, and first published in *The Hopper*, March 2019.

"The Ice Child," by Tara M. Williams, first appeared in the December 2019 issue of *Enchanted Conversation: A Fairy Tale Magazine*.

Quotes in "The Summer on the Brink" are in the public domain, by Rudyard Kipling, "The Islanders," and Paul Varély, "The Graveyard by the Sea." The quote from Germaine Greer is from *The Female Eunuch* (London: MacGibbon & Kee, 1970), 144. The quote in "Nature Morte," by Henry David Thoreau, *Walden*, is also in the public domain.

Preface

Like many creative projects, this book began with a conversation in a bar. It was 2018, on one of those exquisite early autumn days in Portland, Oregon, when our discussion about the need for literary fiction writers to respond to the gravest threat humanity faces—the climate crisis—might have felt theoretical. We were still a year from seeing devastating images of Australia's massive wildfires and two years almost to the day when wildfires raged so unusually close to Portland that we were checking our emergency bags and fearing for our friends in evacuation zones just outside the city. On that afternoon, we were aware of the scientific evidence that climate destabilization will lead to more infectious diseases, but mask wearing and stay-at-home orders to stop the spread of COVID-19 were not yet visceral experiences, to say nothing of the more complex scenarios that would come to pass, such as how humanity's response would cause the Himalayas to be visible for the first time in decades and would expose, in a new way, the deep racial and class inequities in the global health system and economy.

Our conversation became as much, maybe more, about the topic of literature and its role in helping people comprehend the unfathomable. Climate disruption—much like world wars, the nuclear arms race, and genocide—will have profound and lasting effects on our cultures and civilization. Yet humans struggle to internalize the implications of the environmental changes we are causing incrementally, though with quickening speed. As the afternoon light began to wane, we dreamed of an anthology of short fiction by writers with diverse, international backgrounds and artistic approaches, all addressing the question of what the climate crisis means to human civilization—not in the distant future, but now. We brainstormed potential titles, feeling drawn to the word *Anthropocene*, coined by atmospheric chemist Paul Crutzen and ecologist Eugene Stoermer to describe what is now widely considered a new geological epoch in which human activity is so significant it is transforming the earth's ecosystems. We liked the word for another reason too: it reflects our belief that contemporary literary fiction writers and publishers have an artistic responsibility, and a powerful tool, to explore how a crisis of our making is affecting humans and other species in our current moment.

Three years later, this vision has become a reality. *Fire & Water: Stories from the Anthropocene* is a collection of literary fiction from authors who hail from five continents, evoking the lives of people and species across the globe. With this anthology, we also consider another term, *climate fiction*, suggesting that it may be a misnomer. The climate crisis teaches us that human experiences (and those of other species) are myriad, multifaceted, and irreducible to the narrowly prescribed set of expectations that genres often impose. There can be no one Thing with a capital *T* that constitutes fiction about climate disruption, as these seventeen stories illustrate. Showing itself in different, and often inequitable, ways around the world, the climate crisis, and the stories about it, are too diverse to fit within one category.

When we began this journey, we were excited to reach readers through less common angles, but we were unaware of the many lessons the world would soon be forced to face. In hindsight, we see how timely this project is. Literary fiction, reflecting the world as it is rather than a world that is imagined, helps correct one of our society's most serious problems, our reluctance to fathom the breadth and depth of the climate crisis as we are living through it. *Fire & Water* speaks not only to those with the desire to tell stories but to all of us who need to read them.

The climate crisis calls for a sustained, broad, and deep artistic response. We hope *Fire & Water* is but one contribution of many to come.

—Mary Fifield & Kristin Thiel

NICOLE WALKER

Introduction

In his book of nonfiction, *The Great Derangement*, Amitav Ghosh laments the lack of contemporary literary fiction that grapples with climate change. He recognizes that speculative fiction has featured climate disaster since Jules Verne's 1889 *The Purchase of the North Pole* but wonders why the concerns of climate change are missing from realism. Envisioning climate catastrophe has been the bailiwick of science fiction—of worlds so far in the future that we can soberly read about how terrible that would be: thank goodness that won't happen in *my* generation. Ghosh challenges fiction writers who invoke our current times to engage with climate change, not only because climate change is happening before our very eyes, in our current time, but also because mimetic fiction encourages writers to imagine how environmental catastrophe affects existing communities. Speculative fiction invites world building, where authors can create more dystopian or utopian economies, where technology is more advanced or completely destroyed, where Crake from Margaret Atwood's climate change novel *Oryx and Crake* can create for the future pigoons and wolvogs. But when we're restricted by present-day realities, authors must create their characters and communities under existing terms. As Ghosh argues, many people have been living with the insecurity of climate change. Realistic fiction offers the opportunity to show individual lives that will be subject to changes far greater than the disrupted capital markets the privileged fear global warming will bring. *Fire & Water: Stories from the Anthropocene* accepts Ghosh's challenge and embraces these parameters. Here, you will find stories that move at the quotidian level—the daily existence of wrestling with this too-big truth.

Ghosh's own experience with a catastrophic weather event spurs his consideration of why narrative fiction often avoids climate change. In *The Great Derangement*, he describes his own encounter with a storm so brutal that it killed people. He details the rain and thunder dramatically, citing it as a would-be example of how climate change could appear in mimetic fiction. He argues that while climate change may be too large for our present-day brains to behold, we must try in our fiction to make that too-big reality conceivable by the average-size human mind. The ecological philosopher Timothy Morton calls such impossibly gigantic entities "hyperobjects"—concepts too large to seem possible. Whether it be ocean, space, infinity, or global warming, our brains cannot wrap themselves around such massive objects. But as the writers in *Fire & Water* show us, it's the smaller objects, everyday stuff, that shows the earth's climate changes in our present-day lives, how very much we're going to miss the stuff of our regular world, and how the everyday will, for a lot of people, still be a day—but one fully transformed.

This collection reveals how vast a problem climate change is. The stories move across diverse geographies, lifestyles, and relationships. But their commonalities are striking. No story in this anthology is like any other in here, but they share elements that define what some call "climate fiction"—but that perhaps we should call plain "fiction."

The impacts of climate change in many of the stories could be pulled from today's headlines. Jack Kirne's "Escape Out the Back Passage" tells a story of a dried-up aquifer, matching a disturbingly similar story of aquifers in arid regions around the world. As farmers and developers dig deeper wells, looking for water, sometimes, they find none.

> It didn't take a genius to figure out what happened. Drive in or out of town, and you saw them: fields of alfalfa shimmering unnaturally green. Being a rural town in a dry place, we had always drawn our water from the aquifer. People didn't think about it in the past, not really. The water was there, and we expected it to stay that way. But now that it was harder to draw from, you could ask anyone and they could tell you how large it was and its name, the Kirkwood Basin. I used to think of it poetically, as ancient water, moving in slow, twisting roots below us, but now that it was so scarce, I couldn't think of it as anything other than water, always diminishing. When the earth was entirely sapped, the basin would not refill for thousands of years.

As someone living in the southwestern US, I was struck by this story, and related it to what I've observed here. Just as these problems face Indigenous communities first in the American West, they've reached Indigenous populations across the world early. Amitav Ghosh, in *The Great Derangement*, bemoans how industrialized nations dump the effects of their industry on developing countries where the political infrastructure and economic realities make it difficult to complain. And yet local people do rise up to fight against the dumping of toxins and the destruction of forest. Mary Fifield's

"Irene's Daughters" tells the story of Danielle, who took part in and revealed her industry's toxic disposal practices and who fears she and her daughter may be in danger as a result. Danielle finds the disfigurement of the land disconcerting, especially now that she's distanced herself from the company and fallen in love with the place.

Later, she continues the thought about the complexity of the issue, how the local ecology has been affected not just by oil production waste but by the changes in the climate caused by many things.

> It was the very absence of nocturnal frog calls that had started this riparian field trip, and the article on the alarming rate of amphibian die-off from a *Scientific American* that she swiped from a doctor's office in Quito. On the first night in her new house in La Colina, she had expected to be kept awake at night by the croaking toads, just like the first night she'd ever slept in the jungle in a bamboo hut by the Napo River. She'd never heard anything so strangely deafening, both grating and soothing. Here there was almost nothing.

We, too, perhaps only from a distance, after reading about how many species die per hour thanks to human innovation, miss the sound of frogs.

These stories in *Fire & Water* not only sound the alarm. They speak to us in contemporary frequency. Kristin Thiel's "Morse Code of the Yellow Rail" conjures our current voice. We are tied up in this climate change problem. We know it's happening around us. We invent new language for it. We also develop new defenses, some as blatant as throwing a celebration with party favors that cut down on waste, as one character does. We imagine disasters as a prophylactic, practicing our demise as if to prepare for it as Daria does at the beginning of "Morse Code."

> Daria fully expected to die by volcano. Not by lahar, as, say, if the twenty-six glaciers on Mt. Rainier melted under that volcano's heat and helped to create a mudflow so big and thick and violent that it buried everything in its path. Not even by ash clogging the air and trapping greenhouse gases. Even though the United States was second in the world for number of volcanos, Daria didn't fear volcanos in that way. No, what she'd learned from her mother—indirectly—was that volcanos offered foolproof suicide. When the climate got bad enough, Daria would just walk right up and jump. If the fall didn't kill her, the sulfur dioxide fumes would choke her. If that didn't get her, the 1,800-plus-degree lava would, though of course Daria never spoke this plan aloud. It seemed perfectly reasonable to Daria, given the circumstances, but her parents would never understand.

As Daria prepares for tragedy, she mourns the disappearance of glaciers, listing the memories that evaporate with the thaw. List making isn't unique to the stories here; it is a useful trope in both fiction and nonfiction about the impact of climate change. Journalist Elizabeth Kolbert, in her book *The Sixth Extinction*, delves into the five previous extinctions by making lists of the animals that have disappeared. In these stories, we have vivid arrays of the luminous objects around us—the things we love, the things we'll miss, the things that mark us as a unique species.

Jennifer Morales's story, "The Doorman," is an homage to lists—and a book of lists of all the creatures we will miss. Ashley, the main character, questions the truth of climate change, thinking it seems a little far-fetched. But the far-fetched becomes closely realized when his house becomes a portal to another world to which only animals can take refuge. Noah-like, Ashley lists the animals that march past his armchair to the kitchen and through the rathole that will take them somewhere safe.

> He had only just fallen back to sleep when a series of titters and squeaks startled him awake. A family of raccoons hustled in, busting through his cardboard barrier like it was nothing. They were followed a few minutes later by a pair of herons. Several neon-green frogs with poor timing sprang through between the birds' feet, and a heron snagged two of them with its beak.

Certainly, there's a mixture of the fantastical and the realistic, but the animals who are ditching this godforsaken planet do so through the ordinary substance of modern-day life. A cardboard barrier against the window can't keep them out. The refrigerator can't deflect them. They move in a dance formation, the conga line, familiar to all of us American wedding-goers. As Ashley and his neighbor watch the parade of animals go by, it's with resignation rather than surprise. Like most of us climate change deniers (and we all have to deny or avoid the consequences of real climate change at least sometimes, or we'd never sleep at night), we're not really denying that it's happening. We just really don't want it to be.

> A swarm of bees and a mass of centipedes made them both shudder, but that was only the beginning of the deluge of insect life. A sheet of mayflies flew in and covered the refrigerator, their wings pulsing, until their scouts discovered the way to the hole. A conga line of daddy longlegs was followed by a squirming procession of ticks, earwigs, and beetles.
>
> "I liked the cats," said Mrs. Rudrüd, after the last beetle dropped out of sight. "There should be more cats."
>
> Within minutes, a pair of bobcats and a Canada lynx obliged.

> "That's not what I meant," she said, when they were able to breathe again.

If, as Timothy Morton suggests, we cannot fathom the entirety of climate change, then we must envision climate change piece by piece. The authors here take objects of the everyday, places that we venture, measurements we take to stand for that gigantic idea, that overwhelming concept. If we are going to be able to imagine climate change, these authors show us that we'll have to imagine it piece by embodied piece.

Shaun Levin's "A Sea of People" reminds us of the places that were and the places that might not be in the future as his character M finds home and belonging only in the transitory space of a massage table in the middle of a bathhouse in the middle of London, where he lives but still isn't sure is his home.

> This is where we are in history, M thinks. Friends are moving back to where they came from, or away: Sicily, Israel, Greece. Europe is reshuffling its people—you go here, you here, some outward to former colonies, Angola, Brazil. The Portuguese are doing it. Others have been coming from over there to cities like this.

As much as we resist the reality of the climate crisis, stories here make us confront it in the form of characters who mark the change.

All this listing and counting is, to the everyday watcher of climate change, devastating. In "The Rain Diary," J. D. Evans's narrator, C, smashes her mother's rain gauge, not so much denying her mother's haunting measurements that show how the drought approaches but railing against it. All these measurements, calculations, and concerns will be all the more tragic when the counting doesn't matter anymore.

The mother's day-by-day rain records kept her grounded

> and calm and in touch with the seasons. In C's mind, this would become a terrifying list of almost continuous zeroes (the empty set, the truth value "false"), punctuated by short strings of double-digit integers, two, three, four days in a row. Each short string would represent a flash flood here, topsoil erosion there, the destruction of the canola crop, the introduction of fungus, rot, or disease in the vines. The long lists of zeroes would symbolize a crop that never grew, fruit that never set, houses and hay bales and animals burned. C's wife knows that, to the mother, measuring rainfall was a way to stay in touch with nature, with the earth, a way to feel at one with the history of our species.

How else can we certify the change except with numbers and measures? It's a countdown, like a ticking time bomb—a feature of so many of these stories that I might consider lists and counting a feature of climate fiction.

Vivian Faith Prescott's "The Places She Journeys" takes us to Alaska where climate change has already made pronounced impacts that affect Indigenous populations particularly harshly. The main character, Sámi Woman, says, "Climate is affecting the size of sheep, cod, and birds around the world. Local elders used to catch seventy-pounders out by the old city dock, and there used to be big kings at Bradfield Canal. Sixty-pounders used to win the king salmon derby. Now there's no derby. It's been canceled for two years." Counting what is gone is still a kind of counting.

As anyone who reads climate reports knows, the numbers don't lie. The temperatures inch up; the water levels of lakes, aquifers, and reservoirs fall down. The ice melts by the ton. The carbon dioxide in the atmosphere thickens. To conform to reality, these stories must acknowledge the measuring we do. And to provide evidence and embodiment to that hyperobject, they must list the animals that disappear, the borders that shift, the heat that ticks upward. But the stories, and this is why this collection is so impressive and so necessary, remind us that we are still living with and through this. Our ordinary lives mostly go on, indeed changed and threatened, but in tandem with climate change. These stories aren't didactic screeds by which we *should* live but imagined lives as routine and extraordinary as any of our own. To make climate change resonate, we have to imagine ourselves as part of that change. These stories transport us to their moment and remind us that this moment is as much ours as theirs.

Kirne's "Escape Out the Back Passage" describes a dusty, drought-ridden town. First the tanks were low, then empty. Soon enough, people had to pay to use the monitored showers erected in town. The narrator's father, to make money to buy water, has to leave his daughter, the narrator, at home where she monitors the water situation. "The night before he set off, Dad sat me down over a dinner of fish and chips to lay out the ground rules. They were as expected: stay out of the liquor cabinet, go to school every day, there was to be no takeaway except on Sundays, and I was to use the internet for homework and emergencies only." Although the circumstances are unique to environmental hardship, the rules the dad draws up are ordinary. It's always "stay out of the liquor cabinet" no matter what crisis is afoot. The narrator, whose virginity is on the line, finds a way to take a shower and avoid sleeping with a boy privileged with water and the promise of sex. The narrator wins, even if the aquifer itself loses.

If making lists, measuring water, and counting missing species are fundamentals of climate change fiction, so is dinner. No matter the degree of crisis, there will still be dishes to wash. These moments of ordinariness serve not only to make the characters familiar, they underscore an ethic that this collection creates: it is the small things, like dinner, that will keep us together—and I mean together in both senses of the word—with our family and our friends and with our mental wellness to some degree intact. If there is one thing we can count on, these stories seem to say, it's that dirty dishes are forever.

In one of the most conflicted stories, Fifield's "Irene's Daughters," the narrator, who worked for a company that created an ecological disaster for the people who lived nearby, manages to escape accountability for most of the story. She had thought she was safe until one of the women whose children had been hurt by the company's malfeasance insists that Danielle admit her complicity. That night, Danielle attempts to maintain normalcy with her daughter as she contemplates how she's going to escape this disaster herself: "Dinner dishes washed and stacked, lights switched off throughout the house, Danielle curled up with Michaela in her twin bed, gazing over her daughter's shoulder as she silently read a book. Through the electric buzz of the cicadas, Danielle heard only the occasional bellow of a toad." No matter what worries, mothers still clean the house and put their daughters to bed. Still, when we're confronted with environmental disasters, perhaps we can imagine the repercussions best when we consider our daughters with regard to other people's daughters. It's only when we consider all the daughters that there will be any hope to rectify the climate disaster. When Danielle is confronted and her daughter asks why the woman who confronted her seemed so upset, Danielle smooths it over to Michaela but not to herself.

> "She has a lot on her mind," Danielle explained. That seemed to satisfy Michaela, who slipped immediately back into her book. This eleven-year-old girl, who read at the

> level of a ninth grader, had no respiratory problems, no signs of skin cancer. She had not grown up near a poisoned watershed. Danielle stroked her daughter's perfect, soft, brown forearm, finding it hard to swallow and hard to breathe. What Irene's daughters did or didn't suffer, Danielle did not know.

To be sure, nothing about these stories is ordinarily told—we wouldn't be transported to these regular people's lives without the incredibly vivid writing—but it is the ordinary details that make the stories so haunting. We know these dishes. We know this song. We know this bird. These are the objects of our shared lives. That the climate change plots can swirl so deftly around them allows us to see how easily climate change can infiltrate our lives.

Stefan Kiesbye's Carmen, in his story "Smokeland," has been traumatized by a fire that burned down his whole neighborhood, including his house. They rebuilt, but Carmen has nightmares about the neighborhood burning again. And yet his regular life manages to go on.

> Dinner was a disaster. Katie refused to eat turkey, carrots, and peas and instead plastered the food over her face. Then she dramatically fell off her chair, convulsing until she died with a whimper. Devin laughed so hard at her act that he sprayed his peas through his nose across the table at Carmen. Moments after Heather sent the kids to their rooms, the fire alarm went off, and they found Devin standing on his desk chair, holding a candle as high as he could below the alarm.

If there is anything that will make the reality of climate change hit us in the gut, it will be the way we will never look at dinner the same way. It may be the constant by which we organize our lives, but we'll always compare the dinners to our prelapsarian innocent ignorance. Mac 'n' cheese will make us nostalgic just as it does for Ashley from "The Doorman": "'I just wish I could go back to work,' he said to her as she microwaved his mac 'n' cheese. 'Sitting around here isn't doing me any good.'"

What makes these stories so effective and necessary right now is how they recount regular human suffering as part of the climate suffering: Bishop Garrison's "Conscription" marks the distinction between private suffering and planetary suffering. The narrator has fallen into the desperate politics of endless dust storms and other hellscapes. Driving too fast, he's caught by police. The only way to do his time is to submit to being conscripted to fight the storms. He only drove so fast to see his mother one last time.

> When Mom and I reconnected, she promised me through a hacking cough that she was fine. Her doctor told me otherwise. She was far from OK. She was dying. The guilt of the twenty-year chasm between us swallowed me up, whole.
>
> "If you can get here tonight," the doctor told me, hesitantly, "I think you'd have a good chance of saying your goodbyes. Won't be easy for her, but having family at the bedside always helps. The only thing we can do is regulate the pain at this point."

The normal human drama, a man wishing to be home with his dying mother, becomes more heartbreaking with the backdrop of his insignificant offense and the completely unjust punishment. But as this story shows, sorrow will still come, dangerous storms or no.

Anthony S. James's intimate story, "The Summer on the Brink," is about two women who witness change, situating the drying up of rivers among lives full of regret, missed opportunities, misunderstandings: "*Bereavement without death, bereavement by my daughter's decision, mother-killing by email:* It's too late now for any explanation or apology. I don't want any dialogue. *So, all that was us has melted away. While the glaciers are melting, we are killing the glaciers.*"

But within that sea of loss, there's still the delight of imagining possibility, the prospect of future. Even in the flood of climate change, the stones of girlhood crushes and the thrill of attention force the river to go around.

As Levin's "A Sea of People" reminds us, with or without climate change, as the rivers rise too high or trickle to nothing, we will still be looking to quench our loneliness.

> The one escape is sex, a realm without language where the tongue is vocabulary.
>
> Men he meets in places like this, pressing up against each other, almost in slow motion, in sync, the way lovers do after months apart, reacquainting themselves with the body, the person they've loved more than anything. The one true one. Kissing gently, the way he and the German had been doing. Tentative, tender. Fingertips on ribs, along chests. Tenderness is a question mark. Our lives filled with questions regarding desire and its limits: to touch and be touched. By whom? Where?

I don't know whether to take great satisfaction in the fact that we will still be, still are, sad and lonely during climate change. What these stories give me, though, is that sense of constancy—that things will be different but our relationships will stay the same. In Jan Underwood's "Wo Bist Du?" Rolf and Ana wait too long to escape Germany, which has been frozen over—climate change flipping the weathers systems to kick off a new ice age. Their attempt to flee on the freeway dissolves into the usual freeway problem—many people had the idea to flee from the catastrophe at the same time. Rolf's sorrow here is tangible as he leaves the relative safety of his warm car to look for his beloved.

"Ana?"

> Only the wind battering his uncovered ears, and skimming snow off the tops of the burial mounds, and in the background nervous Bach. He tried again.
>
> "Ana? Wo bist du?"

"Where are you?" are words we can imagine crying now or in the dust, snow, rainstorms of the future. The circumstances of loss may change, but the way we search for what we've lost, no matter how bad things get, won't.

Underwood's story, like a few of the other stories in the collection, reaches into the future. Some even reach into the allegorical and speculative, but because they are gathered in this collection of realistic fiction, even those stories embrace the paradigm Amitav Ghosh urges. The futuristic stories don't require whole-world building. Set among the stories of present-day climate trauma, these speculative pieces use as much realism as their fellow stories to convey the real emotions that we will experience in the future. Rolf and Ana are trapped in a yet-to-have-happened new ice age, grieving for the flat they had to leave behind, for the seasonability that used to define their homeland. In "The Ice Child," Tara M. Williams makes the sorrow of the allegorical child she's created hit home. The Gaska-geardi, the ice child whose mother still breastfed her even though she had remarried and had given birth to a regular-temperature child, finally stops receiving food.

> Then one night the mother did not come. Gaska-geardi wrote her messages again and again until the window was layered deep in frost, and she could no longer see inside. And after many days and nights, when her mother still did

not appear, the ice child set off all on her own, for, she told herself, Winter could be no more cold or cruel than these supposedly warm-blooded mortals who had left her there to die.

Loss may be the primary universal emotion of climate change, but abandonment might be secondary. The ice child's story is about the banishment of winter. We won't be able to rely on snow like we used to. Constancy's presence is nature's hallmark. With climate change, we will not be able to predict as we once could. As Karen says to Kathy in "The Summer on the Brink," "The natural world was always *there*, you know? Beautiful or cruel, but always there, always constant, whatever we did. And now it seems sick, diseased."

Even if climate change is humanity's fault, we are sure to feel abandoned, like a child whose parent gets incurably sick. We'll blame the planet itself for the changes in the climate, as the earth becomes unknowable and unrecognizable. And we know, it's always the mother's (earth's) fault anyway. Or at the least, like that nurse-maid child, we'll be too quick to martyr ourselves, as does one of the central, unnamed characters in Carlos Labbé's "On Abyssal Waters." In a grandiose attempt to atone for his own father's sin, he calls a press conference and "unveiled the giant space shuttle he'd christened—provocatively—the Ark, and asked them: where do you think every red cent of the vast fortune my father—the infamous Joe Hazelwood, captain of the Exxon Valdez oil tanker—received from the company's lawyers for taking the blame as the individual solely responsible for the worst ecological tragedy in human history went?"

If the humans are going to feel unmoored by the effects of climate change, Tomas Baiza wonders, in "A Seal's Song," how are the animals going to feel? Epiphanies are not only for the hominid. The whales, seals, even the polar bears, recognize what a mess the humans have made. Not only do the animals seek to rectify it, they attempt to distance themselves from humanlike behavior, but they recognize how complex their task is. We see this in the conversation between Stump the seal and Balena the whale before they enact their plan to save the fish:

> "You sang that to prepare me," I said. "To tell me that what we're about to do might be awful, and that you're not sure how it will end."
>
> Balena's mouth opened slightly, and she nodded. {*it would be wrong to hide that part of the Song from you, half-fin; you of all the little seals must hear it*}

The seals are pissed at what humans have done, but they take their revenge with a wry sensibility. Realism wouldn't be realism without the best part of it: humor. You wouldn't imagine in a sea of climate disaster there would be room for comedy, but this collection is full of snatches of dry wit.

In "Escape Out the Back Passage," Kirne's teenage narrator finds her situation ironic: "It was almost funny, I thought, how this premise was apocalyptic and outrageously dull at the same time. There were no marauding gangs or angry protesters, except Nancy Danaher, who had camped outside the council office for 280 days and counting." In "Reef of Plagues," JoeAnn Hart's narrator responds to tourists wondering what happened to the now-dead coral reef that locals had seen disappear, finding at least a silver lining in the devastation of the ocean.

> "Happened? What do you mean, happened?" another one of us asks. We no longer have to be nice to tourists, so we're not.
>
> Rusted hulks used to sit where they landed on the reef, left as a warning to other mariners. We would collect some fine things from those boats. Our homes are made with so

> much salvage that the priests joke that we live in salvation. But now the tourist board, grown nervous and defensive, tows the vessels out to sea before we can get to them. They say tourists do not want to see that nature's power is greater than their own.

Most of the stories in this collection understand that, really, humans in general "do not want to see that nature's power is greater than their own." Humans' antics to try to appear powerful renders them good marks for teasing. Even in the darkest story, Fifield's "Irene's Daughters," where the protagonist, Danielle, has participated in poisoning, potentially seriously injuring those who lived nearby, there's still the possibility of humor. As she considers trying to escape whatever punishment come her way, she considers the possibilities of leaving.

> She had started to scan real estate websites in Puget Sound and look for research positions at the university, to imagine camping with her daughter on the Olympic Peninsula and speaking English at the grocery store, despite Michaela's protests that she didn't want to move to Seattle because she didn't have any friends there and the mangoes would be terrible.

As Margaret Atwood articulates in *Oryx and Crake*, even in disaster, our habits and proclivities remain our own. Whereas in Atwood's devastation, it's coffee that we'll miss, in Fifield's story, it's good mangoes. The rift between what humans said they wanted and what they inevitably get might be a trope through all great climate fiction. We wanted mangoes. We got mudslides. The inability of humans to imagine the consequence of their desires is the stuff of comedy—and, of course, tragedy too.

These realistic, and sometimes speculative, stories require as much creative work as science fiction does imagination, though to different ends. The world in these stories is seen with a contemporary, realistic eye but one that sees through climate-change-colored glasses. To find humor, to render disaster, to elicit the human panoply of emotion requires concentrated, sometimes even lyrical, imagination.

Jessica Meeker's "Glacier Bear," in which an Alaskan treks from his remote cabin to an equally remote store in a village most people have fled for the season, sees the world with the danger that surrounds him. Nature morphs into other kinds of nature—possibly because nature closes in when survival is at stake or possibly because nature is interconnected, in particular when you're so trapped inside of it that you become it.

> He had become so used to the sea that even now the snow seemed to shift and rise in waves. Rocks were killer whales, harpooned by poachers. Fallen pine needles were their blood. The mice and rabbits that ran atop the snowpack were fish that narrowly escaped the nets. As he walked now like he was carrying a sack full of fish, his muscles remembered the effort of pulling in those he caught.

In these stories, some of the narrators engage with nature so intently, it engulfs them. They become nature. In Prescott's "The Places She Journeys," the main character, Sámi Woman, explains: "She's collected this data all summer, but it's chewing her gut now like she's a skinny bear in hyperphagia, the young ones who've wandered into town recently, tumbling garbage cans and dumpsters and chasing dogs, and searching for salmon in empty smokehouses." As nature pushes her way into our everyday consciousness by staging dramatic changes, our empathy with the creatures who live in nature, without filter, becomes more engaged.

The story of change isn't always catastrophic. As the climate shifts and changes, so do the characters in the story. Adaptability is celebrated, even if it's in one of the more magical stories like "The Ice Child."

> Some days when she visited, the warden was a wolf, other days an Arctic fox or a snowshoe hare. Some days he was a polar bear, or a silvery lynx with silent flat paws, or a velvet-soft harp seal with great, dark eyes.

These stories illuminate that which is beautiful if heartbreaking, asking one of the central questions of the collection: is heartbreak beauty? Just as in non-climate literature, climate literature reveals that it's the small moments where meaning and beauty reside. That the big dramas of life swirl around us but regular sorrows, and joy, persist.

Etan Nechin's "Nature Morte," which the editors perfectly placed as the final story of the collection, incorporates the horrors of climate change, imagination, and humor. This story's lyricism takes the reader in a magical realism direction, where the narrator confronts a pond that should be there but is not. The narrator

> would even get upset, pace back and forth on the pond floor, and shout, "You call yourself a pond? What kind of pond doesn't have water in it? I'll tell you what you are: you are a hole in the ground, a ditch! Why do I even care about you?"
>
> But that was a momentary lapse. I cared about it, I guess, because nobody else did. It just stood there, chained to the ground. Maybe it was dead. Perhaps I should take a shovel and bury it, making it level with the land. But then I would have created another hopeless pit.

Fire & Water does not make a spectacle of climate change. While global warming and environmental damage may be the catalysts for many of the stories, the weight of the stories is in the way the characters encounter new challenges, reconsider their relationships to each other and to their environment, and discover the wonder in the world around them, even as it changes. These stories fly us like a kite in hurricane-force winds through the gamut of emotions brought into specific relief by the devastating realities of climate change. As the climate crisis becomes more real, these stories steeped in realism are pertinent and necessary, heartbreaking and beautiful.

JENNIFER MORALES

The Doorman

Ashley didn't believe in global warming, or climate change, or whatever they were calling it now.

He had to admit, though, that the spring rains had started way too early this year, right at the beginning of March. They were heavy and warm, with fat drops that beat the soft ground into a murky pudding.

When he was stationed on Guam, back in his twenties, he endured rains like this. His first afternoons on the base, he would stand at the doorway of his barracks and smoke while the hot, blue storm clouds spilled themselves out. He wondered how there could be any water left in the sky.

These Wisconsin rains were like that. Since his accident a few weeks earlier—he had fallen on the slick floor of the butter plant, coming down hard on his tailbone and lower spine—he had plenty of time to think about the weather. Ashley still called the place where he worked the "butter plant," although his line was making ghee now, some kind of hippie half-butter the back-to-the-landers wanted.

It hurt to walk, and it hurt to stand. Without painkillers, it hurt even to sit or lie down. He was on disability leave, going to physical therapy twice a week, an agony that the doctors assured would get him back to work-ready condition in three months.

Three months was a long time, he found out. As his pain receded, his restlessness grew. When he got tired of looking out the window at the rain, he watched baseball on TV. It seemed appropriate that the Brewers were having as bad a season as he was. Sometimes he did the large-print word search in the *Foxxy Shopper*. On Mondays and Thursdays, when the medical transport van picked him up for physical therapy, he was generally able to wrangle an unauthorized stop at the KwikTrip, to get beer and a stack of scratch-offs. He told the driver to take a couple tickets for himself, and one time the driver won seventy-five dollars. After that, Ashley didn't really have to ask for the detour. Back home, he smoked and scratched his way through the cards, each scrape of the foil a plea for something interesting to happen.

His visitors were few and far between. His ex-girlfriend, Carolyn, a health aide, came by three or four times in the first weeks of his recovery. She whisked her way through his space, jerking the vacuum out of the closet to give the living room a once-over, cleanly splitting the Chinese takeout she brought into daily portions and stacking them in date-marked containers in the fridge. It felt more like an extension of her day at the nursing home than a social call.

Ashley wanted Carolyn to talk to him—about baseball, her book group, anything—but she seemed content to confirm his medication schedule and rearrange the pillows on the vinyl recliner where he spent most of his day. He missed her. Their breakup the year before had been uncertain and quiet. They didn't fight—she just stopped showing up. Now, here she was caring for him like he was his own weak father. The distance between them seemed to grow with every visit.

"I just wish I could go back to work," he said to her as she microwaved his mac 'n' cheese. "Sitting around here isn't doing me any good."

"It's doing you a lot of good. You just can't feel it yet."

"I fucking hate being stuck. I want something to do." He straightened out the sleeves of his sweatshirt, pulling them hard enough to twinge his back. It felt like the recliner was swallowing him. "Something that matters."

"You could invite some friends over," she said.

"Huh." Who wanted to come hang out at his place? It wasn't exactly Party Central right now. Even he didn't want to be there.

Carolyn delivered his lunch to him in one grand sweep across the open space from kitchen to living room. He liked the way she moved, with long strides and arms spread, as if the world was bigger than it looked.

"Stop showing off," he grumbled, but he smiled at her. "You could come by more often and keep me entertained."

She swatted him on the knee. "Oh, you." Before he could reach for her hand, she had gathered her coffee mug, car keys, and purse. At the door, she peered up at the sky. "Looks like it's going to rain again. Good thing you don't have to go out."

That night, under the pressure of another March monsoon, the edges of the orange sandstone hill behind his trailer gave way. In his sleep, he heard the sand coming, a thick shushing sound, denser than the pinging of raindrops. He dreamed he was pouring out a fat stream of salt from the old Morton's canister in the kitchen of his childhood. He heard his mom yelling at him for wasting salt, but he couldn't stop. In the morning he woke to find the back end of his home clutched in a foot and a half of sand, like a ship run aground. The neighbors on the opposite side of the hill got the worst of it, with sand up over the thresholds of their doors. Parts of the hill, thick with trees and flowers until the storm, were flat-faced and barren. For days afterward, the beeps and grunts of earth-moving equipment constituted the soundtrack of Ashley's thoughts, as the landlord tried to dig down to solid ground.

When the sun finally cracked through the clouds for a stretch, sometime in mid-April, what was left of the yard had been reduced to a foamy mud. Small threads of brilliant-green grass jutted out here and there, giving Ashley something hopeful to rest his eyes on.

The sunny days brought out the birds. They sang lustily, making up for lost time. A pair of pale-brown house wrens courted in Ashley's side yard, rattling their wings and warbling ecstatically to each other. He watched them for a full hour as they hopped and shimmied across the tender ground.

A few days later, as he was shaving for his physical therapy appointment, tufts of yellow fluff began drifting past the bathroom window on the morning breeze. In the minutes he had before the medical transport van showed up, he staggered around to the west side of the trailer to check it out.

The wrens had breached the warped, blue, wooden siding and were emptying insulation out of a hole in the exterior wall, just above Ashley's head. They chattered happily as they pecked away. Bits of insulation littered the grass, a flock of yellow chicks in the deepening green.

"Now, what in the hell am I going to do about that?" He strained to get a look. The birds grew quiet for a moment, as if considering an answer to his question.

Even under normal circumstances, Ashley never felt as dashing or capable as his namesake—his mother was a huge fan of *Gone with the Wind*'s Major Wilkes—but since his accident, little situations like this could make him feel entirely useless. He couldn't swing a hammer or climb a ladder in his condition.

He thought about asking Dakota next door to deal with the hole. Dakota was single, with a lot of time on his hands. With almost thirty years' age difference between them, Ashley had become a sort of father figure to the younger man, giving him advice about dealing with people at work or the cheapest fixes for his truck. The two of them hung out quite a bit last summer, drinking beers, cooking hamburgers, and shooting the shit on Ashley's deck. *Grillin' and chillin'*, as Dakota liked to say.

But Ashley's accident changed the dynamic. He couldn't muster the energy to pull out the lawn chairs or mess with the grill. And maybe the pain was scary for the kid, who was still at that age where a person could think they were invincible. Dakota was spending his evenings elsewhere now. He would come if called, but Ashley had two more months of recovery. He thought he should save his favors for when he really needed them.

So the wrens' creative destruction continued uninterrupted for a couple of weeks. Occasionally, Ashley would hobble outside to pound on the wall next to the birds' crater, hoping to scare them away. But they would only fly out for a moment and wait in a nearby tree, returning the second he headed back inside.

When the wrens began tag-teaming live insect delivery, Ashley knew he was in trouble. He called Dakota, who came over after work.

"What do we have here?" Dakota asked, climbing up a ladder to peer into the nest with a flashlight. The mother wren swooped past

Dakota's face and landed on the shed belonging to their widowed neighbor, Mrs. Rudrüd. The bird cried out, a panicked, repetitive call that was soon echoed by the father from the nearby edge of the woods.

"Are there babies in there?" Ashley asked from the ground.

"Yeah, but not for long." Dakota grabbed the small birds from the nest, eight in all, and shot their featherless bodies, two at a time, into the trees behind the trailer.

Ashley felt the yard spin, and he steadied himself against the wall. The babies piped weakly from the leaf litter. Dakota asked him to hand up a piece of plywood, and he nailed it in place over the hole.

The next day, several woodpeckers arrived, visiting off and on to dig their claws into the siding and peck at the soft spots. When all of them pounded away, the noise inside the trailer rattled Ashley's teeth. He turned up the TV.

As if he didn't know, Mrs. Rudrüd came by to alert him.

"I've been watching. You've got three downies and one pileated. At least. I looked them up in my bird book." She waved the floppy volume in Ashley's face.

He tried to be polite to Mrs. Rudrüd, to listen when she talked. Her husband had fallen over and out of the golf cart somewhere between the seventh and eighth holes the spring before, dead on the green. But her telling him the names of the species hell-bent on wrecking his home wasn't much comfort.

He called the animal control number at the county and talked with Ole. They were in the same class in high school but hadn't talked much since.

"We don't do birds," Ole said. "And anyway, the woodpeckers will just keep coming back unless you do something about the underlying problem."

"Which is what then?"

"Bugs, I'd expect."

Ashley called around to a couple exterminators in town.

"Wood-sided trailer, huh?" one said. "We're gonna have to treat the whole thing."

"With poison?'

"Yeah, poison." The exterminator laughed. "What? You want me to bring my .22 and shoot the bugs? I can schedule you for next week Tuesday if that works for you."

Ashley thought of the baby wrens and their translucent purple skin. The parents had hovered over the wreck of their offspring longer than Ashley could bear to watch.

"I'm going to call around some more," Ashley said. "Thanks."

*

The physical therapy was helping, Ashley hated to notice. Not that he didn't want to feel better; he just wished he could give the credit to something other than the painful treatments. It was getting easier to stand for minutes at a time, and getting out of his chair was no longer a torment.

On an early May afternoon, he got a burst of energy and decided to cook himself a real dinner. He'd been living mainly off of microwave entrees, breakfast cereal, and beer, but his ambitions suddenly extended to a hamburger and a side of pre-cut oven fries. He let the TV prattle on while he cooked, which is why he didn't immediately hear the squirrel.

When he went into the living room to change the channel, he saw it: a chubby gray one, with a black nose and a wise eye that gave Ashley the willies, hanging off the lilac bush and chewing through the window screen near the TV. She bounded in just as Judge Judy was about to render a verdict on the roommates' furniture dispute.

Perched on the windowsill, the squirrel snorted, as if she didn't approve of the trailer's smoke-stained air. Before Ashley could stop her, she leaped off the sill and dashed toward the kitchen, disappearing behind the cabinet door to the left of the sink.

Ashley hit the mute button on the TV. The squirrel thumped once or twice, and then came the manic sounds of gnawing teeth.

"Oh no you don't." He grabbed his heavy-duty flashlight and a half-empty bottle of water from the end table and went to look. He opened the cabinet door and clicked on the flashlight. The squirrel leaped out. Startled, he threw the water bottle toward the beast, but it missed her by a foot and flew into the cabinet.

The squirrel rushed back out the way she came, clambering up the shredded screen and into the lilac. She cursed at him for a good five minutes before disappearing over the roof. Ashley shut the window.

That night, he was awakened from his drug-muffled sleep by a loud smack and a crash of glass. He had been dreaming of hitting a home run, the thwack and shudder of the bat still alive in his arms. He peeled one dry eye open, then the other. In the washed-out glow from the streetlamp out front, he picked out a beaver in the lilac's branches shaking glass from its tail. While Ashley tried to recall how to move his limbs, the beaver jumped through the broken window and waddled toward the same cabinet the squirrel had disappeared into.

"God, no." He turned on the lamp next to him, just in time to see a cluster of bats swoop in through the broken window and head for the cabinet too. One of them wedged its furry body between the door and the frame and held it open for its companions.

"What the hell?"

He picked up the phone but set it down again: It was going on three o'clock. Who do you call at three o'clock in the morning about a beaver breaking into your house?

From his seat in the living room, he had a decent view of the kitchen cabinets next to the sink, but if the beaver and bats were up to anything in there, he couldn't see or hear it. He got up and moved cautiously into the kitchen, pausing to grab a knife from a drawer near the fridge. Standing off to one side, he opened the door wide and waited. Nothing. He leaned over as much as he dared and looked in. Darkness. Silence.

"Hey!" he said into the void. He knocked the knife blade against the cabinet frame. No response. The animals must have found another way out. That was good, Ashley thought, although it puzzled him how he wouldn't notice a draft from a gap big enough to fit a full-grown beaver. He would look more closely in the morning when there was better light.

He settled back into his chair before realizing that he would have to do something about the window. Damp night air was dropping in through the empty frame. He roused himself to find an old cardboard box and some duct tape and sealed it up as best he could. It wasn't a real solid job, and he couldn't bend to pick up the broken glass glittering the carpet, but it would have to do.

He had only just fallen back to sleep when a series of titters and squeaks startled him awake. A family of raccoons hustled in, busting through his cardboard barrier like it was nothing. They were followed a few minutes later by a pair of herons. Several neon-green frogs with poor timing sprang through between the birds' feet, and a heron snagged two of them with its beak.

Ashley felt pinned to the recliner under the combined weight of his fear and curiosity. He tensed, but the animals didn't approach or threaten him. They went straight for the cabinet without a glance in his direction.

It went on all night. Ashley was terrified when a group of rattlesnakes slithered in off the lilac bush and right down the face of his TV, but even the snakes didn't pay him any mind. A soundless parade of fireflies drifted by, some blinking white, some yellow. Next came a bunch of possums, a clutch of rabbits, a long black trail of ants, and then, around daybreak, six eagles.

He was surprised by the awkwardness of the giant birds' gait. He thought of them only in flight, inspiring and majestic, but on his kitchen linoleum, they were clumsy, their feathered shoulders hunched like hoodlums up to no good. Still, he couldn't help feeling that the eagles were some kind of sign, arriving at the start of a new day. He was a patriot, after all. It made him think that, whatever it was these animals were heading off to do, maybe he shouldn't get in their way.

He waited out the day in his chair, half-watching TV. His head abuzz, his thoughts scattered and incomplete, he felt as if he had drunk too much coffee. Ashley was unsurprised by the occasional flick of the curtain as a finch or two slipped in, then a pileated woodpecker. He thought the woodpecker looked like the one that was trying to knock through the wall weeks before, but it was hard to tell. How long had these animals been planning this?

He shook his head. *Animals don't plan, you idiot.*

By early afternoon, his curiosity got the better of him, and he decided to investigate. At least then when help came, he might be able to explain something about the whole ridiculous scene.

He got his headlamp from the hook by the door and went to the cabinet, where he bent down, gasping, to peer into the dark interior.

Two years ago there had been a rat in here. It still rankled with the greasy, sour scent of the animal's waste. Above that he caught a whiff of forest floor and water. Not the mold-riddled smell of the wallboard, damp from the leaky U-trap, but fresh water.

He flicked his headlamp on and then off.

The cabinet had no bottom. The animals had removed it, or their ins and outs had worn it away. And beyond the bottomless space, a light pointed back at him. He stood with the legs of a younger man, breathing fast, and kneed the door shut.

Ashley pulled himself along the counter to a kitchen chair and turned it to face the cabinet. He sank down and let his shoulder blades wedge in between the spindles, his back muscles throbbing from standing so quickly.

He eyed the phone, the cordless handset resting on the counter near the stove. Maybe he should call Carolyn. And say what? He had a zoo in his kitchen? He was afraid of squirrels? At this point, the whole thing was too embarrassing.

Maybe there was water in the cabinet, pooled from the leak, and the light he saw was just the reflection of his headlamp in it. He would feel pretty stupid calling Carolyn if that's all it was. He hoisted himself up for another look.

This time he looked down before turning on his lamp. Sure enough, there was a light down there. It was yellowish and soft, like a good spring day, but far away and small. The forest scent snaked around his face when he leaned in toward the hole, but he barely dared to breathe. He turned on his lamp and ran his fingers along the hole's edge, felt the kind of precise chisel marks made by mice and the spoon-shaped hollows that must be the beaver's toothwork.

The hole appeared to go on for some time, well beyond the layer of gravel spread beneath the trailer. He sat next to the open cabinet and thought. The animals had done this, but why? And where was the light coming from?

Drained by the shock and the effort to get a closer look, he fell asleep. He woke to a rustling sound. It was dusk, and in the half-light he caught the form of a crow on the countertop near the microwave. The bird had found the remains of his morning's instant oatmeal. Pecking at the crusted grains, it sent the bowl toppling to the floor. Ashley reached to turn on the ceiling fixture and cursed.

The bowl was upside down, bits of oatmeal making a ring of mess around it.

"Now, how am I going to pick that up? That's just going to sit there until somebody—"

The bird strutted toward him and tilted its head, as if trying to catch Ashley's eye.

"What, motherfucker?"

The bird straightened up and blinked.

"Did I offend you?"

It seemed so. The crow didn't look at him again as it finished its journey to the cabinet, coming within reach of Ashley's boot. Ashley had half a mind to kick the creature but knew that he'd be risking his back. The crow slid its beak between cabinet door and frame and hopped inside.

Ashley rubbed his face. "I'm talking to birds now, am I?" he said aloud. The evening was getting on. He could have one more painkiller before bed, forget the crow, sleep solidly through the night. He swiped the pill container from the counter and back down again in one motion. He was beginning to wonder if the meds were part of the problem. He knew he wasn't imagining the invasion—there were paw prints across his floor, for god's sake—but the sense he had that the animals were speaking to him directly, that wasn't right. Was it?

He left the bottle and went for a beer from the fridge instead. He drank it sitting in his recliner and waited for sleep, certain that more animals would appear once it was fully dark.

He was right. A half dozen foxes showed up around ten o'clock, gleaming red in the lamplight. Then seven turtles of various shapes and sizes. An entire colony of wasps. A barn owl and a screech owl, arriving separately. Two tiger salamanders, followed by three brown pelicans, their pouchy bills sloshing with water and small fish.

At the darkest part of the night, when a group of badgers nosed their way through the window, their claws cutting into the wallpaper, he began to rethink not calling someone. If he called Dakota, he could come with a board and close up the hole inside the cabinet, just like he did with the wrens' nest.

The memory of the wrens turned his stomach. It was late, anyway, probably two in the morning, and the damage was already done. As long as they didn't break anything else, what difference did a few hours make?

He called Dakota around seven, although he knew he'd be getting ready for work.

"Hey, it's Ashley. Yeah, I need some help over here."

"What's up? I'm heading out in a few."

"I know. It's just that something broke my window, and I could use your help to board it up."

"Now?" His voice was tight with complaint. "I mean…"

"Forget about it. I know you got to get to work."

"You sure? It's probably those damn kids in that brown trailer on the lower landing. Those little fuckers are always breaking shit."

"Yeah, maybe I'll ask their dad to come up and help. You take it easy, man."

Ashley hung up and considered his situation. The carpet, muddy with animal prints, sparkled with broken glass. He could ask Carolyn to come and vacuum up the debris, but then he would have to explain the animal tracks. He should have said something to her and Dakota right away when that squirrel busted in. Maybe then it would seem less weird now, him letting all these animals just march into the house.

The May weather was mild enough. If he pulled the curtain across the opening, he would at least be spared some bugs getting in, and he wouldn't have to look at the damage. And that would have to do until Dakota got home, if he was even willing to help after a long day.

Around lunchtime it occurred to him that if those animals could go into his cabinet, they might, at any moment, all come back out. He hesitated to go to the kitchen to get lunch, but his hunger got the better of him. He decided on ramen, made in the microwave, because it would get him out of there the fastest.

He took a little nap in the recliner after lunch and woke to bright afternoon light pressing through the red curtains covering the glassless window. As he sat there, adjusting to the feelings of being awake, he shivered. The oatmeal bowl, which the crow had knocked mouth-down onto the floor, was right-side-up.

Ashley's body didn't want to hoist up from that chair, but his mind sure did. He flipped the lever to drop the footrest and held himself still while the waves of pain and vertigo settled down. As soon as he could manage, he stood and hurried over to the bowl.

Not only was the bowl upright, it now contained three small stones. River rocks, from the looks of them, smooth and round and blue gray.

Ashley popped one of the painkillers and drank an orange juice while he waited for it to kick in, all the time staring at the bowl. When he felt the trademark cascade of looseness roll down his back, he breathed a deep sigh and bent to pick up the bowl. He rinsed the stones under the kitchen tap and put them, wet, into the pocket of his sweatpants.

Except for PT appointments, he had hardly ventured outside his trailer in weeks, but he made the short trip around to Mrs. Rudrüd's place while the drugs were still tricking him into feeling OK.

"Can I borrow that bird book?" he asked.

Mrs. Rudrüd smiled. "Of course. Come on in while I look for it."

Ashley stifled a groan. Mrs. Rudrüd was a master at turning a quick, neighborly request into an hour-and-a-half social call.

He sat on her velvet floral couch while she rummaged through her bookshelves.

"What bird are you interested in? Wrens? It's a shame about those babies."

He noted the kindness in her delivering this comment while her back was turned, a kindness he knew he didn't deserve.

"No, not wrens. Do you know anything about crows?"

"Right where I left it." She found the bird guide and brought it to him. "I can tell you more than is in that book. There was a special on the other night, a show about a girl—I don't remember where they said, New Jersey or one of those places—and she had a pet crow." Mrs. Rudrüd scrunched up her eyes. "No, *pet* isn't the right word. But anyway, this crow, she had been leaving it peanuts on a tray every day for about a month when the crow started to bring her little doodads, trinkets and such."

"Doodads?"

"Like beads. And an earring someone lost. Links from a chain, some pieces of colored glass. Legos. And the crow would always put it on the tray, just so. And she's not the only one. Other people get presents too."

"What about rocks?"

Mrs. Rudrüd shook her head. "They didn't mention rocks."

"Did they say why they leave things for people?"

"Well, to thank them, I guess. Or, I don't know, maybe they think we eat that stuff. But they're smart, those crows. Did you know they can count?"

"I should go," Ashley said. "I should get back to my place before the drugs wear off. Thanks."

He took the book with him because it would be weird not to after asking for it, but he didn't think it was going to tell him anything important.

Back at home, he took the stones out of his pocket before settling into the recliner. He let them rattle around in his palm, then held each one out to examine it. Nothing special about them. Besides being delivered to him by a bird, that is.

He clicked the TV on, since he did his best thinking with some background noise going. He paused on the baseball game but kept on until he found something mindless: a nature program.

Why would the crow bring him a present? The show Mrs. Rudrüd watched made it sound like it was a quid pro quo kind of thing. What had he done for the crow? Let him eat a few bits of leftover oatmeal?

His line of questioning was interrupted by a terrible noise from the television. The program's narrator said it was the howl of an exhausted polar bear calling her two cubs, urging them across melting ice. Ashley watched for a moment but didn't want to see the babies fall into the water. He turned the TV off.

That was when the deer arrived.

Five of them, a doe, a buck, and three fawns. The doe came first, her narrow head pushing through the curtain before her leap into the room, then the fawns. The buck came through last, a ten-pointer. His antlers caught on the curtain and pulled down the thin rod, cracking it in half. He tossed his head back and forth until his antlers were free of the fabric.

The animals stood blinking at him long enough that Ashley struggled to get up, as if for guests. It was the first time anything larger than a woodpecker had arrived during daylight hours. His heart thumped in his chest.

The buck stepped between Ashley and the young ones.

Ashley held up his hand. "Hey, I'm not going to hurt them." He felt behind him for the chair and sat.

The doe and fawns made for the cabinet, crouching to fit inside. The buck waited until they disappeared to sniff around the frame. He turned to face the living room, and Ashley worried that he was going to charge. Instead, the deer gave a decisive kick that split the cheap countertop in two, collapsing it and sending the coffeemaker and a pile of dirty dishes into the gap. Then he jumped in as well.

From his chair, Ashley felt a breeze rush up from the hole, and with it a scent of the woods. Shaking, he walked toward the wreck of the cabinets and looked in.

He had a wider view now, thanks to the deer's destruction. He was high above another world but how far up, he couldn't tell. Three thousand feet? Four thousand? Below him was an enormous plain bordered by tall trees. A river wound across it and animals moved along the banks. If the deer were down there, they were mere specks from this height.

He braced himself on the edge of the sink and leaned over as far as he could. He didn't see any kind of ramp or ladder or anything. How were the animals reaching the ground?

It was a beautiful day underneath the cabinet, peaceful and

fresh looking. The eagles were making graceful circles in the sky underground. He had an irrational urge to let himself fall in. The animals had jumped and landed safely somehow—he knew they had—and he probably could too.

His half-formed plan was interrupted by the doorbell. No doubt Mrs. Rudrüd had noticed his latest visitors.

She stood on his little stoop, grinding her hands together, the white hair piled on top of her head trembling.

"Ashley." Her expression—eyes shiny and wide, mouth taut—was the face of someone waiting in line for a turn on a terrifying rollercoaster. "The deer."

Ashley opened the door wide to let her in.

"I'm not going in there." She shook her head vigorously until she realized Ashley wasn't going to argue with her. "Am I?"

"Suit yourself." He let go of the door and turned to walk away. She followed.

He had to admit he was relieved to have company. At least if someone else saw the animals, he could quiet the nagging feeling that he was going crazy.

"I saw a bunch of deer come in here. Right through your window." She looked around, her arms crossed. "They're not still in here, are they?"

"Well, yes and no." He pointed to the shattered cabinetry next to the sink. "They're in there."

"What are they doing in there?"

"Take a look."

He pulled his old hunting binoculars off his knickknack shelf and handed them to her.

"Come with me, Ashley." She linked her arm through his, and they inched toward the kitchen.

"Look down there," he said, lifting the binoculars to her eyes.

At first all she said was "Oh!" and, "What in the world?" Then, after a few minutes: "It's beautiful. What is it?"

He led her to a kitchen chair, where she sprawled as if boneless, shaking her head in amazement.

"I don't know what it is. Another world, I guess. Or another level of this one?"

"You got any whiskey?"

"Brandy, maybe."

"It'll do."

He brought her a shot and placed the bottle on the table. She drank it down, poured herself another one, and returned to the edge of the hole.

"What are you going to do about it?" She wiped her mouth. "Are you going down there?"

"No, of course I'm not going down there." He wondered now if she had seen him getting ready to climb into the hole earlier as she waited for him to answer the door.

"Huh." She sat back down. She sounded a little disappointed in him. "Do you think there'll be more?"

Before Ashley could speculate, a plump, gray cat leaped through the window into the living room. Six more followed: an orange tortoiseshell, two Siamese, a couple calicos, and a black one with a white chest.

"Watch," he said, nodding toward the cabinet.

One by one, the cats passed by the kitchen table warily and jumped into the hole.

Mrs. Rudrüd said, "I'll be damned." She scurried back to the hole. "I don't see them. They're not floating their way down there or anything." She leaned over. "Is there a stairs or…oh!"

Ashley pulled her away just as she was about to fall in. A lick of pain shot up his lower back.

"I don't know how they get down there," he snapped. "What I do know is I don't want to be responsible for you falling down after them." He got one of his pills and washed it down with brandy straight from the bottle. "Now, if you're going to stay here and watch, sit at a safe distance."

They sat for hours, Ashley standing every once in a while to stretch and get them soda or a snack. Mrs. Rudrüd only got up to use the bathroom, coming back each time in a rush, asking, "Did I miss anything?"

A swarm of bees and a mass of centipedes made them both shudder, but that was only the beginning of the deluge of insect life. A sheet of mayflies flew in and covered the refrigerator, their wings pulsing, until their scouts discovered the way to the hole. A conga line of daddy longlegs was followed by a squirming procession of ticks, earwigs, and beetles.

"I liked the cats," said Mrs. Rudrüd, after the last beetle dropped out of sight. "There should be more cats."

Within minutes, a pair of bobcats and a Canada lynx obliged.

"That's not what I meant," she said, when they were able to breathe again.

"It's just a coincidence."

"Well, I won't do that again anyway. I'm just going to sit here and take it as it comes."

They sat stock-still when the skunk arrived, until its striped tail dropped below the edge of the hole. A set of minks slipped in so quietly Ashley and Mrs. Rudrüd didn't notice them until they were under their chairs. Next came a few porcupines, another beaver—this one with two babies in its wake—and a mixed flock of songbirds.

"Songbirds! At night?" Mrs. Rudrüd announced each kind with excitement: chickadee, cardinal, warbler, nuthatch, titmouse, goldfinch, and finally, breathlessly, the scarlet tanager and the indigo bunting.

"How lucky are we? They were that close." She glowed, holding her fingers an inch apart. Then her expression darkened. "Wait. They're not all going to go down there. All the birds?" She looked up into his face. "Right?"

He shrugged. It was four in the morning. He was getting tired of company, tired of the questions. Mrs. Rudrüd looked wrung out as well, in spite of sitting on the edge of her seat half the time, her hands on her knees like an eager child in school.

"I think I'm going to head to bed, Mrs. Rudrüd."

She looked relieved herself. "All right. But you need to let me know tomorrow what else shows up."

He saw her to the door and turned on the porch light.

On the threshold, she turned back around. "You don't think it's the climate thingy, do you? The animals"—she gestured toward the kitchen—"do you think they know something we don't?" Her eyes were wide again, and sad.

"People can't change a whole planet," he said.

"Yes," she said, "I suppose that's ridiculous." She descended the steps. "Good night, Ashley. I'll talk to you tomorrow." From the darkness, she called out, "They say on TV it's a hoax the Chinese are playing on us, you know." She waved her hand and disappeared around the corner of his trailer.

He watched from his window until he saw her go into her place, then returned to his chair in the kitchen. Why *were* the animals leaving? It wasn't the climate thing, but something big must be happening to make them act so strange.

He remembered one time when he was a kid out on the farm in Middle Ridge, his dad getting up in the night to shoot a raccoon stumbling around on their front porch. *Rabid*, his dad had said, but Ashley didn't believe it. The animal looked harmless, even as its paws twitched with the onset of death. Years later Ashley learned that sometimes raccoons get drunk on wild grapes fermenting on the vine. Maybe they had just been misjudging nature, what it was doing and what it could withstand, all this time.

Although the wooden kitchen chair was hard and his legs were getting numb, Ashley couldn't seem to make himself go to bed. He drank brandy and turned and turned the questions over in his mind. Around daybreak, he decided that the only way to find out would be to go himself.

Getting down on the floor was not easy. He got splinters in the side of his hand as he used the edges of the broken cabinet to lower himself. He swiveled on the linoleum until his right leg was on the edge of the hole. Only then did it occur to him that if the hole had been widened by the violence of the deer, the floor beneath him might be weaker now too. Maybe it would give way under his weight, in which case his choice was already made for him. The thought horrified and thrilled him.

As Ashley let his leg drop over the edge, an enormous raccoon flew out, knocking him onto his side. It chittered at him, pulling his hair with its hands.

"Ow. What, why are you…?" He tried to protect his head, but the animal had a tight grip. It was clear that the raccoon was pulling in one direction: away from the hole.

"OK, OK." He sat up, and this seemed to assuage the creature.

The raccoon growled once, showing its teeth, then dropped back down the hole.

Ashley pushed himself back from the edge, scraping across the floor to the kitchen table. He hauled himself into a chair and studied the wreck of his house: the torn curtain and shattered window, the filthy carpet, his demolished kitchen counter. The air was ripe with deer musk and the spray of wild cats. The sink, supported now only by a thin sheet of plywood, was leaning toward the hole. It was going to cost him a pretty penny to put things right.

It occurred to him then that he wouldn't fix it. He wouldn't close up the hole. The animals had chosen him, his trailer, for their doorway for some reason, but he didn't need to understand the reason in order to respect it.

He felt a sense of duty stir in his chest and a rightness in this decision that he rarely experienced. He tried to recall another moment like it. Maybe the time he told the other guys at work to stop picking on Elias, who everybody called faggot behind the kid's back. Or the time he turned in a wad of bills he found outside the grocery store, even though he had half a mind to keep it. There was a solidness about those moments, moments when his feet were truly planted on the ground.

His thoughts were broken by a sound from the hole. The raccoon was reemerging, pushing something in front of it. It was the carafe from his coffeemaker, unbroken in spite of what must have been quite a fall. It was dirty, slathered in mud, yet he reached for it once the animal quit nudging it across the floor.

He wiped away some of the mud from the glass with his sleeve then popped open the lid. Inside was a terrarium of sorts, like he made once in fourth grade. At the bottom was a layer of smooth stones like the ones the crow had brought, topped by dark dirt, then moss and a few small plants. A tiny, translucent spider was working up a web across the tops of the seedlings, an egg sac stuck to her back.

There was a pause in which the raccoon seemed to be considering the spider. The animal reached for the carafe, but Ashley pulled it close to his chest and shut the lid.

"She can stay here," Ashley said. "I'll show her where you are if she wants to follow you."

It was not that the raccoon understood his words. It couldn't be that. But the creature did seem almost to nod at him before turning and dropping back through the hole.

JAN UNDERWOOD

Wo Bist Du?

Rolf put his fingers to his eyes and realized they were iced over. He yelped and rubbed them until the tiny frozen tears cracked and fell away and he could lift his lids, painfully. Everything hurt: his neck, his legs. His head hurt, and his face hurt, and his eyes. Limbs so stiff he could hardly move them. He tugged the sleeping bag down to his shoulders. Ana's seat was empty.

"Hey."

He turned, looked in the back. The back seat was less full than it had been. They'd filled it almost to the roof, wisely or unwisely, when they'd left town, the night before, when they knew the big snow was finally coming, when Rolf had finally relented.

"OK," he'd said. "OK. You're right. Let's go."

"Go where?"

"Anywhere. South." Rolf had started rifling through his drawers, pulling out random shirts.

"What are you doing?" Ana said.

"What do you mean?"

"Look."

She had already put their warmest things in suitcases. Already packed candles, flashlights, batteries, a first-aid kit, thermoses. Dried fruit, dried meat. Already. Long before.

It was bitterly cold, but not yet snowing, when they set out. They'd packed blankets, sweaters, sleeping bags. Ten liters of water in one-liter bottles. At Rolf's insistence, they'd taken some books, the laptop, Ana's piano music, their most expensive camera, some knickknacks. Filling the whole back seat, even filling the shelf under the rear window. They could see nothing in the rearview mirror but piles of their own stuff.

The engine had had a hard time turning over, but they got it going, and the tank was full. Ana had made sure the tank was always full.

"How far can we get on one tank?" she said. "Stuttgart? Munich?"

"I think so."

And would it be warm enough in Munich? Rolf thought. And would there be gas to buy in Munich? And would the Austrians let them cross? People had been saying the government, what was left of it, was making desperate last-minute deals with other countries to admit refugees on a temporary basis. Or maybe humanitarian groups would come forward. Churches. Somebody.

*

Now, alone in the stranded car, Rolf gazed over the headrest at the bags of belongings they'd crammed behind the bucket seat.

*

It had been slow going through the streets. Ana and Rolf hadn't been the only ones. Rolf had taken some comfort in the crowds, reflecting that he wasn't alone in his stubbornness. In their green

Renault they'd crept along. A man had rushed up to their window and banged on it and shouted. They locked their doors. People wanted in, people without cars who had no way to leave the city.

"Shouldn't we give somebody a ride?" Ana said. They looked into the back seat. If they took on passengers, they would have to jettison supplies. Rolf sped up.

"Rolf. We can get rid of some stuff."

Rolf came to a stop and waited.

Two middle-aged men ran up to the car. "Please."

"Get in."

"Our mother," the men said. "She's old and sick. We need to go back to the apartment and get her. Will you wait for us?"

"Ja, OK."

The men disappeared into a nearby building.

"Do you trust them?"

"I don't know," Rolf replied. "I don't know what to do."

"I don't either."

They waited. Rolf left the engine running in case he couldn't get the car started again.

"Is there room? What can we let go of?"

"Maybe some books."

Five, ten, twelve minutes went by. They were wasting gas.

"Should I go see if they need help?"

"I don't know."

Then the men appeared. They didn't have the mother with them. They had bags.

"There's no room for more stuff," Rolf said.

"We need it," one of the men said. "We'll hold it on our laps."

"Where's your mother?"

"She's not going to make it," the man said. "We should just go."

Ana and Rolf looked at the two men, standing in the street with their duffel bags. Rolf stepped on the gas. One of the men banged on the roof of the car in protest as they peeled away.

Rolf drove as quickly as he could through the narrow streets, the sound of that fist on the roof reverberating through his nervous system.

*

Now the Renault was no longer full to the roof. Ana had obviously gone through their things and taken some: her pack, some food. Rolf tried to open the car door and could not. It was stiff with cold, like his useless hands. He pushed against it with his shoulder, then wriggled out of his sleeping bag, moved back, gave the door a good kick with both feet, and tried again to open it. Ice creaked and fell into the snow, and the door gave way. Rolf's breath was fogging over the windshield. He pushed his sleeping bag away and stepped into snow. Stood and fell: his legs were not working. Pulled himself up and leaned against the snow-blanketed metal.

"Wo bist du?" His question sounded plaintive. *Wo bist du? Where are you?*

*

The wait to get onto the autobahn had been long. Hundreds of pedestrians were lined along the entrance ramps, pleading. Many vehicles were brimming with people. A car in front of them, not yet full, had pulled to the side and opened the door for a pitiable family of four. But before the four could get settled, other pedestrians had mobbed the car, pushing the family out of the way, cramming themselves in until the desperate motorist had sped down the shoulder of the road, back door still open, just to get away.

"I'll ride in your trunk," someone had shouted to Rolf and Ana. "Please!"

*

Rolf circled the car. The snow was to his knees. No footprints led away from their car, from other cars. Any tracks Ana had left had been covered over. He saw no human figures. Just a field of white on white, the snow-quilted cars in long rows like Viking burial mounds.

*

Rolf had seen the maps on the news scrolling across the walls of kiosks and in the subway tunnels: digital projections of a new ice age that was curling over Europe like a wave. They showed white pixels crashing over the North Sea and creeping down the continent from the top of the screen, covering Scandinavia, Germany, the Netherlands, Denmark, smothering them under a blanket of winter storms, hiding them, altering the map forever.

"We need to get out of here," Ana kept saying. "Let's apply for visas."

But they didn't. To Rolf it had seemed unreal, even as reports of parallel disasters elsewhere kept rolling in. This was Germany, where the trains ran on time, where all the rubbish was recycled. The government wasn't going to let everybody freeze to death. Anyway, what would Rolf and Ana do for work? Where would they live? They had six years of equity in their flat. Were they going to just abandon it?

Already the world map of his childhood was no more, the coasts swallowed by the sea, the continents shrunken, eaten away, whole island nations underwater. Java: gone. Hawaii: gone. Bali: nowhere to be seen. Even more than the terrible video footage of panicked refugees fighting their way inland, this new world map disturbed him. When he was a child, the textbook maps of Pangaea had always made him feel, peering into the far past, a little dizzy, and seeing this new image of the deeply familiar so distorted, the old shapes bitten into new ones, was like peering, dizzy, into the far future. Only the future was now.

Then America had stopped issuing visas, and so had Russia. There are no jobs for you, they said, no resources. And Germans had started going to South America, joining the waves of South Americans themselves fleeing their rising tides, whole coastal cities moving inland, whole coasts dislocated, reset in new shapes on the globe.

"We can go to Italy," Ana said. "We can go to Croatia. Croatia is accepting immigrants."

"What about your piano?"

"They have pianos in Croatia."

"Not your grandmother's piano."

They bundled up. Rolf wrapped the pipes in old wool sweaters, left the faucet dripping slightly.

They used as little gas as possible, slept curled together like cats, kept a supply of canned goods in the larder. Already the gas had been shut off in some cities, rationed for the most vulnerable, or so it was said. The news ran reports of people burning their furniture. For a brief period, it was possible to get a fake visa. Then the other countries began to crack down. Anyway, the images from elsewhere were not promising. Vigilantes waiting outside airports. Mobs in the new inland settlements. Deadly winter storms, even in southern places.

*

Rolf struggled with the passenger door from the outside and managed to yank it open and flop the seat forward. He pawed through the things in the back. Ana had taken the first-aid kit and as many of her clothes as she could wear, he guessed, and much of the water. What she'd left behind was frozen solid.

He sat in her seat, put his head in his hands. Then he shut up the car behind him and began to knock on windows.

"Hallo?"

He started trying doors. Some were locked, some probably frozen shut. His arms and legs were screaming with the sensation of blood returning to them. He wiped the crusting snow away and peered inside. Empty. He moved on to the next and the next. In the fourth or fifth car he tried, he found someone in the back seat, mouth open, mittens curled over the top of a blanket, frozen in that pose of clutching after warmth.

Rolf stared and then began to run through the drifts, checking cars left and right. Ten, fifteen, twenty cars. The cars of the dead, the cars of the missing. Where had they all gone? How long had he been asleep? Had Ana gone for help? Did she think he had died?

*

Rolf tried to remember what had happened. They had left the city, finally. Once on the autobahn, they made better time. Traffic was so thick that they did not move swiftly, but at least they moved. They did not speak. Ana watched in the side mirror the scene at the entrance ramp until it was out of sight. In her lap, her gloved fingers playing an imaginary piano, always. Playing busy inventios by Bach. She probably wasn't even conscious of it. They drove an hour, two hours. They were halfway to Dusseldorf when traffic came to a standstill.

Rolf brought the Renault to a full stop. He idled for a few minutes, and then, when the cars before him did not budge, killed the engine. He and Ana spoke, but not much, about what might be happening. All they could do was wait. By then the snow was falling.

It did not take long for the inside of the car to grow cold. They discussed whether they should turn the engine back on to run the heat. Instead, they got their sleeping bags out of the back and crawled into them and huddled together on the passenger side. They dozed.

When they awoke, their view was obscured by a mantle of white over the windshield.

"Let's see if anyone knows anything."

"OK. But. We need to be careful."

They stepped out of the car slowly. No pedestrians were in sight—they were too far now from any city. It did not seem they ran the risk of being mobbed or having the car wrested from them. To the side of the road lay nothing but fields of snow. Ahead and behind them as far as they could see were lines of cars, all at a standstill. Across the meridian, the northbound lanes of the autobahn were also filled with southbound cars.

*

Rolf returned now to the Renault. He tried to go through every item in the car, systematically, thoughtfully, but his breath came in ragged gulps and he couldn't focus. What would he need? How could he know what he would need? He filled his pack with snacks, a flashlight. He pulled every item of clothing out of the back and put it all on. He had good boots. His feet would be dry. He locked the car, walked twenty meters, then returned and unlocked it. Leaving it unlocked, he set out again.

*

Even at a dead standstill, Rolf and Ana hadn't been too frightened. They had focused on the practical. Ana rummaged for the scraper and cleared the windshield. Rolf knocked on a few windows and asked others if they knew what was happening. No one was getting phone service; no one was getting radio. They did not stray far from their car but returned and tucked into their sleeping bags again.

"What do you think the temperature is?"

"I don't know. Cold."

How cold did it have to get, Rolf wondered, before you froze to death? How long did it take?

"Do you want some food?"

"I'm not hungry."

"We should drink at least."

They hadn't had anything to eat or drink in hours. Still in her sleeping bag, Ana rummaged at her feet until she found a water bottle. She took a sip, passed it to Rolf. The windshield was filling up with snow again. Rolf wondered if they would have to dig themselves out by the time traffic began moving. He wondered if they had brought a shovel. Well, someone would have one.

"At least we're together," Ana said.

"Yes."

The sky went gray, then turned a dusty charcoal color. Still it kept snowing. Rolf grew uncomfortable, the gearshift driving into the back of his thigh, and he moved to his own bucket seat. "Let me know if you get too cold," he said. "I'll come back over."

"OK."

Rolf reclined his seat as far as he could against the items stacked behind it and pulled his sleeping bag up over his head. He drew his knees to his chest, wedging his feet against the gearshift, and closed his eyes. And that was how he woke up, cold and fetal, with eyelids frozen shut and no Ana.

*

The going was slow. He saw nothing. Heard nothing. After twenty minutes of walking, he stopped. Should he leave Ana a note? Rolf stood dumb and still, trying to think, even though to stop was to feel his body temperature drop. He turned and headed back in the direction of the Renault, following his own fresh clumsy path. Why hadn't she thought to leave him one? Maybe she really did think he had died, frozen in his sleep. Tried to wake him and couldn't. What should he say in the note? Rolf realized that he had no plan to communicate. But what was there to do, except keep following the road south? When he came to people, when he came to a town, he would look for her. What else could he do? He didn't need to leave a note to tell her that.

So, Rolf turned and once again set out south.

Maybe she'd simply left him. This was his doing, after all. So many of their friends, their colleagues, neighbors, had left in the months before. His elderly mother had moved to Vienna several years earlier, when the winters were just beginning to grow harder. His siblings had followed to look after her. Ana's parents had emigrated and called every week to beg Rolf and their daughter to come too. One morning it turned out that almost a quarter of the members of the Bundestag had fled, flying to relatives in other places, using their influence or their money to secure safe places for themselves.

Everyone with the means to leave had left. They left their houses, their art, their pets; they left their hometowns; they left their livelihoods. They left almost everything because they preferred to save their skins. Rolf wondered what had been wrong with him that he had looked away and looked away so that he risked losing his skin, and not just his, but Ana's.

Still, why would Ana leave him now? If she were going to leave him, wouldn't she have done it when there was still hope?

Idiot! Why was he walking when he could drive? If he could get the engine started, Rolf could go around the cars in front of him and drive along the shoulder. People ahead of him would have thought of that too, and eventually the way would be blocked. But any distance was better than no distance, and he'd be warm.

So, Rolf turned and trudged north, following his own footsteps, already fuzzy and misshapen with new snow, back to the Renault. He climbed in, pushed the engine-start button. The engine was dead. Didn't even turn over once. Just the tap of the button, and then the silence of the snow.

"At least we're together."

He stumbled out of the dead car and took a few steps. Bach's *Inventio 3*, which Ana had been practicing a lot, was playing in his mind, over and over. How was it that in such dire times he could have a song stuck in his head? It was a frantic little song, a chattering, nervous composition with no soft moments and no clear melodic direction, like a hive of bees or a demonic possession. Ana had played it over and over, many times a day, his caffeinated, nervous Ana, and when she wasn't playing it on the piano, she was playing it on the table or in the air with her long fingers. Now she was playing it in his head.

*

"We need to go," she'd kept saying. "Rolf. Please."

"But the flat."

"The flat is going to be encased in ice."

And still they didn't go. And then suddenly there was no possibility of going. While Rolf had been waiting to see how things played out, waiting for some announcement of a government program, wistfully gazing around their flat and thinking of how they could adapt, all their chances sublimated. The central and southern European nations, to a one, closed their borders. We aren't heartless, they said, but we are inundated. And it was true—refugees were pouring in both from the frigid north and the watery south. Hundreds of millions from the edges were converging on the center. We can't do any more, said France, said Austria, said Hungary. We're overcapacity.

The storm that was going to hit, the news said, would blanket the region in freezing rain, in snow, in ice. The temperature would drop to minus ten centigrade. Gray-faced analysts declared that this would be the new normal and chided the good citizens of northern Europe for not preparing. Human interest stories showed Inuits giving igloo-building lessons, Samis offering tips on ice fishing and food storage.

It was not enough, analysts said. The infrastructure couldn't take it. Power lines would go down. Fuel supplies would run out. The government had bailed. The government almost didn't exist toward the end, and then the news, too, had trickled away.

*

Rolf was shaking, shaking hard. He wrapped his arms around himself and tried to quell the movement, but he couldn't; it was as though an outside force had picked him up to shake him. Trying to knock some sense into him, maybe. It reminded him of the feeling of being very hungry. "Maybe I need a sandwich," he said aloud to the frozen air, and the sound of it made him laugh. "Corned beef on rye, please," he said, and then, "I would prefer the nonfat mozzarella." Then he was laughing hard, shaking with laughter as well as with cold, laughing until he doubled over, and he went down on one knee in the snow. A sandwich. There would be one here somewhere. He began to paw through the snow drifts. *Wait—what am I looking for? A sandwich. No, Ana. Looking for Ana. That's right.* Rolf peered at his hands, smacked off the snow that stuck to the palms of his mittens in concave clumps. He stood. Shaking. Took halting steps. Snow was falling thickly, and the wind picked up the flakes and swirled them in a vortex about his head and confused his memory of which direction to walk. All about him were burial mounds, and the Vikings wanted him to find their ship. If he walked in the proper direction, he would come to it, to a ship with the head of a dragon. That was what he was looking for. No, no, it was Ana he was looking for—that was right. She was here somewhere, but before him or behind him? He didn't remember. His eyelashes were crusted with frozen snowflakes, and everything was gray and blue and white, the gray that was the white of snow, and the blue that was the white of snow, and the white. And he knew then what to do: he should take off this scarf. It made a kind of sense, although he couldn't quite remember his line of reasoning, but he knew he should do it, peel it away and strew it behind him, a semaphore, an arrow pointing the way, so the Vikings could find him when they came looking, and wasn't there something about coaxing blood from your core to your fingertips by thwarting the treachery of your coat, your coat that trapped your warmth in your core and kept it from your cold fingers? It did make sense, and he peeled his coat off and left it in the snow, pointing so Ana could follow him, and his mittens, one and then the other, making a trail to follow like Hansel and Gretel had, a path of pebbles to follow, the pebbles of his sweater and his pants, the breadcrumbs of his boots that would be eaten by the crows. Bach's *Inventio 3* was loud, louder and faster and faster and louder—he wondered if the crows could hear it. Was he still shaking, or was it just the vortex of the wind confusing his directions? He couldn't see. Everything was the gray of white and the blue of white and white. He had to find Ana. He tucked his head against the wind and took twenty, thirty steps, and then his knees began to buckle.

"Ana?"

Only the wind battering his uncovered ears, and skimming snow off the tops of the burial mounds, and in the background nervous Bach. He tried again.

"Ana? Wo bist du?"

His voice didn't carry very far.

STEFAN KIESBYE

Smokeland

He tasted smoke on his dry lips and quickly got up to walk out into the living area. Yes, it was certainly smoke. But the detectors did not sound nor did the sprinklers come on. He walked stiff-legged toward the nine-foot-wide glass doors leading into the yard and pushed aside the curtains. After several seconds, he closed his eyes, rubbing and wiping at the grit. On opening them again, he found he still couldn't see any more than he could a few seconds ago. He pushed open the glass doors and stepped onto the concrete patio. The world had disappeared.

The city had expected the rebuild of the neighborhood to take upward of five years. But after only two, the streets around the park showed barely an empty lot. Most of the neighbors Carmen knew personally had moved into their new homes before him. Twenty-two months after the fires, he'd received his keys. Now it was October again, and wildfires had again sprung up in California, this time since August.

His fence was gone. His bare feet stuck in ratty Birkenstocks. Dressed in gym shorts and a bulky T-shirt, he crossed what had been his lawn. It was dirt now, though he couldn't say exactly how bad the situation was; the streetlights were down. Smoke and cloud layers were too thick to admit any starlight.

His neighbor's lot was badly ravaged, just as it had been two years ago. And the houses beyond that were gone as well. Even though his eyes were not able to cut through the smoke, he sensed the emptiness beyond what he could see.

I'll get Heather, he thought, for he couldn't bring himself to yell or scream. *I don't want to get separated. We need to wake the kids.*

*

"You should have showered last night," Heather said in the morning. "Wow, look at your feet. And the sheets. What were you thinking?"

Heather was not an easy woman to live with. Mornings were not a good time to run afoul of what she deemed appropriate. The crunching sound of protein bar in his mouth could set her off, or their son Devin's snotty nose.

"I woke you last night," Carmen said. "I think. But we never woke the kids."

"What for?" she asked.

It was six thirty. His mind was a jumble. If he wanted to go for a run, he had to hurry.

"The burnt lots," he said and only then realized that through the open blinds of the bedroom—Heather did not tolerate closed blinds after 6:00 a.m.—fences and newly planted trees were visible. He shot up so quickly he felt dizzy and nearly fell to the floor. His feet indeed looked terrible. Black and sooty. Where had he been?

Devin and Katie were not up yet, but Heather had already brewed coffee. Its aroma hung almost visibly in the kitchen and living room. She had pushed the curtains in front of the patio doors aside—or had he never closed them last night? The fence was there, and the neighbor's house, plus an oversize and ugly gazebo from Costco, stood as they had before he'd gone to bed the night before.

But his feet.

Carmen was staring at his black toes when Devin came from his room, messy haired and still wearing pajamas. "Your feet are gross," he said and walked past Carmen into the kitchen.

*

Isolated incidents have no chance of survival in our organized and calibrated minds. We're pattern seekers, and the quicker we detect them, the more successful we are in life. Carmen wrote this into his notebook, a gift from Carlos, a friend who'd been to Mexico City recently. The word on the cover was *Ideal*, and it fit in Carmen's pants pocket, the hidden compartment of his shoulder bag, and under his pillow. He never showed it to Heather, who would want to know what he was writing down and, not being able to read Carmen's handwriting, would insist he read his notes to her. If he loved her.

The fact was that until now he hadn't taken any notes. He wasn't sure what to comment on. He'd never kept a diary. Or maybe he'd used Heather as an oral diary. He didn't keep many thoughts from her. If he dreamed of an old girlfriend or if he imagined his neighbor watering the plants without any clothes on, he didn't tell her. But as soon as he returned from work, he gave a report on everything that had happened. Which battles he'd won, which he had avoided, and which he had lost. He told her about lunch, about what he'd heard on the radio on his commute, and about what colleagues he couldn't stand. He'd never told her about Aspen, his new coworker, and he didn't intend to.

By and large, Carmen was an honest person.

He suspected Heather was too. He wished she had a secret life. At times he wished it so much it hurt. He wanted to come home and see strange clothes on the bed, detect the smell of aftershave on her coat. He wanted to walk in on her screaming in excited tones. He wanted her to commit petty crimes—steal jewelry or write bad checks. He craved bad behavior. So far, he hadn't detected any. They were in their thirteenth year of marriage.

All this he now confided to his Ideal notebook. Thanks to his illegible writing, nobody would ever know what he was thinking. And until he filled ten of the small pages, he hadn't had any idea either. He wanted to walk in on Heather having sex with a neighbor? It hurt to be so shallow.

The notebook didn't help him understand what had happened the night before, but it did help him formulate a plan. The next time he had a dream about a wasteland stretching out in front of his house, he'd take something from it back inside, a memento. He needed to find something, and then he'd be able to show Heather that he wasn't sleepwalking or, worse, being careless about his hygiene. He needed to find proof. In his memories, he fished for something he could have carried back inside his house, but no object materialized. He would have to be more careful next time. Like a wreck diver, he needed to identify what he had found.

As the day dragged on, however, his notes and his plan seemed less important, less clever, even less true. Nothing could stand up to writing invoices and calling up customers to remind them of outstanding bills. Clients called and haggled, offered to pay less, complained about the space they bought in the paper, the intensity of the print. When he walked back to the parking garage, for which he paid by the month, the gray black of the sky and the landscape that was no landscape anymore but just a vast plain of something that had been there and had now been removed felt as real as the possibility of walking in on Heather with another man. He still couldn't explain his black feet, but yes, he had been dreaming. He really wanted to believe that. How easy it made everything.

*

He took the "scenic" route home, past the community park on which work had recently started. Not much of it had been destroyed two years ago, but for reasons he didn't understand and hadn't Googled, the city had decided to replace even the soil and start afresh.

A fresh start—that was what people said when they learned he had moved back to his old neighborhood. They thought a new house with all the modern amenities and slate-colored appliances was enough to make him forget about how his old house had burned down. Only Aspen, his new colleague, had sneered at the notion. "Fuck that," she said. "I'd never move back to that place." It had been rude of her to say that, but Carmen only had eyes for the snake that curled out of her shirt and up her neck. Green, it was, with a yellow tongue. It was an old tattoo, the lines starting to blur.

In the first months after the fire, a woman had put up a tent in the park, posting flyers of people looking for lost pets. It had been taken down, Carmen didn't know when or why. For weeks and months, people had posted messages about found animals to Facebook groups. His neighbor's chickens had burned in the backyard. The man hadn't even opened the cages.

*

Dinner was pot roast and mashed potatoes. Katie was at a friend's house, and Devin was watching videos while stuffing potatoes in his mouth, sometimes missing the opening and smearing the beige paste onto his cheek.

Heather had been given a new conference to plan and supervise, this one in Palm Springs. She would have to travel down south before Christmas to set up everything with the hotel resort and again in March for the event. She was excited, pretty—the grouch from that morning had disappeared. Instead, she was talking with hand and fork about participants, the organization that was putting on the event, the email blasts she needed to create, like, yesterday. Tomorrow she'd meet the board members and get their input for the brochure she would create. She ignored Devin and his smeared face; she didn't mention Carmen's dirty feet. The world had sped up, smoothed out, was moving forward.

Behind them on the kitchen wall, they'd hung framed photographs of their house. The first one was a shot of their old house, how it had been before the fire. That summer, he'd stained the driveway a reddish hue. He'd done the same to the back patio, then had taken delivery of ten yards of caliche stone and redone the backyard. In the photo, he was wearing a plaid shirt and soiled pants. His face was sunburned, his teeth so large and so white. The kids were outside with him, spraying each other with water.

The next image had been taken after the fire. Heather stood to the right. She wore a hat and a bandanna tied over her face, like an old-movie bandit. She looked at what had been there and was now gone. She looked at the emptiness, and Carmen could still feel the hollow in his stomach from when he had taken that picture. The next images showed the empty, cleaned lot. The graded lot came next, the foundation, the finished framing. There were a dozen pictures in all, the last one taken after the landscaping had been done, right before the contractor had handed them their keys.

The next morning, Carmen had changed all locks, just to be on the safe side.

Katie came home at seven, and by eight thirty, she and Devin were in bed, though Carmen doubted they were asleep. But that was their responsibility—he'd given up on checking what couldn't be enforced. You needed to understand your powers, he thought, and flashlights and books, YouTube videos and late-night texts, he could do nothing about.

Heather smoked a preroll on the patio steps with the door closed, and he joined her with a vodka martini. "Hey, lover," she said and elbowed him gently. "You look so hot."

"I do?" he said.

"Yes, you look all cuddly."

"I took a shower."

She leaned over and sniffed him. "You washed all the good stuff off. Hmm, maybe you should do a strenuous workout."

He mussed her hair, and she giggled happily. He didn't mind her smoking, never had, but she became someone else, which unmoored him. She turned slightly loutish, slightly belligerent at times. Like someone who played drunk in a sitcom. Carmen didn't know which of the Heathers was more authentic, the grouchy or the stoned one, and while he was able to grasp the concept of containing multitudes, he liked his life to be steady. Then he thought of his scribblings in the Ideal notebook and blushed. Maybe this version of Heather might be the one he was professing to miss. So, now that he had her, was he happy?

"I think I don't have a propensity for happiness," he said out loud.

She laughed at his words. "Propensity for happiness? Yes, sweetie, you're a pretty gloomy guy."

"I am?"

"You have to think about everything. Constantly. I bet you're still working on a theory about your dirty feet. Right? Am I right? You've been thinking about it all day. You've been thinking about a way to explain it, and I'm sure one of these days you're gonna tell me exactly how you managed to get them so filthy."

"That bad?"

"What?" she asked.

"Am I that bad?"

She laughed a bit too loud and a bit too dirty. "Show me your feet."

He took off his socks, and she inspected his white skin. "They're so soft. How do you get them so soft?"

He shrugged. "Are they clean enough to go to bed?"

She let go of his right foot. "Absolutely. Couldn't be cleaner."

*

His mouth was so dry, he had difficulties pulling his tongue off the roof of his mouth. He got up without waking Heather. The smell was more pronounced this time, and when he stepped up to the patio doors, the landscape was as it had been the night before.

I am dreaming, he thought, *but it's the same dream. And why do I know it's the same dream? Why can I think that?*

Then he remembered his plan: to find something he could bring back from the outside and show to Heather in the morning. So, he slid open the door and closed it again quickly behind him, not to let any more smoke penetrate the house.

He hadn't thought to put on his Birkenstocks, but he didn't mind. Let his feet be dirty; who cared? The ground proved to be warm, hot, really, in places, as though fire had moved through the area just recently. And yet the soles of his feet didn't burn. All in all, it was quite a pleasant experience, as long as he stayed away from debris scattered in his neighbor's yard.

Again, the sky hung low. Smoke and clouds made it impossible for Carmen to see whether the streets and houses on the distant hills were lit. *I should be more upset*, he thought. Then he turned to look at his own house, and it was the only one standing as far as he could see. Only the light above the stove was on, and it soothed him to know that he had a place to return to. He cried, at least it felt as though he were crying, and wiping at his eyes, he moved east, down his street, looking for neighbors, looking for anything alive. He scanned the street for something he could carry or drag back home, when a shadow rose in front of him. It moved stiffly but rapidly, as though in stop-motion, and this made Carmen's heart lurch. He stopped breathing. This thing, whatever it was, had been lying in wait for him, and it would put an end to his life.

The next moment he recognized the shape of a dog, and another second later he could hear the creature breathe. Carmen's heart sank back to its regular spot. He registered relief and disappointment. "Hey, you," he said and lowered himself, holding out a flat hand toward the dog. It looked to be a bloodhound, very large and emaciated, and it sniffed his hand with great caution. Its tongue hung nearly to the ground.

"Come, come with me," Carmen beckoned, and the dog followed him back to his house. Something seemed wrong with his body—every step made it jerk awkwardly—and Carmen had to wait several times to let the dog catch up. In front of his patio doors, he said, "Wait here. I'll be right back with some food."

Carmen tried hard to make some noise in the kitchen. Why hadn't he awakened Heather *before* he had left the house? Was he acting according to dream logic? Or was he just sitting on his brain? "Heather," he shouted now, slamming the refrigerator shut and carrying the plastic tub of Black Forest ham toward the patio doors. "Devin, Katie, look who I found."

He didn't wait for his family to join him. Instead, he closed the door behind him and stepped out. Fine ashes flew past his face. There was no sign of the dog. "Motherfucker," Carmen said under his breath. "Shit, shit, shit." But he didn't need any more proof. Theirs was the only house in the neighborhood that had been spared. He needed to wake his family, and they needed to leave right now. How could he not have had that thought before?

He stuffed some ham into his mouth then marched back into the living room. In the dim light coming from the kitchen, he could see how dirty his feet were. This time, he wouldn't try Heather first; this time, he would wake his kids. And with that thought, he opened Devin's door.

*

"He looks dead to me," Devin said in a voice quivering yet full of conviction.

"I think he's breathing. You have to look at his ribs. What's that smell?"

"Ham. Eww. He's lying in it."

"And look at his feet."

Carmen kept his eyes closed for a little longer, while shame and embarrassment made his limbs burn. "I'm not dead," he said in a flat voice, but it was enough to make his kids run from the room and scream for Heather.

But he didn't wait for her to find him dirty and disheveled in Devin's room. He escaped into the hall bathroom, locked the door, and turned on the shower. He wouldn't avoid needling questions, high-pitched concern, and suspicion, but he could at least face it without evidence of the night before clinging to his body.

He had failed. His whole plan had been harebrained. He needed to wake Heather before going outside into what he thought of as Smokeland. Why had he ever thought that carrying a sooty hubcap or dish home could suffice as proof that his dream was not a dream? The hot water was scalding him; the cheap soap stung his eyes. He knew Heather would be waiting in the kitchen. By now she would have cleaned up the mess he'd left in Devin's room and be questioning his sanity.

But she hadn't cleaned up, nor was she questioning his sanity. She had made coffee but not taken out a cup for him. Her eyes were red, her cheeks wet. "You scared them," she said, after he took a seat. "You scared the crap out of them. I sent them to get doughnuts. What in the world?"

"It's not safe here. I'm not sleepwalking. I'm not dreaming. We need to leave."

"Look outside."

"What?"

"Just look outside," she demanded.

He got up and did as he was told. It was a rather beautiful morning. They'd never lived in a more beautiful place. The sun still had a golden, sleepy hue to it, and he could see the mountains clearly. Their neighbor, whose chickens had burned and with whom they were sharing their back fence, was outside, his small dogs yipping out of sight.

"It's not real," he said. "It doesn't feel real."

"I know," she said. "We're in the same spot; we're sitting on top of what burned down. But Kat and Dev don't need us to be weird about this. They need us to be as normal and steady as we can make it."

"A burial ground," he said.

"If we'd had the money, we would have bought a house somewhere else. But we didn't."

"No, we didn't."

"It will feel normal later on," Heather said. "After a few months, we'll get used to all the new houses. They'll start feeling real to us."

"You really believe that?" he asked and finally summoned enough courage to sit down again and look at her. Her cheeks were wet. He loved her so intensely in that moment, he felt sick.

"I don't know," she sobbed. "I don't fucking know."

*

He arrived late at work, but hardly anyone noticed. Most of the day, he let the answering machine collect messages for him. Instead, he scribbled into his notebook. He couldn't tell Heather what was going through his mind; he couldn't share that. But at the same time, he wasn't sure which was crueler, to tell her or to stay quiet. He would not abandon his search for what happened outside his home at night. He couldn't. And so, he tried to make another plan. One that would allow him to explore what he was waking up to at night.

After work, he went to PetSmart. He'd never owned a dog, not even as a boy. His mother had been a germaphobe with no love for animals. He'd begged and begged, but by the time he got married, he looked at dogs with distaste. They sniffed urine and poop, ate it sometimes.

Carmen bought a red leash, six foot and sturdy. With giddy fingers, he chose a red collar, which he hoped would be big enough. But would he be able to bring the leash to Smokeland? He had failed to carry anything from the outside in. Would it work the other way around?

And where would his dream start? Would he continue where he had left off, or were things happening in Smokeland during his daytime absences? Did that realm have a life on its own, or was he at the center of it? Did he bring it about? If it was his dream, then the dog would be waiting for him at the door. But no matter what, Carmen did not believe for a second that the dog was gone. It would return. Surely it was waiting for him outside his home.

*

Dinner was a disaster. Katie refused to eat turkey, carrots, and peas and instead plastered the food over her face. Then she dramatically fell off her chair, convulsing until she died with a whimper. Devin laughed so hard at her act that he sprayed his peas through his nose across the table at Carmen. Moments after Heather sent the kids to their rooms, the fire alarm went off, and they found Devin standing on his desk chair, holding a candle as high as he could below the alarm. The ruckus made Katie cry and run out of the house. Carmen found her standing in the middle of the street just around the bend in the road, clutching her schoolbag. She was trembling and wouldn't talk to him. She refused a good-night story. Her body was icy cold.

Devin barricaded himself in his room, and sometime after ten, Heather and Carmen gave up, switched off the lights in the kitchen and living room and went to their bedroom. Carmen flossed his teeth sitting on the edge of the bed while Heather brushed hers at the sink with the bathroom door open. She was wearing red pajamas, something they'd bought in the first days after the fire. They were nearly two years old, the oldest clothing item she possessed.

She didn't want to talk, didn't even want to read. By the time he had finished brushing his teeth and gargling, she seemed asleep. She looked beautiful, but her face appeared to be a memory of Heather, something he remembered from a few years ago. He didn't feel like kissing her good night. She was years away.

He didn't shake her either when he awoke later during the night. He didn't feel any urgency to convince her anymore. It had left him like hunger after a decent meal. Oddly, he did remember dinner and his kids' tantrums while his feet were searching for his slippers. He remembered the duffel he had packed just after arriving home last night. A change of clothes, a flashlight, dog treats, collar and leash, two bottles of water. It seemed very inadequate now. His whole plan appeared dangerous and silly. How embarrassing he hadn't come up with something smarter.

While walking down Banyan toward the highway, he wondered if he could have taken the car. That had not occurred to him either and seemed like another odd mistake. Had the car been in the garage? He hadn't even checked, as though the only possible way to enter the outside was through the patio doors.

The dog had not been waiting for him, hadn't come wagging his tail the way Carmen had imagined. He called out from time to time; he was hoping for companionship. Ash flew about. If life in Smokeland continued outside his dream, it hadn't led to anything new. No streetlights shone; nobody else came wandering toward him. The farther he walked east, the less hope he felt about finding another being in his neighborhood.

Then he heard the loud and labored breathing, and something akin to giddiness made him turn this way and that. "Where are you?" he said, and: "Come, I've got something good for you." He set down the duffel, pulled out the treats, and opened the package. The smell was strong. Carmen waved the bag in the air, hoping the dog might be able to pick up the scent.

Just like the night before, the creature seemed to be released from darkness. It didn't come from anywhere, it formed itself from smoke. It sniffed Carmen's bag, then let itself be fed. It didn't like Carmen's hands swooping down toward him; it growled but remained close.

"I got you a collar and a leash," Carmen said. The dog jerked his head at Carmen's touch but held still long enough for him to click shut the buckle and attach the leash. It was a satisfying click—the dog was his now. It belonged to him. He would go home, and his family would finally see that he wasn't dreaming. Not at all. Whatever they had built on top of the burnt land, it didn't exist. It was completely insubstantial, and now they needed to leave. This, this fire-ravaged land, was their real home.

The dog let himself be pulled away. It was easier than Carmen had thought. This was his dog, the monster dog, the devil dog. For the first time since the night of the fire, he felt as though something belonged to him again. "You are my dog," he said aloud, and the dog followed along, taking treats from Carmen's fingers with great care.

"What are you doing?" a voice asked, and it was so low and gentle that it took Carmen two seconds to comprehend that he wasn't talking to himself. He turned around.

A woman stood there, maybe ten years older than him. She wore a raincoat, and underneath that, pajamas. "This is my dog. You can't just take him with you."

"Where is your house? Where do you live? Where is everybody?" He wasn't willing to cede his dog to a perfect stranger.

"You're the first one I've seen in weeks," the woman said.

"The first one?"

"There are others." She pointed behind her into the smoke.

"Where do you live?"

"Here."

"But where?" And when she didn't seem to understand, he pointed ahead of him. "My house is over there, just beyond the bend." And in a mere whisper, he added, "I've been thinking I'm making this up."

"This is my dog," she said and held out her hand. Reluctantly, he gave her the leash.

"If you want, we can walk him together." The woman started in the direction of Carmen's house, the direction he had indicated.

"How long have you been…?" He caught himself, did not add, *in my dream*, or say, *in Smokeland*.

The woman turned toward him, and her eyes seemed to sparkle. Or maybe they were wet. "You should go back. Do you have family?"

"Yes, yes," he said. "What about you?"

She didn't answer, just walked ahead, following the dog, who tore at the leash from time to time, sniffing crumbled sidewalks and pissing on burned-out cars.

"This feels very real," he said.

"Yes, of course. It's very real. We need to find your house. You should really find your house."

She picked up the pace, calling to the dog repeatedly, pulling him along. Carmen had trouble keeping up. And coming around the bend in the road, the same bend where hours ago Katie had stood shaking, clutching her schoolbag, he found his home gone. There was no light, there were no walls, just debris. The darkness was complete.

"Here?" The woman pointed and her hand hung in the air as if detached from her body, her fingers opening to repeat her question, her empty palm turned upward.

*

Heather searched for a note, a few lines explaining where he had gone or why. She opened desk drawers, the closet, yet without touching things, without making a mess. If Carmen had wanted to leave her a message, she'd find it without problem. But no, his pens still lay scattered over the desk. His laptop remained in its bright-red sleeve. Her husband had not left any message on the refrigerator, nor had he left a note on the white quartz countertops or on the dining room table. And—she checked—not on the toilet lid in the hall bathroom either. None of his things, as far as she knew them, were amiss. He hadn't even taken his car or any of his clothes. They were all still here, right here, with Heather. They were all waiting for Carmen to return.

"Motherfucker," she said. She repeated that word for the best part of an hour, her voice echoing in the living room. She made a second pot of coffee and sat down on the brown leather sofa, taking in Carmen's absence. By noon, she knew that she would file a police report in due time, that she might even call hospitals in the area to find out if they had admitted a middle-aged man who fit Carmen's description. There were things that needed to be done to explain her situation to neighbors and relatives. And while she was completing her to-do list by the open glass doors leading into the yard, she understood—not knowing how, but with a certainty that reminded her of morning sickness—that Carmen would not return.

She'd known he wasn't quite happy with their marriage. She wasn't blind. The past two years had been exhausting, eroding subtler feelings, scraping away the joy you felt after cleaning a sink, or after switching on the dishwasher and listening to its sonorous hum. The past two years had eaten at the way they looked at each other when undressing at night. They depended on each other for invoices, hiring subcontractors, hiring attorneys, ordering dumpsters and countertops.

Yet Heather loved Carmen, loved him more after thirteen years of marriage than when they had met. She loved him particularly now, after two years of living in a makeshift home and organizing the rebuild together. That didn't mean, however, that she would deny herself an occasional treat. She wasn't cheating on Carmen, not really, but she allowed herself a "cookie" from time to time, and the men were discreet, not interested in upending their lives.

What a moron Carmen was, to up and leave that way.

By the end of the week, Heather had moved all his stuff into the driveway, and on Monday, the Salvation Army came and picked everything up. He was gone, would stay gone. Over dinner, a very silent KFC dinner, Devin and Katie asked in small voices where their dad was, and Heather attempted to keep her eyes dry while she set down her fork only a tad too harshly and said, "He's not in the picture anymore." Then, as though her words had stirred up a memory, she turned around to that framed photograph with her family in the backyard of their old house. Katie and Devin were still spraying each other with water from the hose. You couldn't see their eyes, they were laughing so hard. They had the whole backyard to themselves.

J. D. EVANS

The Rain Diary

The last thing C did before going to bed was smash the mother's rain gauge against the laundry-line pole. First C swung it overhead, like an axe. She kept missing the pole, so it took a long time to break off the outer tube. When she did, the funnel slipped out and landed on the roof. It is still on the roof. C then batted the inner mensuration tube against the trunk of the mother's young olive tree, horizontally this time, like a tennis racquet. Although she has never played tennis (any more than she has used an axe), she did still shatter the inner tube into sharp, plastic triangles, which bore digits or measuring marks. On the ground, in the dirt, they seemed no different from the small leaves she'd knocked from the olive tree. C poked at them with the toe of her sneaker, and considered cleaning them up, but did not. Instead, she went into the kitchen. She poured an overfull glass of good, aged Barossa Shiraz, which she hates, and drank it, and then two more, while she watched her wife through the window. While C drank the first glass, her wife picked through the fallen olive leaves to find the plastic remains. As C started a second glass, her wife started to drop mixed handfuls of plastic, leaves, and dirt into the rubbish bag she'd taken out with her. By the time she finished, it was twilight. C had the kitchen light on. Her wife watched her finish the third glass and take the last mouthfuls straight from the gold-medal-winning bottle. C held the wine in her cheeks and threw the bottle into the sink. It did not break. C's wife dropped her handful of leaves and dirt and plastic shards, then dropped the rubbish bag. Her shoulders slumped, and she rolled her lips back into her mouth, because she should have been inside helping her wife, not outside tidying up after her. C's wife started back towards the kitchen, but by the time she got inside and slid the screen door shut behind her, C was already under the blanket in the mother's—in C's—in their—bed.

Are you OK? Do you want a hug?

I'm going to bed. That's all. I'm going to bed.

Since then, C has stayed in bed.

*

The mother kept a record of rainfall from the day she moved to her house until she threw herself into a coma. She kept it in a yellow, spiral-bound notebook, identical to earlier rain journals from Gawler and Norwood. She'd taken the notebooks with her from Gawler to the city when she and the father moved and then had taken the notebooks from Gawler and Norwood back to the country when she divorced the father. The mother kept these older notebooks in her bedroom. She kept the current notebook under the coffee table. She had just started the third page of the second volume for Nuriootpa.

When C and her wife arrived at the mother's house, her wife found the current notebook outside. The mother, having jumped into unconsciousness while hanging up the washing, had dropped it under the clothesline. C's wife dusted it off and brought it inside. She took some time deciding where to keep it—back under the coffee table? Or with the other, old volumes in the mother's, in C's, in their bedroom? C's wife knew that she would have to take charge of the rain journals. C certainly wouldn't be involved. C's wife decided to keep the record going and put the most recent volume back under the coffee table.

Thirteen winter days later, she had marked only zeroes. The next day, thirty millilitres. The next day, twenty millilitres. Then nothing for eleven days. On the twenty-seventh day, C broke the rain gauge and went to bed. Her wife might have kept the record for months even without it. The rest of the winter was entirely dry. All of spring was dry. Summer, so far, has been dry.

Why did the mother keep the record so strictly? She wasn't part of some crowd-sourcing experiment to understand rural South Australia's weather patterns. The mother typed with two fingers and jabbed, rather than touched, screens. Even if she had somehow signed up for scientific research, she would not have known how to upload data. She just recorded a number or a dash in the yellow, spiral-bound notebook, every day, using blue or black pen. It was not flawless. Almost every column was marred by crossings-out and overwriting. It was an entirely pointless but fixed part of the quasi-liturgical organisation of her widowed days. First, the rain gauge. Then, changing the date on the celluloid desk calendar. Coffee. Much consideration. Warmed milk and gluten-free cereal for breakfast (or cold milk when it was hot outside). Flick through the *Leader*'s local news section. Yes, there had been weekly interruptions for doctor's appointments and trips to take Grandad grocery shopping, monthly interruptions for seeing a movie or attending a friend's birthday party, and annual interruptions for visiting C and her wife. But still, the mother had kept the record. The neighbours had tracked the rain on the few days that the mother could not, and she got the right readings from them. It was the mother's routine.

Why such a routine? We could psychologize: she needed stability. Eight years after they'd moved to the city for the father's work, and seven years after C had left the state for hers, the father had fallen in love with an older woman. The mother had moved back to the country, so she could choose when and where she saw him, and far enough from where she'd met the father that she could choose when she wanted to remember him. Had the liturgy begun then? Perhaps. But in the interest of psychological theory, we would want to claim that it began after the father died. That would let us see it as the second stage in the mother's disease, or way of life. With her immediate family dead or distant, she felt unmoored, unrooted. The rain diary gave her a way to keep contact with reality, until she stepped down into oblivion and thus avoided our common, otherwise unavoidable alienation.

Or some such similar bullshit. It couldn't have happened that way, because the rain journal is consistently thorough. There is an entry for every day from May 1987 to July 29, 2019, when C broke the rain gauge, excepting only the days between the day the mother's aged brain stopped working and the day C's wife started recording the rain once more.

Or perhaps it could have happened as our theory suggests but can be better said: she was sad, and the old routines made her sadness bearable. But nonetheless, she had started the diary long before the sadness.

What we really want to know is, why did she start to keep the rain diary at all? Or really, why begin anything? And can C start anything, now?

The question presents itself because, since C and her wife came to live in the mother's house, which isn't theirs, but also not entirely not theirs and therefore not so strange, C has often felt that she has taken the mother's place. That is, C feels that she is the mother and always had been. It had to be this way, because all of the mother's objects and experiences need the mother's presence for them to be what they are. The small, plain mirror in the entryway needs the mother's reflection in it each morning in order to be the small, plain mirror that it seems to be. Even more than that, it needs the reflected person's perception and self-understanding to be that of the mother. It needs the reflected person to feel, even if only for that passing second, that the reflected person is the mother. And the brass platter hung on the wall as a family heirloom needs the same thing. And the two pairs of black slip-on shoes and the pair of work boots that rests on the spare square of blue carpet, so they don't muddy the hall tiles, needs the passer-by to be the mother. The reclining chair needs to be tilted back just so each evening between dinner and bedtime, so it can remain the reclining chair it has always been, and the same thing goes for the mother's strangely narrow bed, which needs the mother's hand to caress its carved pineapple finials and needs the mother's weight in it every night, so they can remain the mother's sheets, mattress, pillows, and carved pineapple finials. All these objects and C agreed that, for their sake, C would be the mother. Then, they could be themselves. And the objects agreed to let C be the mother, which would in turn legitimate C's taking possession of the objects and the house that they filled, even while the mother, the real mother, lies in a hospital bed seventy-five minutes' drive south, ignorant of the new sense of self that her objects are imposing on the new inhabitant of her small, clean home.

This kind of impersonation is strange but not surprising under these circumstances. And perhaps it explains what C has started—

explains her going to bed and staying there. Who wouldn't draw a thick, cathectic line between C's first noticing that the blob reflected in the mother's brass platter wasn't C but the mother, and C's decision, a few days later, to go to bed and to stay there? But there's no reason to think that the former caused the latter. C now admits to herself that the shape-shifting is an unconscious response to the mother's catapulting herself into a coma. And the identity diffusion has grown stronger as she has spent eighteen hours a day wrapped up in the mother's grey, pinstriped sheets, so rough compared to C's own bed linen, designed by hand in Brooklyn and made by someone else somewhere else from the greatest organic cotton ever bred, grown, harvested, cleaned, spun, weaved, cut, shaped, and sewn, artisanally. C is now used to her mother's sheets, and they have become used to her. However, C immediately enjoyed the mother's pillows. She is reassured by their down stuffing as she has never been reassured by viscoelastic polyurethane foam. As for the mattress, C's wife finds the springs so painful that she sometimes considers sleeping on the couch, but C has been spending eighteen hours or more on it every day for more than three months, and she has adjusted quite well. The bed does force C to take on the mother's preferred position for sleeping—a tight foetal bundle, on her right shoulder and hip, with her left arm resting gently on the toes of her left foot. In winter, she faced down, with the doona drawn up over her ears and forehead and wrapped under her chin. Now, in early summer, she wraps her body around the bedding instead. The skin between her legs doesn't touch; her legs don't exchange heat. C told her wife that she would be comfortable if she assumed that position every night. But C's wife is a back sleeper.

In any case, C's decision to go to bed was not caused by any wish to imitate her mother. Even though C is now the mother for the sake of the mother's objects, they will remain very different people. The mother liked to keep the roller shutters and blinds closed at all times, for privacy, and to keep the light and heat outside. C always wants them open. When she came to visit the mother, she opened them every morning. The mother would close them before they went out, and then C would then open them again when they got home. C would tell the mother that living in such darkness was unhealthy, and the mother would chide C for being wasteful of air conditioning or heating. Since C went to bed, she has become even more insistent. The blinds cannot be closed until the lights in the house have been turned off. The shutters are never to be closed at all. C must have the minimal light reflected by the moon. She must have some light, at all times, even if only enough for her to see the grainy, grayscale outline of the mother's jarrah vanity. She can accept that, because during the day there will be the warm, calming light of the north-facing windows, and she will be able to inspect the jarrah's grain and the imperfections on the bathroom door and see through to the kitchen where her wife stands to make them food or clean their dishes before she comes back to the bedroom to sit in the Eames knockoff lounge chair and read her cooking magazines or C. S. Lewis books.

When her wife does that, C feels at peace. C's wife has learned not to bring *The Economist* with her into the bedroom, or any other serious news publication. When C sees her wife reading such things, C's peace is encindered.

Unlike C, the mother never pursued a career. She stayed home after C's birth, believing that there'd be more children. There were none. When C started high school, the mother took a job as a bank teller. It kept her occupied, she said, and brought in a little money. When they moved for the father's job, she transferred branches.

She did not try to get promoted. She did not ask for pay raises. C, however, travelled to the other side of the country to feel that she was making progress. She aimed for some position of unassailable power in the administration of some university. Her dream was to go to Melbourne and then return in glory to Adelaide. Instead, she stayed in Melbourne, where she married a professor of logic. Each of them took jobs with greater remuneration. C took jobs with ever longer titles, each incorporating some new duty: Assistant and then full-on Director, of International Studies, Postgraduate Affairs, and New Media Outreach. After some time, C daydreamed about going home, where the real estate is cheap. There, she could work as a bank teller for four hours a day. She could drink good, aged Polish Hill Riesling, which, unlike good, aged Barossa Shiraz, she enjoys. C would throw herself into pottery classes. Her wife would write about conjunctions.

Those daydreams must have played some part in C's decision, in her family's decision, to return home, to do what the *Leader*'s real estate section calls a "vine-change." C had been speculating about it for so many years that even her wife, perfectly content with Melbourne's back-lane brunch spots, started to believe in this idealized better life. And, in its way, this idealized better life was always also realistic. It is true: life in Nuriootpa is unsustainable. The grapes ripen one day earlier every year. Eventually they will not even have time to set, and the vines will slowly succumb to the desert. But this is better than Melbourne. Melbourne's inhabitants will all die soon. Either externalities will be incorporated into the price of cars, petrol, roads, and avocados, or they will not. If they are, food will be prohibitively expensive, and the urbanites will starve. If they are not, the city's inhabitants will die of thirst, as all the fresh water is used to make almond milk. At least in Nuriootpa, C and her wife can get solar panels and a small windmill to power their house and a rain tank to water their vegetable patch. At least here, they know that the population hasn't already overwhelmed the infrastructure. They can know that barriers to prevent flooding have only just been installed and that they were installed in expectation of much higher rates of ever-worse flooding. Whereas anyone who lives in the city must accept that they're implicated in the destruction of the natural and civilized worlds. Of course, C is implicated too, just lying here in bed. And her wife is implicated every time she uses another piece of paper to solve some problem of logic. But there are degrees. The mother's house is carbon neutral. C and her wife decided to move because of their naïve romanticism about life in a small country town. They also moved because of their cynical realism about life in Australian cities.

In any case, just as C and her wife were thinking through these possibilities, Grandad had called to tell them that the mother had cartwheeled into brain damage. The mother, he said, would almost certainly never wake up. Having already buried his own wife, he couldn't bear the idea of burying his daughter alone. *For fuck's sake, your aunt Pogg isn't going to help, is she?* C flew out the next day. Her wife packed and joined C fifteen days later.

Do these differences of career, of expectations, of life experience, explain why C could never start to keep a rain diary but could start to stay in bed every day, apparently for good? No. Why shouldn't the extremely well-paid former Director for, among other things, Inter-Collegiate Events, Expatriate Fundraising, and Post-educational Achievement Indices keep records of the precipitation on a semiarid parcel of land in the driest state in the driest continent on earth? Why shouldn't a woman tired of contemporary workplace trends, a woman sick of the relentless verbal abstraction of management, and of everybody else's self-denial and enhanced productivity, drop it all and take up a habit as concrete, as real-world, as deeply-fucking-racinated as keeping a rain diary? As C's wife said, *Nietzsche did it while writing* The Antichrist, *so we can do it while drunk.*

But C's wife also understands that C couldn't keep up the rain diary. She doesn't explain this by using quasi-Freudian conceptions of the unconscious to reveal that C's fear of becoming the comatose mother by keeping the rain diary is, in reality, a way for C to avoid admitting that she deeply desired to become the comatose mother. She doesn't explain it by saying that C has become too alienated from herself and the natural world through years of administrative employment. She doesn't think C is lazy. No, C's wife knows that C's not keeping the rain diary is perfectly rational. The mother's day-by-day rain records kept her grounded and calm and in touch with the seasons. In C's mind, this would become a terrifying list of almost continuous zeroes (the empty set, the truth value "false"), punctuated by short strings of double-digit integers, two, three, four days in a row. Each short string would represent a flash flood here, topsoil erosion there, the destruction of the canola crop, the introduction of fungus, rot, or disease in the vines. The long lists of zeroes would symbolize a crop that never grew, fruit that never set, houses and hay bales and animals burned. C's wife knows that, to the mother, measuring rainfall was a way to stay in touch with nature, with the earth, a way to feel at one with the history of our species. The removal of the plastic inner tube, the slight head tilt needed to read off the number, the discarding of the water onto the giant, wombat-shaped rosemary bush, the replacement of the inner tube, the recording in the spiral-bound notebook—this whole process, from cock-crow to breakfast, gave a soothing structure to her life. For C, though, it would be a daily reminder that we have entered a new opposition to a new nature, much like the old one, said to be *red in tooth and claw*. Except that the original holders of this view saw nature as simply a given, something that couldn't be and never had been avoided. But for C and her wife and everyone else now, it is something that we have done to ourselves. And although we know in excruciating detail what we have done, how our hunger for energy and profit has belched forth poison—and although this should motivate us every morning to get out of bed and make a difference, should motivate us, even, to revolution—still, on getting up, we inevitably discover that there is nothing we can get to work on after finishing our breakfast. C can start something new by turning on an LED instead of a halogen bulb. At best, she can start something new by not turning on the lights at all.

Measuring rain would remind C that, like everyone else, she is entirely useless when it comes to the greatest and most necessary task of her time. So perhaps it is better for her just to withdraw. Perhaps it is better to just announce it, non placet, and spend time doing literally nothing rather than contribute, merely by eating breakfast, to the destruction of the planet.

C's wife knows that C could never have started a rain diary for one perfectly conscious, entirely rational reason: to start one would have driven her mad with hatred and self-disgust.

CARLOS LABBÉ
translated by WILL VANDERHYDEN

On Abyssal Waters

This will never end, I was reminded, hearing again the sound of the rain: as long as Earth exists there will be sowing and reaping, cold and warm, summer, winter, days, nights. This place will never be condemned because of man. Who whispered this in my ear, hour after hour, despite the headphones or rubber earplugs I always wore, the hum I learned to make with my mouth before deciding never to speak again? Silence.

In silence I stayed until—weeks later—on one of my excursions I found him sleeping with arms spread wide, naked, soaked, and barely visible out in the wetlands that now cover what was once destined to become the launchpad for the Ark. A few months ago, the venerable Joseph Hazelwood Jr. would've been proud to have created a two-million-acre swamp. Now his mind was only capable of insulting the herd of huemules that appeared in the ruins of what'd once been the house's English garden, as if they gave a shit about some old drunk running toward them flapping his arms, screaming:

Silence. And in silence I sat down beside him, bringing the

ultrasonic whistle to my lips whenever an Iberian lynx or anaconda or scavenging cóndor approached me menacingly. Days later, when my older brothers sent the Red Cross, the Salvation Army, the police, and a team from the Wild Life Foundation to find us, I suffered the insults, the judgment in the press, and getting arrested without a word; I didn't owe anyone an explanation for my father's condition. The sinuous steps of a puma stalking its prey sound like a soft, almost-imperceptible rain, and that sound accompanies me throughout my nights in this cell:

Silence. I met them in a noisy trucker bar on the highway to Johannesburg, a place I went to eat steak when I could no longer stand my father's voice, speaking to the whole world via video conference—even on the screens in our own house—about the genocide of chickens being carried out by the food industry. That night, the bar boiled with leather-clad bikers who, without warning, would start fighting each other despite having walked in hugging, with child prostitutes sobbing and locking themselves in the bathroom, with organ traffickers suddenly paralyzed in their seats, overcome with regret for the pain their business caused among the world's poor; and all of it—every fight, every sob, every whispered confession—revolved around that person, whoever they were, sitting in the corner of the bar, not eating or drinking, barely looking up at the heavy man who knelt before them, the traveling salesman spitting insults at them in multiple languages for ignoring him, the drug addict crossing the bar and handing them three baggies he'd been carrying in his pocket, or the little-known singer desperately begging them to marry him. Their answer was always the same:

Silence. I wasn't struck by their beauty. As soon as they saw me approaching, they stood up and resolutely walked out the door, into the parking lot, to my truck, where they waited for me to open the door for them. For once, I enjoyed the silence of the highway, only interrupted by the lights of a truck passing in the opposite direction, but not by the breathing of my companion, who only took their eyes off me when they lightly put their hand on my arm and asked me to pull over. In the fading light, I watched them get out of the truck, slowly cross the highway, and pick up a shaggy body that was clearly bleeding in their arms. It only dawned on me that it was a dog that'd just been hit by a car, howling in pain, when, with a precise movement, their long fingers took what was left of its head and twisted it. Whether it was compassion or cruelty that shone in their eyes, the neck's crack and the body's last breath reminded me again of the voice that wouldn't leave me in peace:

Silence. At the entrance to the park, the precious silence between us was broken; the engine revved so loudly even the flamingos and herons several miles away, on the surface of the artificial lake, were startled into flight, casting visible winged silhouettes across the fading twilight glow. A blink from my companion was all it took, and I drove the truck right to the Ark's hangar, where my father greeted us euphorically, surrounded by empty chairs and long tables uselessly set with caviar and soy milk. The press conference when he revealed the inevitable succession of events, data, and negligence that, in the coming months, would cause the oceans to rise and completely cover the surface of the Earth had just concluded. After, the throng of journalists had been invited to enter the hangar, where in front of the cameras, my father unveiled the giant space shuttle he'd christened—provocatively—the Ark, and asked them: where do you think every red cent of the vast fortune my father—the infamous Joe Hazelwood, captain of the Exxon Valdez oil tanker—received from the company's lawyers for taking the blame as the individual solely responsible for the worst ecological tragedy in human history went?

Why do you imagine that over the past thirty years I bought up small properties across South Africa until I was able to connect them all together into a single park? To what end do you believe I've captured the finest specimens of every extant species on Earth?

Silence. The cameras were immediately shut off, no one asked my father for an exclusive interview, not one of the fifty telephones, with operators standing by to answer the imperious calls of world leaders, rang. Within ten minutes, the hangar was empty; when my companion and I entered, my father was staring, a double shot of whisky in his hand, at the imposing profile of the Ark, ready at last for takeoff. He greeted us with open arms, talked at length about the risky visit he'd made to an illegal zoologist in Madagascar, whom he'd offered an exorbitant sum for the last living pair of dodos, about the stroke of luck that led him to discover a pack of marsupial wolves in a park at an exclusive clinic in Mato Grosso, about his refusal to bring aboard the Ark a unicorn some company—after employing an entire lab to genetically map the fusion of an Arabian horse with a white rhinoceros—had offered him. The same anecdotes he'd told me over and over—as we lunched on the dishes and infusions prepared daily by our Ayurvedic nutritionist and vegetarian cook—were new to me in his faltering, inebriated pronunciation: I'd never seen him drink, I realized, watching him cry out through the tears that it'd been years since the divine voice had spoken to him, never telling him when to bring the animals aboard the Ark to depart for the new planet. Suddenly my companion lifted their head and looked at my father, waiting for him to be quiet. Then, just once, before disappearing into the night, their quaking voice rose above the roll of thunder, fast approaching:

Silence. You're just like Noah: drunk on yourself and you don't know how to listen:

Even now, as I pass what days I have left in this cell, convicted of negligent homicide, I'll let the rain speak for me: Noah's Ark and the Tower of Babel are two versions of the same story; God wanted us to stop talking, to prick up our ears in the stillness, and to hear the rush of the abyssal waters that might drown us at any moment: nothing can block it out, neither my earplugs nor the hum in my mouth nor the persistent sounds I've been making with my pencil on these pages, writing again and again how we were given the rainbow in hopes that we'd give back silence.

BISHOP GARRISON

Conscription

Hellsmouth was the desolate, demolished terrain of former downtown Seattle that acted as a buffer between our camp and the Wild—the battered lands most decimated by the storms. To the leadership of the Emergency Response Department, however, Hellsmouth was no different from some bombed-out city overseas. They didn't care about nuance; they didn't have time for subtlety. In the army, I had the proper time to train and learn the terrain, but my commander never expected me to know everything overnight. Here, they needed me to be an expert. I had a history of adaptability. I'd lived too long in a world constantly collapsing around me. That was all they needed to know. I'd been to hell on earth before—in Syria against the Islamic State Reborn, in Nigeria against Boko Haram, the Natuna Islands War against the Mao Fighters funded quietly by the Chinese government. I could go again.

"Four-five?" a voice shouted into our large bunk space.

"Here, Guard Saunders!" I said.

"TOC with your team and gear in five!"

Clink and Tameer waited out on the small deck with another guard. I walked into the makeshift woodshed that was the Tactical Operations Center. It was crackling and buzzing, busy with analysts receiving reports from the field and around the world. Overlays projected the latest storm patterns. Video feeds on flat-screen televisions provided everything from pundits discussing the government's successes and losses in the Pacific Northwest and California Island to firsthand, live-action video taken from recently returned Rescuers. The scope and scale of the information being ingested and analyzed was immense.

Decker was standing in the middle of it all. He waved Saunders and me over and began immediately to speak. "New materials are finally headed our way in the next shipment. We'll have a proper operation here in a couple of months." He was Chief Guard Greg Decker, the guard-in-charge of Rescue Element 148. Decker was a former infantry colonel in the army who had spent seven years in the Federal Emergency Management Agency, FEMA, before it was dissolved in favor of the conscription structure. He wasn't God, but so far as any of us out in the Wild was concerned, he might as well have been.

I didn't respond. I let him do the talking.

"Dewy Lyle is a fan of yours. He reviewed your rescue record."

Dewy was a shorthand nickname: DEW, as in Deputy Executive Warden Tomlin Lyle. He was the head of Region One. It was Dewy Lyle's job to beat back the fires and fortify against the flooding until scientists could figure out how to control the weather. It was on him to save what life and land he could until the impossible happened. And, if a few Mids died, tragic as it might be, a few Mids died. Still, I said nothing.

He rubbed the stubble on his chin, took in a breath, and exhaled, and I could smell the stale cigar smoke and coffee that floated from his mouth. He put the cigar aside. "Yeah. I wouldn't do this normally. I know you just got back half a day ago, but we literally have nobody else. I would order some of these other newbies to head out into the Wild, but they ain't coming back. And my experienced leaders are spread out all over the place. By the time I reallocate resources, it'll be too late."

"Too late for what?"

He pointed to a large digital map projected on the table in front of us. "See this tower? Old part of downtown in Sector Four. Leonard's team is holed up in there. The area is flooded, and there is a storm hanging there that's not clearing anytime soon."

There was a large, thick, red line along the northwestern border. Fires. A chemical plant exploded a few years back, and the rain in some parts of that area now acted as an accelerant. We used a dirt and soil compound to put out the flames.

"Leonard's team was scouting new dig sites when the flash monsoon hit," he told me.

"And they can't just wait out the storm?"

Decker pressed a button on the table, and several red blobs representing unknown and unauthorized individuals being tracked by the satellite appeared on the screen. Some were moving in the direction of four blue bubbles, representing the rescue team, in the tower. Our uniforms all had trackers woven into the fabric. He was pointing to violators of the Seattle Evacuation Act. News called them bandits or gangs. The guards just called them assholes. Some were the original residents of Seattle and adjacent areas; some were Canadian border jumpers. They crossed the Northern Barrier hoping to eventually claim whatever was left of the land once the weather was stabilized.

"A couple of bandits probed the tower for hours before they took them out. The team will run out of water and ammo before this storm lifts."

So went the Wild. They were sending people guilty of speeding and stealing food for hungry families into a wasteland. They hoped that occasionally an idiot with my background might stumble his way into the wrong place at the right time. And here I was at the gates of hell. I wanted to walk away. But, as I often did, I thought of my mom. I owed her a debt that could never be repaid. Maybe other people had debts they could settle if they made it out of here alive. Maybe even one of those four bubbles on the screen. There was a chance they could find happiness or make amends in a way I could not.

"I can't order you to go. Dewy Lyle would have my ass. But believe it or not, I don't send people to their deaths, Parson. My teams have had the fewest casualties of any in this region. The rest of this country may have forgotten, but this is human life out here."

"I'll go."

"You sure?"

"Yeah, but I get to ask my guys to volunteer on this one," I replied. "They are people I think I can trust. As much as I can trust anyone I've known a few months, I guess. I'll see if they'll go."

"If they won't?"

I shrugged. "I'll go solo. I'll move faster like that, anyway."

"I couldn't ask you…"

"Don't worry, Chief Guard," I told Decker as I headed toward the door. "You didn't."

*

All conscripts carried something extra out into the Wild. Regret, anger, fear, hopelessness. I brought along guilt. Guilt that I'd been so stubborn as a kid that I had run from the only home I knew just to fight in the wars of other men. Guilt that I'd left a mother whom I knew was too drunk to make it through the days. Guilt that I knew there was something more to her drinking, even if I couldn't rightly see it at eighteen. It took my mother being on her deathbed for me to reconcile what really happened. She had shielded my brother and me from my father's abuse, and after years she was able to force my father from our home and lives forever. Sometimes it's hard for the son to see his father as the monster. I had blamed her for it all.

My adulthood—nearly twenty years of estrangement between us now reduced to a half dozen or so remaining hours. My older brother, who remained in contact with her, finally brought himself to call me. We hadn't spoken in years. In the past I would never let him mention her. Now he had the opportunity to tell me the truth.

When Mom and I reconnected, she promised me through a hacking cough that she was fine. Her doctor told me otherwise. She was far from OK. She was dying. The guilt of the twenty-year chasm between us swallowed me up, whole.

"If you can get here tonight," the doctor told me, hesitantly, "I think you'd have a good chance of saying your goodbyes. Won't be easy for her, but having family at the bedside always helps. The only thing we can do is regulate the pain at this point."

If I could get there tonight? Not a chance in hell. She was in Miles City, Montana. I was standing in the middle of my hole-in-the-wall bar in Des Moines. After the army, I'd moved to the Midlands, just as everyone does, and put all my combat pay into a bar I now owned and operated.

"I'm in Des Moines. What's that? A half a day drive?"

He went quiet on me. I imagined some stocky, middle-aged man rubbing the silver hairs on his chin. "Well, son, she could maybe make it to morning. She talked about seeing her boys for some time. She's determined to do just that, but the odds are only about 50 percent on it. I'm sorry to say that's the best news I can give you."

Fifty-fifty. A goddamned coin flip.

Plane tickets to Montana were astronomical. I didn't have that kind of cash. And driving, if I even made it in time, she'd likely be gone as I pulled into the parking lot. But I felt like I owed it to her. I owed it to her to try.

I ran back to my apartment, packed a small bag, and hit the road.

After the storms appeared on the East and West Coasts, the people who could afford to make the move to the Midwest did so and quickly rebranded it the Midlands. The sprawling urban landscapes of Iowa and Nebraska didn't really begin to disappear until I neared south-central South Dakota, the outer edge of the Isolation Zone, the Iso, as we called it. The signs alongside the highway were illuminated in a soft, halogen glow with everything from religious rhetoric to legal mandates.

Repent now! For the Storms Signal the Second Coming of the Lord and Savior!

Followed by a more official warning from the Montana & North Dakota Highway Patrols beginning a mile or so down the road:

You are now 100 miles—50 miles—25 miles from an area of heightened criminal activity. Penalties for all criminal actions are dramatically increased in this region. Be advised!

I was officially entering the Iso. Five minutes away from the Montana state line, a good thirty miles into the zone at that point, I'd been driving throughout the night. I was out near a town called Sully Springs and was too tired to be driving. The adrenaline was coursing through my veins, colluding with an abundance of caffeine. Although I was alert, I wasn't at my best, wasn't being as careful as I knew I needed to be. I was just speeding for a few seconds, but one second was really all it took.

The red and blue lights were in my rearview before I had time to think about the brakes. I slowly pulled over to the shoulder of the road with the police car tightly in tow. The patrolman was alone, but I could hear swirling routers of a drone hovering somewhere above. He slowly approached my side of car. The sun was in the distance, beginning its climb into the sky behind us. I could see in the side mirror the officer had his hand resting on his sidearm.

"License and registration," he flatly requested.

"Yes, of course." I handed over the documents.

He mumbled a laugh under his breath. "Middie, what the hell are you doing speeding out here? They don't teach you to obey the goddamn law in fancy-ass Des Moines?" There was a sneer in his tone. A little bit of spittle escaped his lip. He wiped it away with his free hand.

I'd only heard the slur once or twice before in person. A guy from the Iso had just moved to Des Moines and used it when a young woman refused his advances. It was what people from the Iso called us, those who relocated to the middle of the country once the storms began to intensify and tore both coasts apart. The storms appeared due to our government's continued lack of action in confronting global warming. Those in the Iso saw the rest of the country as children running scared and unwilling to fight for them. We were leaving people behind who didn't have the means to get away from the wasteland themselves. It didn't matter if you were originally from there, like me. Now you were a part of the "metropolitan Midwest." We were all the same. We were all cowards to them.

"Middie?" It was a reflex, a momentary lapse. There was something in his tone—part slur, part accusation. It didn't matter that he and I had the same dirty-blond hair, or that his eyes were just a shade off my own deep blue. I was a Midlander, an "other." I was different to him. Not a someone, but a *something*. It was easy to resent a person when you saw him as less than human. For thirty years that was what the people of the Iso had been conditioned to do, and before that, Americans did it to people they deemed to be outsiders for the entirety of the country's history. They were told we saw them as something different, so they should feel free to reciprocate.

I wanted to apologize. I was going to steer the conversation in a more hospitable direction and explain what I was doing there in the first place. That was when he ordered me out of my car at gunpoint. Seconds later, my face was pushed against the asphalt as I pleaded for a reprieve. I remember hearing the siren of another police car approaching just before feeling the butt of his pistol striking my temple, knocking me unconscious.

I knew better. I should have known better. I'd pay a lifetime for a momentary lapse in judgment.

*

From the TOC, we walked back toward our recently upgraded living quarters: Compartmentalized Housing Units, CHUs, resting on a nearby hill just out of the way of any standing water. The guards patrolled the Rescuer area, but, to date, only three people had ever attempted escape from a conscription camp. At least, those are the ones who made it into the record. It was commonly believed that many more were killed on the spot out in the Wild for dereliction of duty. If you wanted to run, you could try, but the nearest habitable area was hundreds of miles away through the worst conditions possible. If another team or guards didn't get you, the Wild definitely would. You were better off trying to stay alive patrolling through Hellsmouth as ordered. At least then you had a chance of surviving long enough to enjoy your freedom, if freedom ever came.

We stood out in the open area halfway between our bunks and the TOC. I explained the situation to my teammates, Clink and Tameer. Clink jumped at the chance to sign up. Anything for him to pass the time, he told me. Tameer was a harder sell because he had common sense. He could probably just ride out his time supporting the TOC or joining scouting missions for dig sites. Why the hell should he risk his life—of his own volition—for some jackasses who got caught in the storms and who should have known better?

I didn't have a good answer or enough time to draft up a decent lie. So, I went with a hard truth instead. "Because they wouldn't do it for you."

"What?"

"They would not do the same for you. A lot of people out here lost their humanity, and the rest of the nation doesn't want to think about our existence. They're dealing with enough of their own shit without having to go through the pain of thinking about us too. So, they just don't. Empathy is always the first thing to go. The government just made it easier, making all of us convicts."

"Hell, then, Four-five, why would I turn around and go help people that wouldn't help me?"

"Because you're better than they are. You've survived this long, and you'll survive some more."

Tameer stared at me. The tension around us was palpable. After a while he told me to get lost and headed for the CHUs. Fair response. He barely knew me, and none of us knew the scout team at all. It was a gamble, and I was just unlucky. Just as he began walking away, I thought I would try a Hail Mary.

"If nothing else, there's probably some time served wrapped up in it."

He didn't say anything. He continued walking as though he hadn't heard me. I thought to repeat it but figured it was best to just let things be. I turned back toward the TOC; a light drizzle had begun. Clink was in tow behind me, making a bunch of noise. We were almost to the porch before I heard Tameer shouting.

"How much time served?"

"Three years if you make it back." Decker appeared in the doorway, the sun beginning to rise in the distance behind him.

"You'll put that in writing?"

"I'll do you one better. I'll approve it right now." Decker lifted a tablet in his hand.

Tameer stood, silently considering the offer. After a few moments, he responded. "Respectfully, I want to see you authorize it on a tablet with my own eyes, Chief Guard."

"Smart man," Decker told him. He let Tameer catch up to us before he continued. "Current conditions are slow moving, and you'll be carrying extra ammo, water, and MREs. It could take you up to a half a day to get out there, even slower coming back. Important thing is to get to the team. They're running low on power too, so we may lose radio contact. Move as fast as you reasonably can."

Decker punched a few buttons on the tablet and presented it to Tameer. He quickly read through it and placed his thumb against the bottom left corner. Decker did the same, and the device chimed. "Good luck, gents. We'll be in touch."

As we followed Guard Saunders to the gate, Tameer leaned over and asked me, "Do you really believe all that empathy and humanity horseshit you were selling, Four-five?"

I shrugged. "If I'm going to make it out here, I've got to believe in something. It's been raining here for a month straight. The rain can't last forever, right?"

"I'm not so sure," he told me.

In silence from there on, we marched toward the gates leading out into Hellsmouth and the Wild.

*

I woke up as I was being jerked out of the back of the squad car in Miles City. Moments later a medic was tending to my wound. He told me I had suffered a minor concussion while resisting arrest. No real damage done. I would be fine to see the magistrate. A glimpse in the mirror and a light touch of the bandage displayed wet, crimson on my fingertips. But by their standards, I was OK to see the judge. I was marched to a nearby Plexiglas telephone station. A woman I didn't know sat opposite from me. She introduced herself as my court-appointed counsel. I could wait and get my own lawyer if I wanted, but it might delay the timing for my case. I'd overheard rumors of the artificial backlog the Iso purposefully maintained to encourage defendants to relinquish rights to move them more quickly through the system. I wasn't going to go sit for a year or longer in arguably the worst jail in the world to wait on an attorney I couldn't afford. A public defender was fine.

Mine was around my age, with large brown eyes and a grimace. Pam Winters. I told her the full story. She leveled with me, saying I was likely screwed, but she'd do what she could. The entire conversation lasted about three minutes. Guards pulled me and a group of other defendants out of lockup and ushered us into a courtroom with faux-wood laminate paneling on the walls and onlookers whispering in the gallery.

Senior Magistrate Georgina Howard of the Montana Criminal Court: she was in her midsixties maybe, a Black woman with dark-brown skin and chestnut hair transitioning to deep silver. She stared harshly at each of us through round, wire-rimmed glasses. The Montana Emergency Response Act, informally referred to as the Conscription Act, meted out draconian penalties for once-mundane violations. In turn, the law provided that defendants could opt to serve a dramatically reduced sentence at the needs of the state in battling the effects of severe weather.

Legislators argued that this court existed to expedite processing and ensure that the potential influx of criminal defendants would indeed receive a speedy trial. What the corporations lobbied for, however, was the fastest possible increase of able-bodied men and women to maintain a stable pool of healthy emergency responders known as Rescuers. With the climate drastically changing the way it had in many parts of the country, the storms and the fires and Mother Nature were all winning. Time was money, so anything that would get people into the field faster to protect corporate interests was good for the bottom line. Multiple corporate entities from social media firms to textile manufacturers and large pharmaceutical companies owned a stake in the plethora of private prisons established in the wake of Conscription. Stocks of the prison industry were a part of everyday portfolios. Retirement funds and savings for college tuition were tied to the profitability of American incarceration like at no other time in history.

I was one of ten in a block-format trial deemed constitutional by the Supreme Court. The magistrate technically handled our cases independently, but for the sake of time, she would read her procedure out to all of us collectively and go down the line for questioning. First came the pleas: in unison, not guilty. This initial hearing was simply a pretense to weed out physically unacceptable candidates. We were all healthy, and some of us just severely unlucky. We then went through a second round of individual questioning between the magistrate and our representation. Then my turn came.

"Defendant Bryce Parson, you are changed with the vehicular crime of speeding beyond the posted limit exceeding ten miles per hour as well as—"

As well as what? I thought.

"—resisting arrest. The arresting officer reports that you initially failed to obey orders to exit your vehicle?"

He called me Mid, and I responded. An affront to his authority. I knew better. Before I could reply, Winters lightly patted me on the arm and responded.

"Magistrate, may it please the court?"

"By all means, Miss Winters. You have something to address with respect to this charge?"

"With all due respect to Officer Wright, the fine representative of the law we all know him to be, my client was in a distraught state given the exigent circumstances that brought him to our community. He simply requested clarification of the officer's request. It was not meant as an action to resist arrest in the least."

Magistrate Howard gazed down as she scrolled through the tablet with the tip of her finger. She glanced back up to us momentarily and then down again at the pad. Still affixed on the device she asked, "Exigent circumstances, you say, Miss Winters? I see no mention of them in the record."

Winters scrolled through her own tablet's notes. "Yes, Your Honor. The defendant was traveling to see his mother in Miles City.

He was informed by her physician, Dr. Michael Reese of Miles City General, at approximately seven last evening, Central time…"

"Central time?"

Oh, shit.

"Remind me, Counselor, where is the defendant from?"

Winters cleared her throat. "Iowa, Magistrate. Specifically, Des Moines."

"Goddamn Middie!" someone shouted from the gallery.

Magistrate Howard slammed her gavel. "The next outburst, offensive or otherwise, I will immediately clear this courtroom, and the perpetrator will find themselves in contempt of my court." Then, back to Winters, she continued: "Defendant Parson is from Iowa, but his mother resides here?"

"Your Honor, Defendant Parson is originally from Miles City but enlisted in the army at the age of eighteen. Following his honorable service, he relocated to Iowa. He and his mother maintained a strained relationship but had begun reconciliation in recent months. He was not made aware of the severity of her illness until very late in its progression. An email with biometric signature submitted in the file as affidavit one from Dr. Reese supports this fact."

Magistrate Howard leaned back in her chair for a moment, closing her eyes in an apparent act of contemplation. She removed her glasses and massaged the bridge of her nose. Returning the spectacles to their position, she waved to Winters to approach the bench. Then she pointed at me.

"You too, Defendant Parson. Come on up."

A bailiff moved closer alongside the bench but remained out of an earshot.

"You're a vet and grew up in the zone? Miles City?"

"Yes, Your Honor," I answered.

"You knew better than to speed through here, Mr. Parson."

"I did, Your Honor. I didn't mean to. I didn't want to rush at all to get here, but he said it was a fifty-fifty shot she'd make it to morning."

She nodded. "Do you know how long you've been in custody?"

"About three hours, ma'am."

"What does that mean for your mother's chances?"

I shrugged but couldn't fight the tears welling up. My voice was cracking under the pressure of the moment. "I…I honestly don't know. It was a coin flip to start. She may already be dead."

Magistrate Howard nodded once more. Winters stared down at the floor.

"Do you know how this criminal court works, Mr. Parson?"

"I have an idea, ma'am."

"You'll note there is no prosecutor assigned to or present in this courtroom. The way the MERA was written, even though under the color of law you're innocent until proven guilty, there is a certain presumption that, faced with a possible mandatory sentence, you will choose to enter into the Emergency Response Department program instead. You're free to decline the option I'm going to give you, but if you do, there will be consequences, Defendant."

I got the message. You're free to plead not guilty. You're fine to challenge the state but do so at your own risk. Fight the system, but you should know that the system will fight you back, hard.

"I understand, Your Honor."

She pursed her lips and glanced to Winters, who was still fixated on some imaginary spot at her feet, then back to me. Finally, with another wave of her hand she ordered us to return to our positions.

"Defendant Parson, given the severity of your crime but the lack of a prior record, it's the recommendation of this court that you receive the minimum sentence of five years in a facility operated in conjunction with the laws and procedures of the Montana state penal system."

Five fucking years. Six months for every mile over the speed limit. Justice served.

"By my authority as a duly appointed magistrate of this court, I am obligated to offer you an alternative to your time of incarceration. Under Title 102 of the Montana State Code, also known as the Montana Emergency Response Act, you are offered a term of service to the state as a Rescuer in support of activities combatting the extreme weather conditions experienced by our neighboring states in the Pacific Northwest."

That was how the states made their money: selling off our term of service to their sister states fighting through the storms. She took a moment to look down at her tablet, but I surmised she recited this speech regularly enough to have committed it to memory. The action was more theater than necessity.

"Conditioned on passing both a physical and psychiatric exam, should you agree to participate in a term of service within the program, I am authorized discretion in determining the appropriate length of that term. The location of the term of service, however, will be determined by the penal system at the needs of the Department of Emergency Response. Should you decline this opportunity to serve this state and your country admirably, your case will be remanded to the municipal court and scheduled in accordance with the procedures and laws of Montana. You have two minutes to confer with your counsel and provide this court with your response."

There it was. Conscription. Its single, constant selling point for the masses was redemption. If you made it through your term—or all of them, if you were a multi-termer—you'd be lauded, respected as a champion having served his or her time in service back to the nation. If you remained on a "criminal's path," however, there would be no acceptable place in society. You were a pariah, shunned, doors slammed in your face. You could die a hero out in the Pacific Northwest, ravaged by the increased severity of storms, or die on the streets of the Midlands as a coward following years of imprisonment. Where was the choice in that?

Winters leaned in to whisper something to me, but this time it was me patting her on the arm.

"I accept the term of service, Your Honor."

Without emotion, Magistrate Howard replied, "Acknowledged and so ordered. You are hereby remanded to the custody of the state of Montana, which will determine your service location in a period not to exceed thirty days following examination."

Magistrate Howard read something on her tablet, then paused, perhaps out of pity or exasperation over my carelessness or some combination thereof. With a deep breath, she looked me straight in the eyes and began again.

"Given the exigent circumstances, your previous service to this nation, and your lack of any criminal record whatsoever, I'm going to go out on a limb for you, Defendant Parson. The typical term of service for a minimum five-year sentence is two and a half years. I'm giving you one year. You make it through your term, and your criminal record will be expunged. Your emergency service record, however, will remain intact."

That was unheard of. No one's criminal records went away, not anymore. It was easier to get longer terms of service for repeat offenders. Yearly recidivism rates had a very real effect on the stock market now.

"Your Honor?"

"You heard correctly, Miss Winters, but don't get used to the mercy of this court. Your client with his very specific history and situation has found me in a welcoming position. You may not find me so warm in our afternoon session."

"Understood, Your Honor, but may we have one small request from the court?"

Magistrate Howard nodded.

"Defendant Parson's mother. We'd like to see if the court might allow him a brief, supervised visit to be at her bedside before he departs for his term of service."

"I'm sorry, Miss Winters, but the defendant's file was just updated in the last couple of minutes. You'll have it on your pad momentarily, I'm sure. Mrs. Parson passed away a couple of hours ago. I'm sorry for the defendant's loss."

Winters and the magistrate had another short exchange after that. I'm not really sure what they said. My mind was elsewhere, far off. I don't know where exactly, to be honest; it just wasn't in that courtroom. One of the deputies came and took me by the arm, and Winters said something else to me. I think it was an apology, and something about the best anyone could do. I thought that was what she said. Again, I was there, but not there.

*

A tactical wet suit with full internal biometrics kit and temperature control. Five MREs broken down into main meals, bread, and all the jalapeno cheese I could scam. I hated myself for loving that garbage so much. Waterproof boots. Standard-issue universal camouflage uniform with smart thread technology for pattern changes on the fly. Waterproof watch cap, gloves. Smart goggles with the Heads-Up Display. I kept my Rescuer identification card in my right breast pocket per SOP, a family photo in a resealable bag in my left. It was faded, edges torn. A trip to a lake whose name I could no longer remember. My mother and my father and my brother and me. We're all smiling. We were happy. Only picture like that I ever remember seeing, before my father decided it was easier to find work and survive without a family to feed. Before I blamed my mother for his disappearing. Before I took the first chance I could to do the same thing he did. The guilt of that act was strapped to me just as securely as the rifle. I marched forward for her, for me, hoping that I could forgive myself if I could ever make my way out of the Wild. Hoping that there was a better day on the other side of it all.

ANTHONY S. JAMES

The Summer on the Brink

All across Britain—or so the evening news said each day—travel was disrupted by road surfaces melting in the heat and railway lines buckling as the glare of the sun expanded and twisted the metal. *And this is the country that invented the Industrial Revolution.* The words kept repeating themselves in Karen's head like a tune that intruded and irritated her. Sometimes the phrase was so insistent that it frightened her with the throbbing apparition of mental illness. At other times she felt a grateful relief that they had no plans to travel anywhere and no wish to travel. Last summer the hottest day ever had been recorded in Britain, a record that stood only until this summer. The world revolved and revolved, parched and grinding, around them and past them, as they sat in a garden, vulnerable, isolated…

*

Kathy had taken to sitting naked in the garden in the afternoons and the evenings as the heat of the July days went on and on. Karen made faintly disapproving jokes and kept circling back to the refrain, "Really, we are two sixty-one-year-old women…" Kathy just laughed at her. Karen herself could never go further than taking off everything except a thin, loose cotton dress, although she knew quite well that they could not be seen in this corner between the tall wooden fence and the back of the house. Sometimes they left the radio or television on inside the house beyond the half-open glass patio doors. They talked or read and sipped wine. Sometimes Kathy looked at musical scores, some of them compositions by her students.

Now she looked up and wrinkled her nose at the book Karen held. "*The History of Man*—a nice, nonsexist, enlightened title…"

"Yes, well, I started reading it when I was a kid, and I've never finished it."

Karen looked away, gazing at the big trees at the end of the garden, trying to press her thoughts into words. The sunlight coming through the leaves was green and seemed even hotter because of it rather than being softened and cooled. *Panoply*… Yes, the trees were in the full panoply of summer leaf—they immediately suggested that word to her mind. She suddenly knew that the next time she walked down a street on a bitter winter day and the word *panoply* came to her, she would see an image of green leaves and trees in summer. She went on: "I never finished it. But the book excited me—this American anthropologist starting with early prehistory and going on right down to the present day, well, the 1960s, the present day when he wrote the book. And he could explain it all—stone axes and atom bombs, the Catholic Church and cave paintings—by exactly the same methods."

"And that's when you wanted to be a historian?" Kathy was leaning forward, tracing the rim of a wine glass with one finger, not merely being polite but genuinely trying to understand. Always the seriousness, the awareness, the sensitivity toward others: *total Kathy*. She looked totally comfortable with her own nakedness too, in a way that Karen could not be, not out here.

"The book was part of it. It was summer 1971, when we went to Wales, because your parents let me come along."

"I got ill for three days. They were terrified it was meningitis—all that fever and vomiting. No one ever found out what it was." Kathy took a sip of wine, and a droplet fell just above her breasts, weaving its way down until she wiped it away with her thumb.

"Yes…that summer, and just like this summer, *our boys*, our national team, *our heroes* were somewhere or other, expecting to win by some kind of divine right and living on the memory of past glory." Karen tilted her head back at the room inside the patio doors where the television seemed to be muttering to itself, making fragments of the early evening news just audible.

"'Then ye returned to your trinkets; then ye contented your souls/with the flannelled fools at the wicket or the muddied oafs at the goals,'" Kathy quoted.

"What made you think of Kipling? He's been de-platformed, like Germaine Greer—except that he's dead. Anyway, students won't put up with him these days. It's part of our new freedom. He causes students stress."

"Strangely, someone set some of that poem to music. Some of my students performed it. But yes, you're right, that was thirty years ago, before we became so free."

"He *was* a racist bastard, of course. But very few people said harsher things about this country than he did." Karen looked down at the book she held. She had touched up the creases in the blue-and-black paperback and covered it with clear plastic…published in 1969… And the price on the back: 10'6, *ten-and-six*, ten shillings and sixpence...the old, pre-decimal currency of Britain, incomprehensible to the rest of the world and occasionally used to cheat American GIs stationed in London during the Second World War. She looked up at Kathy almost fearfully, almost in panic. "I think I feel as people must have felt in the summer of 1914 or in the summer of 1939—on the brink."

"That bad? A group of overprivileged right-wing bigots exploiting the anger and fear of those who feel left out and left behind? Everything will get meaner, poorer, and less efficient of course. But you think it's that bad?"

Karen was not really seeing the book in her lap anymore...but there was the road to Akureyri, eight hours with a three-year-old by bus, the long-distance bus with the strangely high wheels for driving through stretches of floodwater on the road. And the treeless, deep-plunging green upon green of the wild meadows of near-Arctic central Iceland, pricked by the yellows and whites of flowers and cut by swerving and on-gushing streams, white-silver, down into the valleys, down from the uplands, underground steam rising distantly on moorland. The mountains were sharp in impossible dream shapes as they drew nearer to the northern coast, like a legend or a story of another planet. Finally, away east toward the interior, blank white against the black basalt, there were the glaciers... In Akureyri, as at Thingvellir, the summer sunlight shifted over the land, appearing and disappearing like a smile, and in June the wind from the Arctic brought winter chill into summer warmth. Then the chill blew away and the heat of the sun returned... *"My earliest memory, Mummy, is you climbing up the rocks alongside a waterfall in Iceland."* Emily. Emily. Bereavement without death. *Your earliest memory, twenty-nine years ago. And for the last five years, I haven't heard your voice or seen your face... Bereavement without death, bereavement by my daughter's decision, mother-killing by email:* It's too late now for any explanation or apology. I don't want any dialogue. *So, all that was us has melted away. While the glaciers are melting, we are killing the glaciers.* Karen looked up and saw that Kathy was watching her, still waiting for a reply.

"I *do* feel we're on the edge of something, yes, here and all across the world."

"I see." Kathy bit her lip, then spoke with absolute solemnity. "Well, you are the historian."

"Do you remember the river near the place where we stayed in Wales? There *used* to be a river. We walked along it in summer..."

"Yes, that's right..." Kathy stared at the shafts of green light from the sun through the leaves igniting a little core of brilliance in the wine in her glass. "There was the beautiful boy, older than us, always mending his boat."

"It's not just the overprivileged right-wing bigots." Karen was struggling to make herself understood, shifting direction. "It's not just the political stuff. The natural world was always *there*, you know? Beautiful or cruel, but always there, always constant, whatever we did. And now it seems sick, diseased. The light seems poisoned. On the morning I gave birth to Emily, there was a frost... All through that winter it had been damp and almost warm, as if the world was running a fever. And *that* was more than thirty years ago."

"Well, look at us sitting in a garden. We're not saving the world."

"I suppose we can say we've reached people during our lives, young people." Karen, pausing just at that moment, did indeed look at the two of them. She felt as if her consciousness was lifted upward toward the roof of the house. Two women, aged sixty-one, friends for more than fifty years: Kathy, with the sunlight catching her butter-on-brass hair, never yet touched by gray, lounging naked, the life enhancer, never speaking cruelly about anyone; Karen, in her white cotton dress, her coffee-and-ash hair cut in a severe bob, an aging, scathing-tongued academic, long feared as a ferocious bitch by her male colleagues who were relieved to see her slide into semiretirement.

"And meanwhile, 'The wind rises, we must try to live.'" Kathy shrugged her bare shoulders.

"Another poem set to music?" Karen felt a quiver of uneasiness crawl along her ribs as a gust of wind did rise just then; a few early fallen leaves came rustling over the paving stones. The wind was hot, like the air that rose into her face when she opened an oven door.

"Yeah, translated from French… It took *us* a long time to live as we wanted to."

"We didn't know how we really felt." Karen was now calm, contented. This was The Conversation, and they had it frequently. It had become almost a ceremony, a ritual.

"I knew. But you got married, twice, and you had Emily to consider. And I knew how you really felt too. That evening you came over to my place to tell me about that young woman Molly, your student. You were furious that she had been labeled schizophrenic. I was wearing a miniskirt, and you kept looking and trying to see if I had any knickers on under it."

"I did not!"

"Well, today, at least," Kathy said, "you don't have to look very hard to ascertain that fact."

*

Karen had often walked with Kathy by the river in the valley that opened just beyond the tiny rented cottage. The shallows of the river receded into drily whispering reed beds in places, or the banks shelved down in little beaches of pebbles. There was an old and picturesque wooden bridge. In the fresh and blue-white and glittering mornings, they had several times passed the youth with the boat. He was very tanned and had skin that was satiny with the moisture of sweat and river water, dressed only in a pair of cutaway jeans, working and working away at mending or improving an old wooden rowing boat, proud, engrossed. He was perhaps seventeen. Karen and Kathy were just approaching fifteen. He always ignored them, but Karen repeatedly felt the need to look down and quicken her steps as she passed him... It was the summer in which she felt both defiantly confident and vulnerable, her feelings flayed raw, cringing from any further hurt and humiliation.

At the end of term examinations, Karen had come far and away top of her year in history and English in the girls' grammar school she and Kathy attended. Then there was the matter of the presentation she was chosen to give to the entire school assembly. And there was the matter of Miss Ritchie, the English teacher Karen adored: tall, beautiful, with a sophisticated narrowing of her eyes, a naughty pucker at the corner of her mouth, and a dramatic way of sweeping back her long black hair. Miss Ritchie praised Karen, treated Karen almost as an equal, and Miss Ritchie supported Karen enthusiastically and seemed to understand her. She also understood that the women's movement and women's liberation seemed to be in the news every day and in the very air, as was the sudden awareness of how much the earth, the oceans, and the air were being poisoned. Karen had discovered Germaine Greer's *The Female Eunuch* and brought her battered paperback copy to school. Of course Karen should go ahead and give the presentation on women's liberation. Miss Ritchie would give Karen her full support. Feeling invincible at home in her bedroom, Karen stood in front of a mirror and read and reread her presentation aloud, a girl in a school uniform, white blouse and dark skirt, hair tied back, her face earnest and severe. She quoted from *The Female Eunuch* and pointed out the link between the beauty and garment industries and the liberation of women. She steadily read the passage about cruelty to baby seals, moles, muskrats, and other animals. Karen read out loud: "...the eyes of a Biafran child have an unmistakable message. But while electronic media feed our love for our own kind, the circumstances of our lives substitute propinquity for passion."

Then came the morning of the presentation, a blue June morning already touched by the gray powdering of a heat haze. It was just before morning assembly, and Karen was tensely arranging her notes in her form room. Miss Ritchie was also Karen's form mistress, and just now she was perched stylishly on her desk at the front of the room, one leg swinging, almost one of the girls. Then the headmistress arrived unexpectedly. Miss Mathews, a short and athletic woman with round glasses, always showing the edge of her underslip below the hem of her skirt, something of which she seemed quite unaware, habitually speaking rapidly, hurriedly, looking just beyond the girl she spoke to as if she was already on her way to somewhere else, now came straight over to Karen. She picked up Germaine Greer's *The Female Eunuch.*

"Just why have you brought *this* book into school?"

Karen looked over at Miss Ritchie expectantly and with a glint of triumph. A long pause.

"Dear me!" Miss Ritchie said easily. "I'm afraid that Karen is taking being mature and grown-up rather far these days."

Karen felt suddenly alone, as if everything and everyone had dissolved and she stood in a huge, featureless desert.

Now it was the third day of Kathy's mysterious illness, and she was at last improving. Karen came down to the river alone in the Sunday evening stillness. The sun was low, but the heat still pressed on the air; it was still too hot for the mosquitoes to start biting. Even the sound of the river seemed quieter, softer because of the heat. Karen walked on and on, her own thoughts spinning around her. The wooden bridge rose up further ahead, black against a lilac sky. Shadows were deepening here down in the valley, getting thicker. Karen came around a bend in the river and stared—blinking, startled, confused—at an open stretch of short grass beyond the pebble beach, now in deep shadow. For a moment she thought she was looking at some large animal, perhaps a black-and-white cow, down on its side on the grass. Then she knew. The youth who tinkered with his boat, his cutaway jeans now removed, and a young woman were on the grass. The white patches were underwear lying on the grass, or pushed up or down, still clinging to their bodies. The young woman was perhaps twenty, two or three years older than him. Karen stared at her with fascination, feeling that she could not turn away or turn back or even lower her eyes. What startled Karen most was that all the movement, the energy and the passion came from the young woman, while the young man lay still beneath her. For more than a minute, Karen watched the couple, who were completely unaware of her. She had the sensation of vibrating wires fastening her feet to the ground. In those moments she also felt her body change physically. When she finally turned and ran back the way she had come, she felt that she was no longer the same person. She knew that she could never forget what she had seen. She also knew that she wanted to kill Miss Ritchie, quite calmly and seriously. She never would, but she wished to—she would go on hoping that the English teacher would die violently and painfully. These twin forks of knowledge, red and black and jagged, thrust their way into Karen's consciousness for many years afterward... She and Kathy returned to the river and the valley in the summer of the following year. To her relief, or was there also disappointment, she never saw the young man with the boat or the young woman ever again. By the following summer, the wooden bridge had collapsed.

Forty-five years later the river began to dry up every summer.

*

Karen, sitting in the garden of Kathy's house, became aware that Kathy had gone inside and turned off the television but had now returned with another bottle of wine. Some music was playing very softly. Karen thought that it was Elgar but could not be sure. She looked down at the book in her lap again: 10'6—*ten-and-six*—ten shillings and sixpence... Then she thought of the wooden bridge that had collapsed long ago. And the river that was a dry bed of stones each summer, just as her life as a mother had been declared over without her death, declared void by her daughter's email.

"There's no way back anymore," Karen said. After waiting a moment, she looked up at Kathy. But Kathy was asleep, naked and content, one hand trailing beside her deck chair.

The sun was lower now, and the panoply of summer leaf had turned black green against the sky. Another restless tug of wind and the early fallen leaves moved in a whispering scuttle over the ground. This had been the house of Kathy's parents. Long ago, Kathy and Karen had climbed into one of the trees with their teddy bears and dolls, playing Noah and his wife escaping the Flood with all the animals of the earth.

VIVIAN FAITH PRESCOTT

The Places She Journeys

Sámi Woman approaches fishermen with a star map traveling across her face. The dock rocks beneath her rubber-booted feet, and she hollers down the finger to the man tying an aluminum boat up to the cleat on the bull rail. From a distance, she holds up her waterproof clipboard in the light rain to let them know she's a familiar fish technician collecting data. "Hey, how are you? Catch anything?" she yells.

She knows better than to approach anyone nowadays without asking permission, even though it's her job with the Alaska Department of Fish and Game where she's worked every summer for a decade. Sámi Woman pulls down her cloth mask, the one her auntie made for her early in the pandemic, and she smiles like a shapeshifter emerging with an old story ready to tell. She pulls the mask up over her mouth and nose again, and as she speaks, the gold stars on an Alaskan night sky appear to dance.

The fisherman doesn't answer her, and Sámi Woman slow-walks toward the boat, passing the old troller with the peeling white paint and the rain-filled skiff with the crab pot next to it with the rotting bait inside. *Note this life history*, she thinks. Recent declines in salmon body size impact ecosystems and fisheries. Trollers and permits are for sale. People are moving off island. *Salmon are part of your story—remember how the woman in your oral tradition slipped into the sea and became a salmon. Recall the narrative you're recording now. Learn how the salmon and this rainy summer story link through major selective forces like climate change and harvest.*

Sámi Woman approaches the aluminum boat cautiously, and the fisherman with a red bandana over his face holds out his hand like a traffic cop and says, "Stop. We have an elder at home."

She stops. "OK," she says. She points to her mask and cocks her head as if to reassure him. He shakes his head.

Sámi Woman knows better than to push. These people she lives among are like the salmon; they're integral to her ecosystem components and contribute to her well-being, primarily as sources of her food security and cultural connection. They are *her* people. The fisherman is likely a cousin's cousin. Her family has been here for six generations living among the Tlingit.

The fisherman keeps his bandana up, and she imagines he's smiling back. He holds up three fingers, then two, then one. He says, "Three fish: two halibut and one salmon."

She asks for measurements, and he gives her a typical gesture with widespread arms. She laughs. Elders have told her that salmon are getting smaller. Local fishermen complain they're losing money now; there's less flesh recovery rates. More skin and bones and viscera, less muscle. Body size is important for reproduction and fitness, and there's predator-prey dynamics—there's an increase in resident killer whale pods around these islands, and they're preying on larger salmon. Climate is affecting the size of sheep, cod, and birds around the world. Local elders used to catch seventy-pounders out by the old city dock, and there used to be big kings at Bradfield Canal. Sixty-pounders used to win the king salmon derby. Now there's no derby. It's been canceled for two years.

The fisherman yells the fish lengths back at her, and she jots down salmon measurements, notes the species in her chart. Sámi Woman asks about missing adipose fins from hatchery fish, if any, despite not being able to get close enough because of COVID-19 to set eyes on the fish. She senses irritation and thanks him and turns, waving away the mist and the small black flies and the smell of the stinky crab pot at the same time.

Sámi Woman shakes the rain from the sleeve of her raincoat. She loves working outside of a four-walled office, and the job allows time off in the winter so she can make her traditional medicines.

She looks down at the clipboard with a familiarity of interpreting patterns—king salmon have declined an average of 8 percent in body length and coho over 3 percent, and then there're the pinks and the sockeye that're declining in size too. Somewhere, someone, later, will interpret this story like a noiade—a shaman—to reflect the large number of populations sampled from diverse habitats across Alaska, from temperate rainforest ecosystems in Southeast Alaska to subarctic ecosystems farther north. It's coming—the winter king fishery will likely be shortened, the catch limited, then the summer fishery will be no longer, and worse, maybe someday salmon will be extinct. Hopefully, after she's long dead.

Sámi Woman turns from the data collecting and walks toward the red lawn chair she's set out to await the scows and the skiffs and the runabouts and leisure yachts. Her stomach growls, and she senses the link between the salmon, human, and the bear, her relatives who understood the forces of nature. She's collected this data all summer, but it's chewing her gut now like she's a skinny bear in hyperphagia, the young ones who've wandered into town recently, tumbling garbage cans and dumpsters and chasing dogs, and searching for salmon in empty smokehouses. This gnawing and knowing are familiar. It's an ancestral knowledge inside of her, but she doesn't know how to name it, only knows how it feels to seek out knowledge from long ago without any guidance.

She sits in the lawn chair and removes the inhuman mask and sighs, trying to shed her hunger for community, this loss. Understand the magnitude. Understand the consistency of size declines. Evaluate causes. Quantify consequences. Maybe she'd be able to see this data clearer through the knowledge collected by a noiade's otherworld travels if most of their drums weren't kept behind museum glass. She inhales the sea-scented air, and she knows it's just a matter of time—the Bow Man symbol painted on the drums stands ready to shoot the Polar Star and end the world. Now, everything within her lingers like needlefish flashing beneath the green harbor's surface.

TOMAS BAIZA

A Seal's Song

Act I: Plan

It was me and Balena who came up with this.

We were forced early on to accept our limitations—orcas being fully aquatic mammals on the one flipper, and seals mostly aquatic mammals on the other—if we were to get this project on the ground, so to speak. We would need help. We would need the damn bears.

We hate the polar bears because they're idiots and eat us every chance they get. It's been that way forever. Sure, everyone accepts that Circle of Life stuff, but still, it's hard to enter into negotiations when you barely escaped last week's ice-hole ambush. Out of gratitude to Balena, I sucked it up. You know, for the greater good.

And the orcas. They eat us too and bat our dead and dying bodies through the air like some sick game of water polo. Don't let their strangeness fool you, though. They're the smartest and toughest things in the Sea. If this were a water fight, those behemoths would run the table, a frothing red tide from horizon to horizon, nothing alive that they didn't say so. Those clicks and whistles and teeth... How could the Sea conjure such flawless beasts?

Sometimes it's like their purpose is to remind the rest of us of our imperfections—or maybe give us the opportunity to be better than we are. I didn't have much to lose, even before Balena found me. Ever since I could talk, the cows called me things like petulant, disrespectful, and contrary. The other yearlings called me worse things. I admit that I can be difficult, but I was able to convince Whiskers and Balls to do this. I'm trying not to feel guilty about that.

But even those two know that this isn't about me, that it's about the fish. The orcas eat the fish and us, and the bears eat us and some fish and the occasional orca that washes up, and we eat *lots* of fish. The one thing we all have in common is the fish. Without fish, the system's off, and when the system's off, we die—whale, bear, and seal alike. Men like fish too, apparently. Every day they go out in their boats and toss out their deadly, drifting clouds and scoop up more fish than my colony could eat in a year. No matter how much I've thought it over, looked at it from different angles, I can't make what the men do right in my head.

The truce started with the nets. We and the orcas tried breaking them, but too many of us were shot from the boats or caught in the nets. Too many died. The men acted as though we were trying to steal *their* fish. The Old Bull claimed it was a plot, a part of Balena's master plan to do away with us, once and for all. I tried to convince him that without us, the orcas would suffer. Go figure that's when the fat bastard faked like he was deaf and sent me packing.

The cows say I have a special talent for getting into trouble and bringing the wrong kind of attention to myself. It's not like I'm trying to cause problems. It's just that they don't try hard enough. For them, good enough is just fine. And lately, not enough will also do. I can't accept that.

My time to prove them wrong came a half-moon ago. Just my

luck that I ended up getting snagged trying to break a big, heavy net. I thrashed so hard the men decided to cut the whole thing loose. For days I fought to get my hind flipper free until that last time I came up and knew it was over. I took one last gulp of beautiful air and made my peace. The net pulled me farther down than I'd ever been before. It was dark. My lungs burned. I didn't want it, but I was ready.

That's when I heard it, the whistles and clicking. The terror we call Balena.

I'm not sure I can do her justice. When she passes above, between us and the surface, I swear it's like one of those human submarines blocking out the moon and stars, the only difference being that she actually belongs to the world and those man-whales don't. She eats *a lot*, but we've always known her to be fair. She's living proof that it's possible to be feared and loved at the same time.

That far down the water grew eerily still and my head felt thick, as though a huge set of jaws closed gently on my skull. Balena's singing rose from the nothingness. Old cows told stories of this. Balena's Dream Song. We'd always thought they just made it up to scare us pups, but it's real. By the Sea, it's real.

The old, gray cows always said that the seal who heard the Dream Song was either dead or would be soon, that only the most ancient orcas shared the Song with the prey they valued the most. They said it was an honor to be eaten at Song's end, and then they would snicker at us behind their flippers when we shivered in fear and threw our heads back to wail at the night sky.

Balena's song was the most beautiful sound I'd ever heard, more beautiful than raindrops pattering the waves, than the wind blowing sand across a beach, more haunting even than the gulls' cries as they ride the gusting air above the colony. Balena's moans and whistles came to me from farther than the stars in the sky, stars I found that I could see clearly in the void, so divine that I almost forgot I was drowning. The Dream Song conjured the star shapes we all learned as pups: the Blue Whale, the Shark's Tail, the Gyrfalcon, the Kelp Grove, the achingly beautiful Two-headed Swan.

Then the star-points swirled into new shapes. Fish, countless numbers, schooled around me, flitting and dancing. I grinned in the blackness at the sight until, slowly, the fish-stars began to disappear, snatched away by webs of light. The webs—nets, I realized—pulled and heaved until all the fish were gone and I was left alone in the depths to sink.

No, not alone.

I opened my eyes as wide as I could, the blackness so deep it had a presence. The Dream Song became substance, as large as the Deep and as wise as the Sea. The Song changed pattern, its moans eliding into chatter that tickled my neck. She was close, close enough to touch. In the dark, a flash. Something white. Teeth. Many, many teeth.

{*quite the predicament, little one*}

Balena whistled at me, gently poking her jaws through the net that would be my death shroud.

{*you fought well—i've been watching*} she clicked.

It's a blessing and a curse that we seals can understand orca.

"Please sing again. I'm ready," I gurgled, using the last of my air. Carefully avoiding the net, she brought her great eye up to my face. Her teeth. The last thing I'd see would be her rows of perfect white teeth. All fifty-two of them. I closed my eyes.

{*no, not yet*}

I hardly felt it when Balena's jaws separated me from the rotting half of my flipper, the half caught in the net. Next thing I knew, she was pushing me up up up, escorted by her harem of hunter-killers. I wanted to escape, not to safety, but down, back to the Song. It hurt to have been so close and then have it taken away. Instead, I would become a plaything for their young, slowly nibbled to nothing for sport.

Screw the Circle of Life.

I awoke to the soft, uneven rhythm of lapping water. My hind flipper throbbed. I looked down and saw my own blood staining the ice where I lay, half of one flipper bitten cleanly off. A short distance away, three big polar bears eyed me, noses raised high. No doubt I smelled delicious.

A splash behind me.

Just off the edge of the ice, several orcas bobbed, occasionally rising high enough out of the water to make sure the bears knew they were there. In the middle of them, Balena's great bulk lolled and floated. She rolled an eye upward and looked at me for a long time before saying anything.

{good, half-fin! call to the bears; call them to you}

I frowned at the rough-looking trio of ragged bears. "I'd rather *you* eat me than them," I coughed.

{they will not eat you; i will not let them; call to them; we need their help}

That monster. A mix of revulsion and admiration sent a chill up my spine. "You used me as bait," I growled.

Balena bobbed high out of the water and looked straight at me. Is it even possible for orcas to smile?

*

I was the one who thought to use fire. The polar bears knew about it, but it was obvious that Balena and her guards had no clue. They all listened as I told them about the fishing boat I'd sunk last summer, when I was still technically a pup. I had snuck aboard at night to steal back some of the fish they'd taken and accidentally knocked over one of their fire boxes, the things men use to make light because they're so helpless in the dark. I managed to snatch one fish before slipping off the rear deck. From the water, I watched the fishermen jump overboard to escape the glowing tongues of flame, marveling at how the fire had followed the amber liquid wherever it spilled, like a seal chasing a school of sardines. The violence and heat in that yellow light was terrifying and thrilling. Even the men fled from it.

Balena came up with the rest of the plan, with me translating for the moronic bears. It seemed like a long shot, but if we could pull it off…

She charged me and the polar bears with recruiting our best and bravest. We would meet at the rocky beach east of the fishing village at the next full moon, which was only seven nights away. The bears complained that they didn't live like seals—"nose to ass," as they put it—and that it would take more time to collect the numbers necessary to destroy the village.

With a patience that came from her many years, Balena reminded the bears, again, that they would not destroy or even enter the village, but rather blockade the docks to keep the men from reaching their boats. That would allow us seals to do our work.

The bears grumbled at this. They'd dealt with men before and had ample experience with their guns. "Coward sticks," they called them. We knew of them too. Sometimes the men came to our rookery. We would flee into the water. Not everyone would make it.

The big male bear and his companions turned to leave. "We're hungry *now*," he snarled over his rolling shoulders.

Balena and her guards rose high and blasted spray from their blowholes.

{go, half-fin! full moon, bring your best, ones like you who know what is at stake}

Act II: Colony

It wasn't so much the rejection as the laughing. The fat, vain sea cucumber actually laughed at me.

The Old Bull easily outweighed me five-to-one. His mane glowed golden in the moonlight and his teeth flashed when he spoke. Even so, it wasn't hard to look him in the eye. How could he frighten me when I had been face-to-face with Balena herself?

"And this is how Her Terribleness has rewarded you for your loyalty?" the Old Bull said while aiming his snout at my missing flipper. His luxurious mane bristled in disgust.

"This is our one chance! No more nets. We're going for the boats themselves. The orcas—Balena *herself!*—and the bears, they've agreed to do this, but they need our help." I searched his face.

"Think of the fish," I pleaded. "Think of our pups!"

The Old Bull huffed and grumbled, shaking his mane and flashing his canines. "Go back to your new queen, *Stump*!" he growled, his bellow echoing across the colony. "A seal's life is hard enough without having to worry about when the orcas will convince us to swim straight into their mouths. Best to live and die as we always have—by skill and luck. Why race willingly into the jaws of the Sea?"

He lifted his face to the starry sky, imperious and dismissive. His way of saying, *We are done here*. When the Old Bull realized I was not leaving, he wrapped his jaws around my neck and dragged me into the surf. My flipper caught against jagged rock, and I fought not to cry out.

"Go!" he roared. "Before I lose my patience, Stump."

I felt my missing flipper more keenly than ever. Stump. That's what they'll call me now. *Half-fin* has more dignity.

I swam half the distance to the narrow beach where the colony rested. I felt the pull, that instinct to crawl into the musky seal scrum and lose myself in the collective vibration, that buzz that told us we were home, appreciated as one of the many, a part of something larger and more important than ourselves.

It was a loving, numbing anonymity that I'd never completely rejected but that never felt totally right, either. Sure, we each had names like Harelip, Sand Flea, Snagtooth (and now Stump), but ultimately, our only value was to the colony. The only seals who rose above would be the bulls of the rock and their chosen mates, their queens, those haughty cows who lorded over the rest of us and sometimes didn't even go out to hunt for themselves.

The only way a female like me could hope to earn a shred of respect would be to live long enough to have a cove full of pups, acting flattered when bulls warred over me and then acting just as compliant when one of them came to claim his prize.

I bobbed in the water, behind me the lordly and overweening bull, ahead the roiling mass of the colony. The familiar sounds of home came to me over the gentle waves. Chuffing, barks, growls, snores. Within that mass of muscle, fur, and fat were the pups, their squeals occasionally piercing the steaming murmur.

What the sounds didn't say was that we were slowly starving. Each season there were fewer pups because there weren't enough fish for the parents. Fewer of them make it to weaning, and even fewer to yearlings. Every one of us knew it was because of the fish and no one had the courage to say or do anything. And in just a few months, I'd be expected to bring more pups into our home.

Exhausted, I pulled myself onto a spit of sand at the quiet end of the colony, away from everyone else. It would be cold, but at least I'd be able to lick my wounds and maybe even sleep in peace. I spun in a circle to carve myself a nest in the pebbly sand and curled up tight. If any seal had ever earned some rest, it was me.

"We heard everything! Tell us about it!"

Slink, Grace, and Drip wagged their heads at me from a few feet away. I was so tired I didn't even notice them following me.

"If you heard everything, why do I need to tell you about anything?" I snarled, not even trying to be polite. The only things I had in common with these three were that we were all older yearlings and expected to start adding to the colony in a few months. "It's not nice to eavesdrop," I said, sitting up.

"Oh, we didn't eavesdrop." Slink grinned. She'd earned her name because she was skinny and twisted like an eel when she swam. "The whole colony heard. You know how the Old Bull's voice carries at night."

Grace gave me one of her smug smiles, like she should be praised for having the patience to deal with seals like me. "I'm glad you're not hurt…Stump."

"Really, must you call me that?" I said, yanking my half-flipper away from Drip's constantly running nose.

"That's what the Old Bull named you," Grace said. "Those are the rules."

Head low, Drip crept slowly toward my half-flipper again.

"Get away before I tell my friend Balena how good you'd taste."

Drip yelped and hid behind Grace.

"Must you always be so…*abrupt*?" Grace said, nuzzling Drip to settle her down. Grace was always the most dignified and appropriate of all of us. She had this regal air that all but guaranteed she'd end up with one of the ruling bulls. I never liked Grace, but I could never bring myself to hate her. Grace was how things were *supposed* to work and, if I'm honest, how things *did* work when times were good, when fish were plentiful, when the men didn't make it so that all of us—seal, whale, and bear—had to fight harder to survive. But if Grace was part of our system, she was also part of our decline. In seals like her, the system became personal. None of us wanted to swim away from the herd and listen to the Sea and accept that things had changed. Seals like Grace forged ahead, defiant in their belief that everything was fine, or would be, if we just kept our heads down and stayed the course. Maybe I could change that.

"Grace," I said. My flipper throbbed, and I tried my best to rise to her height and look proper. "You're smart." OK, a little lie for the greater good. "You must understand that we're in trouble. That we need to do something."

Grace glanced at Slink and Drip, nervous and flattered that I'd singled her out. "I don' know what you're talking about, Stump."

"The fish, Grace. There are fewer and fewer every new moon."

"The old cows tell us there have been hard times before. We'll be fine," Grace said smoothly, more for Slink and Drip's benefit than mine. Oh, you will make such a handsome queen, Grace.

"It won't be fine unless we *do* something," I said. "We need to *act*."

Slink and Drip chuffed nervously and shook their necks. Grace nuzzled them. "You know, Stump, you are not without your talents," she cooed, her eyes darting to my flipper. "You could have a good place in the colony if you understood your role in the order of things."

"I'm not like you," I snapped, my patience gone. "I'm not some ambitious, bull-crazy flirt willing to pump out pups who'll end up starving on the beach!"

Slink gasped and Drip crouched further behind Grace.

Grace blinked at me and spoke slowly. "Stump, look at them," she said, tossing her head in the direction of the colony. "They need to believe that there will be a tomorrow, and a next day, and then another. Order comes from confidence, and confidence from stability. All this talk of men, orcas, bears, and starvation undermines that stability, which upsets the order. This will not do. It's why the Old Bull won't listen to you. It's why you lost your flipper."

Slink inched forward, head low. "Don't worry, Stump. We can cover that up. The old cows can do wonders with seaweed and shells. I know that Whiskers and Balls kind of like you. I don't think they'll mind how you look now. And that Whiskers, he'd be quite a catch."

I stared at the three of them, the worst things I could think to say flashing through my head like a school of herring. I sat there until I realized I was crying and had nothing meaningful to say to them anymore. Cold water lapped at my wound, and I turned to let the surf pull me away. I headed for a small rock just off the beach, where the cows send their pups when they're acting up. I could be alone there.

*

The stars twinkled, and a pink glow had just begun to spread over the colony when I awoke. I rested my chin on the rock and tried not to think about my flipper and the things the Old Bull and Grace had said. I closed my eyes and tried to remember the Dream Song. Images of Balena and her harem danced and swirled.

"Do you think she's dead?" I heard from the water below. That was Whiskers.

"I don't know. Go and check," said another. That was Balls.

"No, you look."

"You do it!"

"For the love of the Sea, would you both shut up?" I groaned.

Two heads bobbed in the dark waves. "May we?" Balls said.

"You may," I said.

Whiskers and Balls hauled themselves onto the rock next to me. It was high tide and there was just enough room for the three of us. I had to admit it felt good to have two warm bodies against mine. I gazed across the water at the teeming mass on the beach, all that seal-heat. So many pups.

"We heard what the Old Bull told you," Balls said.

We called him that because when we were pups, he found a ball on the beach, some man-toy that had washed up. He and that ball were inseparable. He swam with it, played with it, even slept with it until the Old Bull decided it was silly and tore it to pieces. The ball is gone, but the name stuck. All those months with it had made him the most dexterous seal in the colony. What he lacked in pure intellect, he more than made up for in agility.

"I guess I'm Stump now," I said, lifting my tail.

"I like it," Whiskers said. "It's not one of those regular cow names like Sea Foam or Shell."

"Or Grace," I snapped.

Whiskers rolled his eyes. "No, definitely not like Grace!"

He was Whiskers because his were the longest in the colony. Eyelashes too. It was all the yearlings and cows could talk about. Even though his whiskers never did much for me, I had to admit that he was a good seal, and a *big* one. Big and loyal were the two best words for him. Everyone knew he would be there for you until the end.

Someday Whiskers and Balls would be full-fledged bulls, maybe even the kind who would compete for the colony. That morning on the rock, though, we were still just young enough to call one another friends.

We huddled together as the stars faded and the sun rose behind a smattering of high clouds. I'd just started to doze when Whiskers rose and bent to inspect my flipper.

"Did Balena really do this?" he asked.

I lifted my half-fin to his face and nodded. "She saved my life."

"Why?" Balls asked. "Not that you're not worth saving, Stump." He shot me an apologetic look. "It's just, you know, not something they usually do."

I sat up and looked out over the colony. "She knows something needs to change. She needed me to help her. And I'm going to."

"How?" asked Whiskers.

"I'm going to talk to every able-bodied seal out there," I said, nodding at the crowded beach. "I have six nights until Balena expects me to come with help." Whiskers and Balls exchanged a worried look. "May as well start now," I said.

"Stop. Wait," Whiskers said. He put his large flipper on my back.

"You can't, Stump," said Balls.

"Why the hell not?" I growled.

"The Old Bull," Whiskers said. "He'll kill you, or exile you, if you're lucky. And you won't be," he added, looking at my flipper. "Lucky, that is."

"And Grace has already started talking about how you're 'consorting with killer whales' and 'bargaining with bears.'" Balls shook his head and spat on the rock.

"They're all idiots," I said.

"They're all *scared*," Whiskers said with a long, steamy sigh. "They know everything is wrong, and then you go missing and come home injured and ranting about Balena and the Dream Song and bears and attacking the village."

I tossed myself into the surf. "Is that what I do now?" I shouted.

"Rant? Am I like one of those senile old cows the Old Bull leads away from the colony and gives to the Sea?"

All of us were silent, Whiskers and Balls shuffling uncomfortably on the rock while I bobbed in the water.

"I have six nights until the full moon. If I can't get anyone to join me, I'll go myself," I said quietly.

Whiskers shook his head. "Stump, I'm no genius—"

"No argument from me," Balls said.

"—but it's obvious the Old Bull will never do anything to risk his throne," Whiskers said slowly, glancing at Bull Rock in the distance. "Balls and I are already associated with you, and, no offense, that's not good for us."

"Nope, not one bit," Balls shook his head vigorously. "You're political poison, Stump."

Whiskers glared at Balls and then lowered his snout toward me. "Yeah. And you're probably the cleverest seal in the colony. And you're our friend. And"—Whiskers rumbled and cleared his throat, embarrassment spreading across his broad face—"we'd never forgive ourselves if you went off into the dark alone."

Balls nudged Whiskers with his snout. "Hey, there, buddy, uh, this isn't part of the script. We were s'posed to talk her outta—"

"We're going with you, Stump."

"What's that now?" Balls said, bug-eyed.

Whiskers rose to his full height and looked down on Balls. "We're going with her."

Act III: Part of the Whole

It wasn't hard to slip away from the colony.

The full moon rose above the coastal mountains, bright enough to cast shadows. The Old Bull and his cronies were bellowing and snorting on their rock as wave after wave of seals returned from the evening hunt. No seal was reported missing and hadn't been for many days.

"The orcas are keeping the truce," I said. Whiskers and Balls shifted nervously.

"Last chance to back out," I said.

Balls looked Whiskers up and down and shook his head at me. "Nope. As much as I hate this idea, doing something is better than nothing." He scooped some sand with his flipper and playfully flung it at Whiskers's face. "If King-size here and I are ever going to fight for the colony, there needs to be a colony to fight for. I can't have him coming home a hero while I just rolled in my own piss on the beach!"

"Plus, the three of us will get more done than one, and, no offense, Stump, you're still not moving so great." Whiskers gave me a sympathetic look with his big, weepy eyes.

We took a moment to gaze out on the colony and then let the high tide gently pull us off the rocky beach.

*

{*only three, half-fin?*}

Whiskers and Balls pressed hard against me, trembling.

"You said to bring our best," I answered. "That's us."

Balena responded with a jagged stutter of clicks that seemed to rummage through my head and heart. I wondered whether she could tell from the inside out that I was bluffing, that Whiskers and Balls were all I could scrounge up.

We floated in the surf, a ways out from the beach. Tall black dorsal fins cut the water, circling us. Balena hovered just ahead. She shook her snout, as if to say, *So be it, then.*

I squeezed out from between Whiskers and Balls. "Shall I tell the bears the plan?"

Balena nodded, her toothy mouth opened wide. *{go; be wary; make them understand}*

On the shore were maybe twenty bears. The three large ones I recognized from before, but the rest were the most emaciated, run-down, ragged creatures I'd ever laid eyes on. Sagging skin hung from protruding bones, their once-glowing fur now a mottled blend of white, gray, and a sickly rust. Desperation seemed to drip from their eyes.

Approaching the beach, I began to feel sorry for them until I remembered that a skinny bear is a hungry bear, and a hungry bear is an unpredictable eating machine that probably shouldn't be trusted. But we had no choice.

Whiskers, Balls, and I glided onto the sand, making sure to keep ourselves half in the surf for a quick getaway. The polar bears approached warily, noses high and chuffing in the cold night.

"Is that all?" the lead bear grumbled, scanning the water behind us.

Balls wagged his snout. "Like you all are much to look at!"

I turned and bit down hard on his neck to shut him up. For his part, Whiskers was mostly holding it together, the deep growl caught in his throat barely audible. I had to keep this under control.

"We need to hurry," I barked at the lead bear. "Balena and her guard are waiting."

"What good will the big fish do when we face the men?" the bear sneered.

"She's right over there. You're welcome to swim out and ask her yourself." I scooted aside, as if to welcome him into the surf. Just then, a sleek, lethal shape arced gracefully out of the water and splashed hard onto its back, sending up a great spray that sparkled in the moonlight.

The bear spun round and roared in frustration, "Get on with it then, gimpy!"

I took a deep breath and explained to the bears that they were to move quietly to the edge of the fishing village, nearest the boats.

"Then we attack the town," said a thin, twitchy bear in the back.

"No," I said. "Pay attention."

I explained that from there they would wait for us to take up our positions on the docks. I explained that three seals on the docks would draw little attention if we were seen, but the bears might cause an uproar. They grumbled and postured at that, apparently flattered.

"And then we attack the town," another bear said, "to eat their trash and any slow ones who get in the way."

"No!" I shook my head and spoke slowly. "All of you will block the way to the docks once we start our work, to keep the men away. When the boats are on fire, then you run into the night. Swim if you need to. The orcas will let you pass and might even help you get back here. If we do this right, none of you gets hurt and there will be fish for everyone so you can get nice and fat again."

They looked at one another with sunken yellow eyes and licked their lips, hot, stinking breath curling from their slack mouths. It almost hurt to see how hungry they were.

A couple of grunts from their leader and the bears were trotting toward the twinkling lights of the village. I nodded at Whiskers and Balls before shuffling into the surf. Balena moved in easily beside me.

At first Whiskers wedged himself between us, but she just nudged him away like he was nothing. I was impressed that he even tried, given how terrified he was of her. Maybe the future-bull had a protective streak.

The massive orca cruised near my half-flipper. I felt proud to no longer be gripped by fear at the sight of Balena, yet there was something unfathomable about her, deep and impenetrable. In the dark water, even my eyes couldn't quite make out her dimensions, her flank a field so perfectly black and vast that I might fall into it if I gazed long enough.

She pulled up next to me, and without knowing why, I dove. Balena shadowed me as we sped downward. Whiskers let loose a panicked bark before everything else faded and soon it was just the two of us speeding through the dark. Balena's side brushed mine, and my fur tingled. This close to her, it was almost as though I didn't have to swim and I could simply let myself be pulled along by her momentum.

"Sing me the Song," I begged, water flowing over my face faster than I'd ever known possible. "The Song, Balena."

A shiver ran down her side, and we slowed until we hung motionless in the murk. Balena turned her head and brought her eye up close. Her mouth parted slowly to reveal her perfect teeth. From somewhere deep within came a sonorous, swirling moan. I wanted to flee, but I was frozen before her, the bone-melting sound more powerful and terrible than a thousand cows wailing over their starved pups, the roars of bears forced to eat their cubs in the hope of another litter next year, the mourning-songs for orcas so skinny they were little more than swimming skeletons. Paralyzed by the Song, I began to sink.

{*i have you, half-fin*} Balena clicked, tucking beneath me to hold me up.

Flopped over her head, I looked straight into her eye. "Why?" I asked. "That wasn't the Whale Song."

{*there are many, many Songs, half-fin, all of them part of the whole*}

"But that one was awful," I said, beginning to feel my body again. "Hideous."

{yes, all part of the whole, sad and terrible, joyous and carefree; every Song is necessary}

I let her carry me up, the glow of the starlight slowly growing brighter. I rested my head against her, and that's when I saw it. In Balena's eye, bottomless pits of sorrow, innumerable caverns of tragedy, the farthest corners of which were hidden to me. I slid away to face her, just beneath the surface.

"You sang that to prepare me," I said. "To tell me that what we're about to do might be awful, and that you're not sure how it will end."

Balena's mouth opened slightly, and she nodded. *{it would be wrong to hide that part of the Song from you, half-fin; you of all the little seals must hear it}*

I thought of the corners of Balena's sorrow that were too dark to make out. "You didn't sing it all to me."

Balena wagged her jaw, almost certainly a wry smile. *{goodgood-good, half-fin! now you know that even I cannot see everything; how pointless the Song if we knew where every tide, every current ended?}* She nudged me gently, playfully, with her nose, but I could still see the sadness in her eyes. *{the Sea keeps her secrets, and we deserve to not know all of them}*

We both came up for air and lingered to gaze at the stars. Not far away, Whiskers and Balls bobbed in a grove of swaying dorsal fins. Beyond them, the sparse lights of the village and its docks.

"I think I'm ready, Balena."

At the shallow water our group slowed, and I turned to the whales. Balena glided up close and nudged me with her great snout. She opened her jaws wide, and I was mesmerized by her teeth, white and flawless.

{good tide and clear water, half-fin—strength}

I spun and swam hard the rest of the way. The orcas would see that we were not afraid. I wanted Balena to know, most of all.

My courage began to drain when we crawled onto the main wharf, its planks smooth from many years of use. There were four piers extending from the wharf with four docks each. Most of the docks berthed fishing boats, some of which I recognized from our hunts, their nets forcing us farther and farther out. I thought about what it would mean for the colony if these boats no longer stole clouds of fish from the Sea.

Whiskers and Balls huddled close, and we listened and sniffed. The boats pulled lazily at their creaking ropes, the occasional thump of a hull against an old rubber tire or bell clanking. The smell of too-old fish, man sweat, and the sickly sweet tang of oil I remembered from the burning boat.

I turned to Whiskers and Balls. "Do you smell that? It's what we need to start the fires. Come with me."

Shuffling toward the nearest boat, my flipper began to throb, so much so that I had to bite my own tongue to keep from crying out. The sight of shadowy polar bears trotting down the main wharf toward the village helped to distract me from the pain. Even though it was according to plan, doubt nagged at me. Would they do what they'd agreed to? Would they remember that this was about the fish and not revenge?

The gangplank bent under our weight as we boarded the first boat. The deck was littered with rope, netting, and fish the men had carelessly left to die. We scooped as many as we could into our mouths, ravenous. Still chewing, Whiskers and Balls followed me around the boat until we found several lanterns resting on the deck.

"Here, see these? What's inside will burn, even on the water. We need to find as many of these as we can and spill them onto the boats." I tipped over one of the boxes with my snout and stepped back as the amber liquid spread out across the deck.

"Where is the fire?" Whiskers asked, edging backward.

I groaned. That was the part of the plan I hadn't thought of yet: how to start the fire. I had hoped we would find a lit lantern on one of the boats, but now I wasn't so sure.

"Go, both of you! Find as many of these as you can. Spill them on the boats and leave a trail down the ramps to docks and down the docks to the piers. We need a trail that will end here so that the fire will touch everything. Like this," I said, taking up another lantern. Carefully, I tipped it over and shuffled down the ramp, leaving a line of acrid-smelling oil behind me. Whiskers and Balls put the pieces together and followed, each with a lantern in his mouth. Balls balanced a second lantern on his nose as slid down the slick ramp. They passed me quickly on their way to other boats as I traced a thin line of oil toward the main dock.

My flipper screamed in pain, and I paused to rest. From my spot on the wharf, I watched Balls lay a stream of oil down the walkway with one lantern while balancing the other on his head. I couldn't help but laugh. Show-off. Whiskers was already boarding the next boat over in search of more lanterns. My heart swelled. Balls was brash and enthusiastic, whereas Whiskers was more cautious and methodical, but they both went about their work with a sense of purpose. They were here for the colony—but if it weren't for me, they wouldn't be here at all.

A noise to my right caught my attention. In the darkness, the polar bears had set up a ragged picket line between the village and the docks, knowing that the instant they were seen there would be a commotion. They were to weather the storm long enough for us to spread the oil and start the fires.

Rather than sit quietly, the starving bears stalked to and fro, shaking their heads and huffing challenges into the darkness. One bear, a lean adolescent with a rust-colored back, trotted to a large trash bin next to one of the men's structures. With a swipe of his paw, the garbage can went clanging across the narrow street, its contents spilling out across the dirty snow.

Several bears growled and jumped on the trash. Lights came on up and down the street. Nearby a door opened, a man's shape silhouetted against the yellow glow behind him. One of the bears raced toward the door. Before the man could slam it shut, the bear burst in and disappeared into the structure. Screaming pealed through the night, and as if on cue, the bears roared and raced into the village.

"Hurry!" I barked at Whiskers and Balls, no longer worrying about being heard. "The men will come soon!"

Whiskers's head popped up from a boat two berths down. Balls was sniffing at the door of a shed at the far end of the wharf. They both looked at me briefly and then returned to their work, a frantic desperation in their movements.

Ignoring the pain, I shuffled down the wharf to the next pier and boarded the closest boat. Quickly, I found a red container that held enough oil to reach the wharf.

The village was crackling with shouting and running feet. No one had time to worry about the docks. Yet.

At the other end of the wharf, Balls hopped upright from the shed with three red oil containers, one on each flipper and the third on his head. Whiskers took one of the containers from him, bit off the stopper, and began to spill more oil down the nearest dock. When my container was empty, I set it down and froze. There, right in front of me, was a man standing on the dock. He was stretching, facing away from me, arms extended and back arched slightly. It never occurred to me that any of them would sleep on their boats.

As I considered rolling off the dock into the water, the man stiffened up. Shouting and crashing sounds drifted to the boats from the village, and he took two steps toward the wharf. Without thinking, I scooted up from behind and head-butted him into the water between the boats.

The man looked up at me in disbelief, sputtering and cursing in what I could tell were rage-filled words. He paddled clumsily to a dock pile and began pulling himself up when it happened. From beneath a dark, glassy mound of water rose up. A black fin broke the surface, and with barely a ripple, the man was gone. No shout or struggle. Just gone. I'd seen it happen a hundred times, a poor seal—sick, wounded, foolish, or perhaps just young—caught from below by a hungry orca, but never this.

This was not supposed to happen. No one was supposed to get hurt. I vaguely wondered whether this man had pups of his own. Whether they would miss him.

I stumbled to the wharf and dazedly picked up an oil container Whiskers or Balls had left. With it I oiled two more boats and the dock they shared. At the dead-end of the wharf, Balls was rummaging through the shed looking for more containers while Whiskers rushed to finish the last dock.

It occurred to me that at some point I had begun to hear shooting from the village. I bounced between anger and pity at the thought of men using their guns on the bears. How could the men not understand that they had helped to make this happen?

Or was I the one who made this happen?

I forced myself to concentrate on how we would turn the foul-smelling oil into fire. A bear tripped into the open at the village end of the wharf, covered in blood. Two men with guns chased him. He stumbled toward the small sandy beach and collapsed at the edge of the water. The two men raised their guns and watched the bear long enough to confirm he wasn't moving before turning round and running back into the village.

I roared at Whiskers and Balls, "Look for a fire! Any fire! We need to light the oil!"

The three of us bounded up and down the wharf, no longer worried about the noise.

"Nothing!" Balls shouted from the end of the wharf.

"Me neither!" Whiskers answered from somewhere between us.

At the end of a gangway, I heard a voice behind me. A man stood on the deck of his boat pointing at me.

"Какого черта!" he shouted and stepped heavily onto the dock. He held a mean-looking cudgel. A small, white stick dangled from his mouth. The smoke curling from the stick's glowing tip tickled my nose.

"Убирайтесь отсюда!" He yelled again and raised his club, expecting me to flee. Instead, I lunged at his leg and pulled him off balance. His body slammed against the oil-slicked wood. As if in a dream, I watched the small, glowing stick leave his mouth and spin end-over-end through the air to land on the pier.

The oil ignited in a *whoosh*. The man screamed, jumped up, and started to run for his boat, but the line of flame beat him up the ramp. When his pant leg caught fire, he turned and jumped off the dock.

This time I didn't look down into the water.

I watched the orange flames trace a line down the dock to the pier, turn left, and then sprint toward the wharf, where it turned again and lunged at the shed Balls had just left. Whiskers rolled out of the way and barked at Balls, who had just enough time to get free of the shed before it exploded, the sparks and embers rising into the predawn sky. The remaining bears were stumbling back to the small beach. Boat hulls and dock boards and pilings cracked and groaned.

The growing flames forced me to the edge of the pier. "Time to go!" I barked. The fire crept toward me and I realized, numbly, that my fur was slick with oil. Through the crackling flames and smoke, the reduced, tattered squad of polar bears hit the water, chased by the men with their guns. I looked back to Whiskers and Balls and let out a long, deep call.

"Go!"

*

And now I feel them. The bullets.

The first one snaps past my head, but the second, third, and however many more thud into me. For a second, I'm sure they'll pass through like Balena's clicks and whistles, but they slap wetly into me and stay, angry and burning.

I sway. "Go!" It comes out as a croak. The fire reaches me, and the reek of my burning fur fills my head. Maybe I see two seals pushing through flames toward the water when more bullets tear into my side. Maybe not.

Go!

The heat bends the night so that everything twists and quivers. I stumble toward the end of the pier, my flippers sizzling and muscles clenching down on the bullets. With a desperate push, I throw myself into the pure, cool Sea.

I swim as though I have never done anything else. The water behind me glows orange, and the concussions from the explosions punch through me. I swim hard enough to leave the village far behind, far enough to no longer see the unnatural light or feel the blasts.

Whiskers and Balls. They got away. They must have. Please.

I swim through kelp and jellies and then into the open deep where the floes begin to dot the water. But I don't stop to rest, to cool my charred hide or simply let my blood spill out onto the ice. That would be the wrong way to do it. I know I must keep pushing.

I swim for you, so that you will see how strong I am.

I swim until my mouth sputters above the water line, my half-flipper dead and the others moving only through sheer will and pride.

I swim until even the burning in my muscles has left me, the only sensation the water rushing over my face.

I swim until I take one last bite of air in the weak morning light and then slowly sink. I have done my part. You will come now. You must.

Before I can begin pleading, I hear it, the Song. This time it soars to bring down the stars and spread them across the Deep before my fading eyes.

In the quiet darkness, glittering images flash. The Sea is a spinning galaxy of fish. The Old Bull is gone. In his place sit two silhouettes on Bull Rock, one hulking and steady, the other sleek and graceful. They are scarred, well-fed, and wise. They remember me with fondness and respect. The colony is whole and prosperous. And who can sleep for all the pups!

{*half-fin…*}

From the depths something massive rushes upward, so fierce the water flees before it. Its Song both swaddles and pierces me.

All I wanted was to change things, Balena. To make a difference. To be a part of something before the end.

{*every Song is part of the whole; you and I shall sing your ending, half-fin; sing with me*}

My open mouth makes no sound in the blackness, but I know

she can hear the music in my heart. I sink like a stone. She is coming. I am ready.

Breaking through the cloudy murk, her teeth, her perfect teeth.

TARA M. WILLIAMS

The Ice Child

Long, long ago, when the green world we know yet slumbered beneath thick glacial sheets and a comforter of snow, the ice child was born.

Her mother, belly hot and heaving, had ventured alone deep into the forest where, under spires of pine and a chipped glass sky, she lost her way. While crossing a frozen stream, she fell to her hands and knees, pushing and groaning, the snowy owls echoing her grunts and cries till the child emerged at last, transparent and perfect, connected to her mother by a silvery rope of ice. With her sharp-edged fishing knife, the mother severed the ice cord. She opened the front of her coat, fashioned from the skin of a winter wolf, and cradled the ice child upon her breast. The infant's blue lips suckled eagerly, her tiny ice hands cold and grasping, and the mother's love flowed like warm honey from her heart, crystallizing where it touched the child, whom the mother named Gaska-geardi in the ancient language of her people, ancestors of the tribes of the far, far North.

Winter was the ice child's father. Weeks before the birth, the mother had fled his frigid embrace, fearing she too soon would find herself among the frozen maidens piled in stacks outside his palace walls. His attractions to mortal women were intense as they were brief. Yet the mother loved her ice child, as all mortal mothers love the beings their bodies bring forth, though the child, she could already see, more resembled her father, his elemental nature, his austere beauty, his icicle touch. And for a time, all was well with the mother and the ice child. They hid in a cave in the womb of a mountain, where the mother kept a small fire to warm herself while the ice child slept in a snowdrift.

But one day a man came upon them, a herder of reindeer of the mother's tribe, and the mother and the ice child returned with him to the village. The mother was welcomed back with joy, for until that moment the villagers had believed she had perished in a winter storm. The people of the village were wary when they saw the ice child, whose strange appearance, they feared, marked her for calamity and some dire fate.

The herder and the mother married. They went to live in a wooden hut with a roof of tin, a hearth, and windows. The mother, happy there and warm, bore another child, a mortal boy. And the hunter grew angry as the mother continued to suckle her ice child alongside his pink-faced son.

"Thief!" he thundered, accusing the ice child of stealing his son's rightful milk. Enraged, the herder struck Gaska-geardi away from her mother's breast with a heavy blow that left a crack in the perfect transparency of the ice child's chest. Then he opened the hut's front door and tossed the ice child out into the frozen night, telling her never to return or he would lift his iron axe and shatter her in pieces and toss her shards into the hearth's hot flames.

For a time, the mother continued to feed Gaska-geardi in secret.

"When you are hungry," the mother told the ice child, "write a message on the window, and I will come."

And so each night the ice child waited, watching from where she stood in the darkness outside the hut's window as the herder dandled the fat baby boy on his knee and the little family laughed their laughter of belonging and tenderness while the crack in the ice child's chest would ache. When the father and baby boy fell asleep, the ice child would write a message to her mother on the window in frost, and the mother would steal out and nurse Gaska-geardi until the ice child grew drowsy in her mother's arms, though each morning she would awaken to find herself alone in the snow's cold embrace.

Then one night the mother did not come. Gaska-geardi wrote her messages again and again until the window was layered deep in frost, and she could no longer see inside. And after many days and nights, when her mother still did not appear, the ice child set off all on her own, for, she told herself, Winter could be no more cold or cruel than these supposedly warm-blooded mortals who had left her there to die.

The ice child discovered she needed little to sustain herself. Away from her mother, her hunger dwindled. The cold she found invigorating, the howling wind and driving snow a tonic to her frigid soul. She grew to young womanhood, sleek and slender, a figure of glass-like grace, and the crystalline crack diminished as she grew till it was no more than a forgotten childhood scar.

One day her father found her by cold magic. She was swimming with the narwhals, white unicorns of the northern seas. "My child," Winter sighed, and wrapped her in his iceberg arms, and Gaska-geardi wept, surprised by the sudden hot mortal tears that welled and melted furrows in her perfect cheeks, which her father's silvery fingers instantly smoothed and healed. He took the ice child back to his palace and taught her the language of wintertide, a hundred words for snow alone: the soft snow one's feet sink into while walking; the hard, icy crust that melts under a sun's warmth and refreezes in the night; the soft, sticky snow that falls thickly in great flakes; the snow that blows up from the earth in fine gusts; the old snow; the fresh snow; the empty space between snow and ground.

He revealed to her the secrets of the blues of ancient ice and sky. Enchanted, she traced them through the palace's sculpted corridors, its silvery ballrooms and banquet halls set with lavish tables, sconces alight in cold blue flames. The changing light of day and night, refracted through the frozen architecture, wrought endless variations of image and reflection, every surface a gallery of shifting display, and she was certain, in all her travels, she had never seen anything more lovely.

There was only one place in her father's palace where the ice-child-turned-woman was forbidden to go: the wing that held Winter's impregnable prison, where three inmates had been sentenced to languish for eternity. A shape-shifting warden guarded this prison day and night. When Gaska-geardi first saw him, he wore the form of an enormous winter wolf, asleep at the foot of a wall of blue ice which bore no door, no lock nor key. As the ice woman bent to stroke the wolf's white-silver fur, she recalled her mother, whom she hadn't thought of in quite some time, and what was left of the old crack in her chest creaked and ached.

Startled from his slumber, the wolf nipped her wrist. Her ice hand broke off and lay between them on the white marble floor.

"You're a brittle one," the wolf said, his round golden eyes gazing into hers until she grew drowsy. Then, with a great effort of will, Gaska-geardi looked away, picked up her severed hand and took it to her father.

"Disobedient child," her father chided even as he healed her. "I should leave you to suffer the consequences of your actions, but I am too fond." The ice hand, reattached, shimmered seamlessly at the end of her arm as before.

"Father," the ice woman said. "What do you keep imprisoned in that far wing of the palace? Your power is great. Your might rules the land. What remains for you to fear?"

Winter regarded her gravely. "Are you happy here, my child?"

"As happy as an ice being may ever hope to be," she replied. "Father, you have been most kind."

"Then you must promise never to return to the palace prison wing."

And the ice woman promised, a promise she would not keep.

Some days when she visited, the warden was a wolf, other days an Arctic fox or a snowshoe hare. Some days he was a polar bear, or a silvery lynx with silent flat paws, or a velvet-soft harp seal with great, dark eyes. Some days he was a man in a white fur coat, and on these days, she loved him least, yet she was enthralled by his endless variety, and he by her transparent adoration. And thus, they went on meeting at the juncture of enchantment and prohibition, until the day Gaska-geardi asked the warden to reveal to her what it was he guarded, what lay on the other side of the blue ice prison wall.

The warden refused. "You will not survive it. And if I should lose you now, I would surely die of a great loneliness of spirit."

"As would I, should you leave me," the ice woman assured him. "But I must know what my father fears."

The next time she saw the warden, he had taken the form of a large snow goose with sleek white feathers and black-tipped wings. He bent his pink legs, and the ice woman climbed upon his back. "You may look down," the snow goose said, "but I cannot land." And in a rush of wind and feathers, her slender ice arms wrapped tightly around the goose's long white neck, Gaska-geardi was quickly aloft, the snow goose soaring toward the top of the blue ice wall.

As they crossed over the wall and the snow goose circled in flight, "I understand now," the ice woman whispered. For below them stretched Summer, pulsing lush and hot. The ice woman's eyes were dazzled by bright fluttering butterflies. Her ears rang with songs of birds of every hue. Her nostrils filled with a thick perfume of blooming flowers and ripening fruit. Summer's long-enclosed heat, magnified, reached up and enveloped them, and the ice woman felt the surface of her frozen skin grow moist and slick and slippery until, with a small cry, she lost her grip upon the snow goose and plummeted downward through the fecund, heated air.

The snow goose watched in horror as his lover fell and was caught by the branches of a lilac tree, where she hung, helpless and stunned. A creature of winter, the snow goose could not land. Instead, he retraced his path, returned to the winter side of the blue ice wall, and alighting, assumed the shape of a man. He retrieved an axe and wielded it desperately, chopping a narrow passage through the doorless ice wall. He squeezed through the opening, disentangled Gaska-geardi from the lilac tree where she hung. He carried her fast-melting form in his arms, back into the palace, then sealed the breach in the prison wall with snow.

But it was too late. Summer had escaped, scorching its exit through Winter's palace. It could no longer be contained. The two remaining prisoners, Spring and Fall, assaulted the breach in the blue ice wall, broke through and freed themselves before Winter could intervene.

Furious, Winter banished Gaska-geardi and her lover. He seized the warden's skins and feathers and burned them so the warden could shapeshift no more. Trapped in the body of a mortal man, the warden grew old. Gaska-geardi, much reduced in size from Summer's melting, wept yet again her mortal tears as her lover froze in her fatal embrace, and there was no one now to heal the cracks and furrows that marred the perfect surface of her face.

Winter, much diminished in power, forfeited his dominion over the land. Summer gained ascendancy, allied itself with Spring and Fall. Winter kept only his most far-flung territories, and some say a time is coming when he will lose them all.

The ice child found her way back to her mother's hut in the far north village, but years had flown, and her mother had long since passed away. Yet, on the coldest nights, they say, the ice child searches for her mother still, writes on warm windows her ancient runes in frost as she waits outside, bereft, having lost all she loved, her heart an aching crack.

JESSICA MEEKER

Glacier Bear

A small cabin just beyond the Alaska Range shuddered under the weight of fresh snow. It had been falling for days, but finally, today the sky would clear. The sun would hover above the mountains for the first time this winter, allowing Ivan to travel away from the cabin without a flashlight.

He pushed open his front door into the snow, sweeping away the snowdrift on the other side. After clearing the path, he tucked his shovel back inside and closed the door. There was no need to lock it since very few ventured out in this temperature.

Ivan strapped on a pair of rusted snowshoes with worn straps but pulled one too roughly and nearly snapped the leather off. He cursed and tested the grip to see if it would last the trip. Satisfied, he began to clamber over the snow pile surrounding his house. At one point he had carved steps into the snow, but due to a warm wind from the south, parts had melted and refrozen, making climbing difficult for an old fisherman with a rough knee. At the top, he scanned the twilight landscape. Behind him, nameless mountain peaks rose from the earth. On one, a bald area of exposed rock and fallen trees showed evidence of an avalanche. It was probably not even a few days old since it hadn't been masked by the relentless blizzards that tormented the range.

Other snow-covered cabins and trailers were barely visible under the piles of white. Thin lights showed through the windows, and a few shadows of people moved within. He wished they too would be buried deep in snowpack, returning the landscape to its ancient state before the humans colonized. Most of the others out here were like him. They had worked in big towns, earning enough money to hide in the mountains come winter. He had worked for over thirty years at a commercial fishing business in Anchorage, forever leaving him with the stench of salt in his skin, his hands rough and cracked. He had become so used to the sea that even now the snow seemed to shift and rise in waves. Rocks were killer whales, harpooned by poachers. Fallen pine needles were their blood. The mice and rabbits that ran atop the snowpack were fish that narrowly escaped the nets. As he walked now like he was carrying a sack full of fish, his muscles remembered the effort of pulling in those he caught.

Ivan had only been outside for a few minutes, but the frost had already begun to accumulate on his eyelashes and beard. His cheeks were turning purple, and he had to rub his gloved hands against them to ease the numbness. It was a painful feeling, trying to wake the nerves. It was like shocks of electricity, sparking under his flesh, but it was a sign that frostbite had not set in.

The snowshoes helped him walk through the deep snow, but he still sank to his knees. Ivan hadn't wanted to leave his shelter for a few more days, but he was nearly out of canned food and salted meats. The snow fell early this year, cutting preparation time short. Today was probably the safest day to go out according to the radio. The temperature dipped to fifty below and would remain constant for the next few hours before dropping farther into the negatives. He didn't want to be out when that happened. He had to keep flexing his fingers and toes to keep them from going stiff.

The store was only a mile walk from home, but it took him over an hour to get there. It was one of the larger and older buildings in Coback, made of red brick and wood-trimmed windows. Someone had cleared out the front entrance, leaving the only tracks he saw, which led to the door. They were already crusted over with ice and snow. The doors had been left open, allowing snow, and probably a rat or two, to find the way in. The store wasn't in operation during the winter—only a few locals dared stay—but the owners kindly left the doors unlocked, expecting people to leave money for what they took. Ivan knew it was late into the season and supplies would be scarce.

Ivan followed the prints of the last poor, cold soul who was here, hoping it was the safest path down to the door. He couldn't risk getting injured. Not when the only way out was by snowmobile or helicopter, which wouldn't get to him for hours. Many people died out in the tundra and mountains of rural Alaska, all because they weren't mindful of their surroundings. Ivan's own cousin fell into the Tanana River while ice fishing and wasn't discovered until spring broke the ice up.

He took off his snowshoes and leaned them against the brick building. Before he went in, he looked back at the mountains where the sun was sliding down, then made his way inside. It was a tight squeeze between the wood and metal, but with a little sucking in of the gut, he was able to push through. Inside, a thin fog hung over the aisles of wood shelves and glass freezers. It smelled of moldy fruits and vegetables that probably rotted last fall. On the keepers' desk, a stack of coins and bills rested. Ivan, himself, would leave whatever he had on him. He opened the drawstring bag he had stuffed into his pocket before leaving the house and began to scavenge. This year there seemed to be less food than usual. The locals were known to be selfish, taking more than they needed. At least he was able to get a few packets of dried meat, fish, and a small strip of leather for his shoes. He passed quickly by the rank produce bins and down the canned aisle, grabbing things that would be filling, like lentils and the few cans of soup that remained.

The twilight that haunted most hours of winter started reclaiming the land. He grabbed a few dollars and coins from his pocket and left them near the register, then beelined for the door. Once again, he sucked in his stomach and passed through. He turned to pull it shut to prevent any more snow from getting in. It was more effort than others made, but it was his small thank-you to the owners. In this hard season, he didn't take access to a store, even this one, for granted.

Outside, the world was so quiet that he could hear the crackled breathing of frost-ridden trees. Carefully, trying not to rip the old leather strap, he put on his snowshoes. He began to climb out of the store's entrance. Going up put less pressure on the knees, but it took more energy. He struggled to pull himself and his supplies up the slippery hill. Suddenly, the silence was disturbed by the sound of snow crust crunching under the weight of something heavy. Ivan's whole body throbbed with his heartbeat as he strained to listen. It was coming from the west side of the building along with grunts and huffing.

From the immense size of the creature, he thought at first it was a grizzly, but after a minute he realized it was a black bear. No matter what, meeting one in winter meant it was hungry, dangerous, most likely scavenging and drawn by the smell of rotten produce. Its long and narrow head told him it was a female, but something was off about her. In the dwindling light, her black fur cast shades of dark blue, her stomach colored a light silver. Each move she made was like the shimmer of the moon on water. Ivan was stunned. He had heard about these blue bears, often referred to as glacier bears by the native Alaskans. They were close relatives to the black bear but much larger. He'd never thought he would see one in his life, especially here. Glacier bears lived in the eastern part of the state and were rarer than a blue moon.

Instinctively, Ivan reached for the hunting knife he kept in his left pocket. The metal felt cold through his gloves and heavier than usual. If this were a grizzly, a knife would barely be able to pierce the thick skin, but for a female glacier bear, it could be lethal. Having grown up in Alaska, he'd faced bears in the past, even the famed Kodiak bears that can weigh over one thousand pounds and stand eight feet tall. He had occasionally seen them crossing the permafrost tundra and mountains. But this was the first time he had faltered in front of a bear since he was a boy.

When he was working along the Cook Inlet and Alaskan Gulf, he would see dozens of bears scouring the rocky shores. They were searching for food, and Ivan remembered one day, maybe sixteen years ago, the sea had blessed them. A large humpback whale washed onto the land, west of Chisik Island. It must have been dead in the water for weeks, its body already bloated and misshapen. Its skin was a sickly gray, marred with decay.

Ivan first spotted the whale early in the morning before the sun had fully risen above the horizon. Dark shadows of wild animals surrounded it. Ravens, eagles, and magpies were plucking at its flesh when a group of larger creatures started to tear at it. After a closer look, he could tell there were bears, dozens of them. A few nipped and shoved smaller ones away, but each one was persistent in getting a meal. Other fishermen joined Ivan, some carrying rifles. They looked out at the whale, lifted their weapons, and fired. Despite the breeze, the gun smoke seemed to linger in the air for the rest of that day.

The bear trudged steadily, moving her head side to side, smelling the air. Ivan tried to remain as quiet as possible. He avoided shifting his weight for fear of falling through the snow's crust. But he did not realize his grip had loosened on his bag. A single can slipped; he watched it fall, sliding down the hill, clanging against the store's door. A tingle ran down his spine, and he turned to look at the bear. She had raised herself onto her hind legs and was now watching him, her cool, brown eyes full of sorrow and starvation. Ivan pointed the knife at her. She shifted slightly, and only now did he see what was hidden between her legs and what caused her struggle: a single cub. It was big enough to be a yearling, but it was dreadfully thin. Its spine and ribs visible through its skin, the cub breathed slowly and raggedly. Like its mother, its fur was blue and silver except for a few patches of black against the muzzle.

He stepped back, his right foot breaking through the crust. The mother bear's body now rumbled and shook as she growled, exposing her large canines. She leveled on all fours and charged. Ivan fell against the ground, losing his hold on the knife, which slid out of reach. He felt her hot breath and smelled her pungent odor, but the sow didn't make contact. She seemed to linger for a moment, taking in Ivan's own scent, before turning away. His head buzzed as the adrenaline traveled through his body. Though his eyes swam, he could see that the mother was already back at her cub, covering it with a large paw.

Ivan knew no mother and cub should be out here this time of year. He glanced away and looked up at the mountain. It was possible that their den had been crushed by the avalanche. That would have forced them to move into a lower area, but it did not explain why they had come this far. Maybe the mother and cub had not stored enough winter reserves to make it through. But bears were hibernators by instinct and evolution. Under normal conditions, they knew what it took to survive till spring.

He felt a lump rise in his throat. He almost didn't care if the bear tried to attack him—he knew she and her cub needed food whether it be from the store or from his flesh. He was just an old man, a retired fisherman who hid away in the deep Alaskan wilderness. He'd killed plenty of black bears in his time; now, for the first time, he saw their desire to live. He knew what they wanted, and he wanted to give it to them.

He didn't want to frighten them again, so he quietly removed his snowshoes. The mother seemed to flinch with each of his movements, but did not charge. He slid back down to the store entrance, and with what strength he had, he pulled the doors until the opening was wide enough for the bear. So that they would feel safe entering, he moved several feet away. They hovered by the corner for a moment, but the smell must have been enough to convince the blue mother and cub to move. The cub struggled through the snow, but luckily it did not sink far into its grasp. It let out a low grunt of protest when the mother paused at the entry where Ivan had once stood.

"Let there be enough for the both of you," he said.

He watched them pass through the doors into the darkness. Then he grabbed his snowshoes and walked toward home. After he had gotten a good distance away, Ivan glanced back to see if he could get one last look, but like the glaciers they resembled, they had already melted away from sight. All he could hope for now was that they would live to see another freeze.

JACK KIRNE

Escape Out the Back Passage

Dad left early on a Sunday morning. It was the start of summer, and for the next four weeks, I would be alone in the house where my family had once been happy. Dad didn't want to go back to driving trucks, but he was desperate. Our well was dry, and the cost of getting the water trucks to fill our tank was prohibitive on the wage he made bartending at the local pub. I was sad to see him go. Although we struggled for conversation, we had grown close in the wake of my mother's disappearance, following each other from room to room, eager for the company. But also, I was seventeen. I liked the idea of being in control of my life for once.

The night before he set off, Dad sat me down over a dinner of fish and chips to lay out the ground rules. They were as expected: stay out of the liquor cabinet, go to school every day, there was to be no takeaway except on Sundays, and I was to use the internet for homework and emergencies only. ("Use it too much, and I'll cancel it," he said.) There were to be no boys over whatsoever, which was fine by me—I was plain and mousey; they wouldn't come even if invited. He looked old, I thought. The orange linoleum tablecloth amplified the sickly mustard light, and as we ate, the signs of his premature aging seemed to announce themselves. He was nearly bald but for a few wisps of grey hair he combed over; moisture gathered in the crow's feet that pinched the sides of his once full face. Sometimes strangers asked, always in an embarrassed hush, why I lived with my grandfather.

Dad reached out and put a hand on mine and said, "I shouldn't leave you." But he did.

*

I did not go to school, even after my teachers left long messages on the machine. I was sure they phoned my father too, but when he called to check in, he did not mention it. Maybe he felt guilty. I spent those first days alone watching old DVDs of *'Allo 'Allo!* on the couch. We had five seasons, and I found the show's predictability comforting—cowardly Renée always being roped into increasingly harebrained schemes by the French resistance, the naff accordion theme that bracketed each episode. My favourite character was Michelle "of the Résistance" Dubois, whose catchphrases, "Listen very carefully, I shall say this only once" and "I will escape out the back passage," I found endlessly amusing. I liked that she was single-minded and fierce, not romantically attached. She was always let down by the incompetence of others. I loved this about her most of all.

I spent a lot of time in the house managing the water situation, which was this: we had no water. The trouble started three years ago, shortly after we moved in. First, we noticed silt in our water, which seemed harmless enough. Then, one day, Dad had run a bath and gone off to do another chore, only to return to find the faucet spitting out a coffee-coloured sludge. This alarmed us, but soon after, the water seemed to return to its former, slightly soiled state. Months later, our neighbour, Grace, was knocking on our door, asking if our pump was pulling up anything. Her house was the first in the area to go dry.

It didn't take a genius to figure out what happened. Drive in or out of town, and you saw them: fields of alfalfa shimmering unnaturally green. Being a rural town in a dry place, we had always drawn our water from the aquifer. People didn't think about it in the past, not really. The water was there, and we expected it to stay that way. But now that it was harder to draw from, you could ask anyone and they could tell you how large it was and its name, the Kirkwood Basin. I used to think of it poetically, as ancient water, moving in slow, twisting roots below us, but now that it was so scarce, I couldn't think of it as anything other than water, always diminishing. When the earth was entirely sapped, the basin would not refill for thousands of years.

What I hated most about living in a house without water was the maniacal modes of saving Dad enforced. The tank had been dry for months: everything we used came from a bottle, and so if we weren't drinking it, the water was being recycled somehow. We reused the water we did the dishes with to flush the toilets and used greywater from our washing machine to mop our floors. When there was water in the tank for us to shower, we put clothes at our feet, to double up the usage. With Dad gone, I allowed myself a certain wastefulness. I pulled out plugs and let the soapy water run down the drain. I poured half-drunk glasses of water onto the parched garden, rather than drinking them myself. This was an outrageous thing to do. I felt powerful.

A week passed, and again, I found myself rewatching *'Allo 'Allo!* from the beginning. It was Lt. Gruber, the show's token homosexual, who alerted me to my problem. "It was very lonely on the Russian front," he said. I sat and considered the empty cups and dirty towels around me, thought, *Yes, that is me: I am here, in this wasteland, waiting for the weather to kill me.* But what could I do? There was no point leaving the house. For a hundred kilometres in any direction, it was as dry and miserable as here.

I might have stayed in the house until Dad got back if not for the other problem. I was beginning to smell. Most of the time, I was oblivious to it—but occasionally, there was a whiff of my odour, a putrid onion stench that reminded me of a Four 'n' Twenty meat pie. I needed a wash, a real one, not done with a sponge over the laundry sink. There were enough bottles of water in our basement to last two months, but if I wanted a shower, I had to ride into town, where the council had set up a series of stalls that blasted you with cold water for two minutes and forty seconds. The only other option was waiting for unlikely rain. After three days of patience, the sky turned dark. Pausing *'Allo 'Allo!*, I ran to the window to find the dark was caused not by rain but dust, which pelted the house like a brief but angry hailstorm.

On Friday, I dowsed myself in deodorant and rode the ten kilometres into town. Hoping to avoid anybody who might ask where I had been all week, I set out midmorning, figuring they would be in class. The ride was easy enough, the road flat and straight across the landscape. I pedalled past the Ryans', the Medlicotts', the Wrights'. I had heard they were considering abandoning their properties. They couldn't sell, after all. Nobody wanted to buy a home that had gone dry. My father hadn't said a word, but I knew that if the drought didn't break, we would meet a similar fate. It was almost funny, I thought, how this premise was apocalyptic and outrageously dull at the same time. There were no marauding gangs or angry protesters, except Nancy Danaher, who had camped outside the council office for 280 days and counting. But nobody paid much attention to her, on account of her being somewhat unusual. (She had, for some time, kept a chicken that she walked on a leash.) Of course, in town hall meetings there was the yelling and tears, and reporters sometimes stopped in from the city to take unflattering photos. Otherwise, the focus was on getting on, surviving. I passed a sign that read: *40km per hour, Earth Fissures Possible.*

I arrived in Greenwell at eleven. The day was warming up, and the beige concrete shone in the dry heat. The portable showers had been erected in the carpark of the Coles supermarket. To my relief, they appeared almost abandoned, except for Ms. Holland, who sat in a small wooden hut reading a newspaper. She was in charge of the showers and took her duty seriously, never surrendering more than a single water token, even if offered a bribe. The paper's headline read: *Terror from the Air*. Beneath, a photo of the thousands of pigeons that had descended on Dookie the week before.

"All that town needs now is Tippi Hedren," I said.

Ms. Holland peered at me over the paper.

"You know, *The Birds*."

"*The Birds*," she said, keeping the stare up. "Hilarious." She went back to her paper.

"Can I get a token?"

She licked her finger, turned the page. "Water's out. There was a big truck coming in this morning, but it hit a fissure."

"How's the driver?" I said.

She chewed her lip. "Well, she's dead."

Ms. Holland's tone was cold. We talked a while longer, mostly about who'd gone dry, who hadn't, before I said goodbye and set back out into the blaring morning. Without the shower, there was no reason for me to be in town. But also I did not want to go home, where I would be alone.

I found myself drawn to the supermarket. As I approached, the doors parted with an exaltation of arctic air, and I hurried inside. I had no intention to buy anything, but I liked to loiter in that tiny universe of goods. I had recently seen a documentary on SBS that explained how the CIA had once airlifted a fully stocked supermarket into Yugoslavia. This was during the cold war, the CIA wanting to preach the possibilities of free enterprise. I imagined those famine-starved Communists felt a little like I did now, astounded by the wealth of so much stuff. It replenished me. There was no sign of anything awry, the broccoli firm, the cans neat and fully stocked.

I ran into Matthew in the confectionary aisle shoving a king-size Mars bar into the crotch of his jeans. Matthew was in the grade above me at school. He was attractive, I suppose, tall and thin with wiry muscles. His bone structure was impeccable. He was a good footy player and moderately popular. Some people hated him because his father had made it big when the corporate farmers moved in. He owned a drilling company, and these days there was always a new well to be sunk as everybody raced to the bottom of the basin. We locked eyes, and I could see Matthew trying to figure if I'd squeal.

"It's you," he said.

I nodded. "Why aren't you in school?"

Matthew looked up and down the aisle. "I had better things to do," he said.

"Yeah, I can tell."

He considered this for a while and then said, "Are you sick?"

"What? No, I'm not sick."

"Why aren't you in school then?"

I shrugged. "I guess I don't feel like going."

This was a half-truth. I was avoiding Mr. Hedd. He taught maths, science, and German—subjects I loathed because he taught them. He was a thin, pretentious man, a dead ringer for Herr Flick. A few weeks before my father had left, Mr. Hedd had leaned in close to correct my German spelling. His coffee breath was musty warm, and I had the urge to bat him away like a mosquito. That was when he sniffed of my hair. The grovelling inhalation had seemed loud to me, but nobody had noticed.

The Mars bar bulged against the front of Matthew's jeans, and realising that I was staring, he grinned and gave it a suggestive stroke. "You stink," he said.

"Well, thanks." I tried to affect an easy sarcasm, but I could feel myself going red. "I rode in to shower, but the water is out."

"That's too bad," Matthew said. "Really." We stood there a while longer, and I could feel his eyes moving up and down my body. I wanted to turn and run. Just as I was about to say I had to go, he said, "You could come to my place. Dad's just had the tank filled."

He sounded almost ashamed as he said this, his voice higher and more boyish than usual. I felt nervous at the prospect of going with him and even more nervous at the prospect of being naked in the same house as him. He was more or less a stranger. But I did really want that shower.

*

His house was square and white and massive on the landscape. Its windows were tall and narrow, which made the building appear as if it could have housed prisoners or a cult. Everything inside was black, white, or chrome, except for the chandeliers, which were gold. Matthew appeared confident in the space, throwing his car keys into a bowl by the door and not seeming to notice how his footsteps boomed on the black-on-white marble tiles.

"You want a drink?"

"Sure," I said, following him into the kitchen, which was all marble countertops and Smeg appliances. When he said drink, I thought he meant water, so I was a little surprised when he pulled a bottle of gin from the freezer and tonic from the fridge.

"I make them pretty strong," he said, filling the glass halfway with gin.

"Are you a big drinker?" I said.

"I've got a pretty high tolerance," he said. "Stronger than most."

He dropped a cucumber slice into each glass, then passed one to me.

"Thanks," I said, although the already-sweating glass worried me. I was not a drinker, had been drunk only once. That was at Jessica Eyre's sixteenth, and while nothing terrible had happened (I had skulled four Lemon Ruskis and fallen asleep in the garden), it was agreed by all that I had embarrassed myself.

"Cheers," Matthew said, clinking his glass against mine before knocking his drink back in three long gulps. I wondered if Matthew knew the story and, if not, whether I should tell him now. He wiped his lips with the back of his hand. Was this a dare? Wary, I took a sip and bit my lip to keep from bursting into a coughing fit, the alcohol burning the whole way down. The second sip was less awful, but still a challenge. I felt his eyes on me as I drank, watching, judging.

"You don't have your bathers in there, do you?" he said, pointing to my backpack.

I said I didn't.

"Shame," he said gently. "We have a hell of a pool."

"Oh yeah?"

"Yeah."

He led me through two French doors and out onto a tiled patio. He was right—the pool was fuck-off impressive. Standing at its edge, I thought the whole scene was resort-like, the pool cerulean and seemingly without an edge at the far end, creating the illusion of the water being impossibly suspended above the yellow-brown expanse of open land below. Around the edge were banana lounges and sturdy umbrellas that tilted in the middle to manage the sun at any time of day. It was far nicer than the local pool, which had not been filled for the last two years due to water restrictions. He said, "You know, I wouldn't mind if you went without your bathers."

My heart thundered, and I started to shiver, although it was tremendously hot. "I bet you wouldn't," I said. I skulled the drink, and the rush was extraordinary—a cool surge like a spotlight at the front of my mind. I didn't want to sleep with him. What I wanted was to swim. Perhaps it was stupid of me to pull the shirt over my head and kick my shorts off. A lusty disappointment flashed in his eyes when I kept my underwear and bra on. I took two steps, then ran into a dive as I plunged into the water that closed and pressed around me. I held my breath and stayed weightless in the blue depths. It was cold, almost painfully so, and this was exactly what I wanted. When I surfaced, Matthew was shirtless on the deck. He looked afraid, arms clutched across his chest as if hugging himself.

"You're coming in," I said, not quite phrasing it as a question.

Matthew started to undo his jeans, then reached into the front and drew out the Mars bar. It had gone limp in the heat and flopped about as he shook it in the air.

"You hungry?" he said, peeling it open. It was turd-like and sloppy in his hands.

"Gross," I said, as he made to eat it. A cheekiness came into him then, and he cocked his arm to throw it.

"Don't you dare!" I said. "I swear, if you throw it, I'll go straight home!"

Matthew laughed and tossed it aside. Then, he stripped off his jeans and dived to join me. In his near naked state, he appeared fragile, not yet complete. Each bone of his spine jutted out with such clarity that they appeared like a range of mountains running down his back.

"You bastard," I said.

We swam for an hour or two, climbing out of the pool when we got too cold. When the water fell from our bodies, it looked like falling light. We chatted easily, probably due to the alcohol. Matthew talked about his parents mostly. His dad worked across the country now and was rarely home; his mother was visiting her sister in the city. The gang of boys Matthew hung with at school were a rough bunch—a few were expelled the year before for growing pot in the school's communal vegetable garden. But poolside, Matthew was different, sweeter. When I told him about *'Allo 'Allo!*, he listened with patient interest, even though I knew I sounded mad trying to explain why the Nazis kept forging *The Fallen Madonna with the Big Boobies*. He said it sounded "really funny." He went inside to make us a couple more gin and tonics, and as the day strolled toward evening, I started to feel light and relaxed in my body. Then, when I went to stand, I nearly fell flat on my face but caught myself at the last moment, skidding my hand on the tiles. Before I could make sense of what had happened, Matthew was leading me inside and draping a towel over my shoulders.

"When did you last eat?" he said as he sat me down on a cream leather sofa.

I had to think a little about this. "Last night," I said.

He threw his arms up and laughed. "Classic mistake," he said. "Drinking on an empty stomach."

I wanted to tell him it was his fault—he had started off this drinking—but he was already out of the room. While he was gone, I looked at the DVDs stacked on a black bookshelf by the telly: they had box sets of *Friends* and every Bond film. On the wall there was a framed poster for *Titanic*. I thought this was very classy. Matthew returned a few minutes later with toasted cheese sandwiches and two beers. I devoured the warm sandwich, burning the roof of my mouth with the broiling cheese. I didn't care; it was delicious. Meanwhile, he flicked on the television and surfed between channels before settling on an old *Seinfeld* episode. In the blue of the TV screen light, his face appeared hollow and waifish, with deep pockets of shadow beneath his bold cheekbones.

"I'm so glad you came over," he said.

"I'm still waiting for that shower you promised me," I said.

I immediately regretted saying this, as it triggered that lusty flash in his eyes. But this time, I felt less afraid. I had not had sex before, and I wondered if I wanted to, right now, at this moment.

"The upstairs bathroom has two showerheads," he said. "If you're interested."

"I think you're the one who is interested," I said.

He chuckled. "God, it's never straight with you, is it?"

"I don't know what you mean."

"I can't tell if you're here to use me or to hang out."

I felt annoyed by this. He was the one who had invited me, who had plied me with alcohol and encouraged to swim. And that euphemism, *hang out*. Like we were old chums. "Can't I do both?" I said.

And then, his hand was on my thigh—a gentle ambassador, moving up my side. He paused. When I didn't brush it away, he leaned in to kiss me. Why didn't I push him away? My entire body was alive with want. He placed his hands all over me, and beneath him I felt small. I could feel the moisture moving between us, through our mouths. *This is how the earth works*, I thought. Then, he went to grab at the top of my underwear, and I panicked. I snapped up and pulled myself away.

"What?" he said, his mouth all wide and thirsty.

"I have to shower," I said. "Trust me."

"I don't mind if you smell," he said. "Really."

"Well, I do."

He huffed as he led me to the other end of the house. The bathroom was all white tiles, with a clawfoot bath at the far end. There were ferns on the windowsill, and the fittings on the pristine faucet were a faux-eighteenth-century design. The shower was to my left. There were no buckets. Matthew plodded over to twist the shower taps, allowing water to slap against the tiles. I couldn't help but think this was barbaric. Sweetly, he leaned in and kissed me.

"Do you want me to stay?" he said. I could not see or feel his erection against me, yet somehow I knew it was there. I thought about my hero, brave and tenacious Michelle "of the Résistance," what she might do. All I wanted was that shower. But I needed him gone.

"Where's your bedroom?" I said. I saw the excitement move through him as he led me out the bathroom door and pointed to the end of the hall.

"I'm a virgin," he said.

"Wait for me there."

I went back into the bathroom and closed the door. Steam was filling up the room fast, and I sucked at the humidity as I stripped. The noise of all that water crashing against the tiles was enormous.

*

More of the town went dry, and most people just up and left, sometimes leaving their possessions behind. "Let the banks deal with it" was a common refrain. For a while a class action lawsuit gave us hope the town might survive, but by the time it made it to the courts, even the farmers' wells were dry, and those who had profited had declared bankruptcy, having split their companies and squirreled their wealth into Cayman Islands accounts. I went to study biology but soon switched to arts. I did not go back. My father was one of the few to remain. He is happy there, I think. He calls in the middle of the night, sometimes, to tell me what he has plundered from the abandoned houses: old fridges, jewellery, and once, a ceremonial sword he sold to a private collector for $30,000. He makes a good living this way, and I suspect he will stay out there until he dies.

Sometimes, not often, my mind drifts to Matthew, all those years ago, lying in the dark as he waits for a girl he barely knew. In my mind, the lights are off, and he lies atop the covers in his jocks. He listens to the sound of water dancing on the tiles; his muscles are perked with want. When the shower quiets, he positions himself to best show off his features. When I do not emerge, he creeps down the hall to stand at the door. He listens, then shouts (cautiously at first, and then again, full-voiced), "You all right in there?" And when I do not answer, he opens the door to a window left ajar and a bathroom full of steam.

MARY FIFIELD

Irene's Daughters

At quarter past the hour when she was supposed to meet Ricardo Salinas, former-mayor-turned-real-estate-developer, Danielle leaned against a cinder block wall and fiddled with the used iPhone she had just bought from her landlord. Everyone at home already had one, but anything with an Apple logo on it cost an arm and a leg here, and she was not exactly flush with cash these days. Besides, her policy from the very beginning had been not to call attention to herself, to the extent that was possible as a six-foot tall white woman with red hair.

The day was soupy and hot, exactly the right conditions for a tropical squall that she suspected would not materialize because storms during this rainy season had been few and far between. She moved to the shade cast by her neighbor's canela tree and dragged her finger across the screen. Would she ever use half the stuff on this thing? She slipped the phone into the woven wool satchel she'd been carrying around since her Peace Corps days and zipped it shut.

A shiny black Ford Expedition careened around the corner and slowed as it approached. Under the right wind conditions, she could detect the hum of that chassis half a mile away. Her breath caught in her throat.

As the passenger window slid down, a man with coiffed salt-and-pepper hair and a trimmed mustache leaned over from the driver's seat. "Señora Daniela?"

She clutched the strap of her bag with both hands. "Who are you?"

"Ricardo!" He smiled broadly.

"Oh…yes, yes," she stammered, embarrassed for overreacting. But then, she hadn't expected to see that particular model of car ever again, certainly not up close. "Of course. I'm sorry."

He pushed open the door. "Pleased to meet you. Excuse me for keeping you waiting."

"That's fine." Climbing onto the leather seat, she quickly regained her composure. It surprised her that he even mentioned being late; he must have assumed she was one of those resident foreigners who still lived on American time.

As he closed the window, sealing them in a climate-controlled pod, she involuntarily recalled the last time she'd ridden in a vehicle like this—two years and three months ago, when she gave a British reporter a tour of the abandoned, unctuous tailings ponds after he assured her anything she said would be deep background.

"Nothing on the record," Danielle insisted. "I've got a little girl."

"I give you my word. I'll hire a car." A car, as it turned out, nearly identical to the company's shiny black SUVs, better to avoid suspicion.

That was in the chaotic months after Danielle had resigned from Repsol and before PetroEcuador took over the oil concession, after the village president filed a human rights suit with the Inter-American commission but before the president's husband took a bribe from the state. In fact, it wasn't clear exactly when her husband had taken the bribe, but she ended up on television, dressed in traditional regalia and looking angry and mortified, claiming the government was trying to frame him. Danielle had watched from an overpriced hotel room in Coca and felt sorry for the young woman, whom she'd met once when she and another scientist explained to the community how the soils would be tested before and after drilling. The president—the first woman ever elected in that village of Kichwa families—stood steely gazed and poised, asking when they would see the report and reminding the company that by law it had to be translated into Kichwa. "We are not fools, you know," she warned in Spanish. Danielle nodded, fully aware that the company would never go to the trouble and the government wouldn't require them to.

"The city is upgrading the water system out here." Ricardo gestured to the mounds of dirt piled on the sides of the street where crews were excavating to lay sewer lines. "Finally."

"Um-hmm," she muttered, distracted by fragments of her conversation with the reporter that kept slipping out of the folds of her memory:

Does the produced water get dumped here directly, without any kind of treatment?

Usually.

And do the chemicals leach into the soil?

Into the topsoil, yes. The subsoil is clay, so it's more impervious…

Humming, Ricardo commanded the four-wheel drive over the perennially under-construction road to the far edges of La Colina, where Danielle and her daughter, Michaela, were currently renting a flat. The town on the western edge of the rainforest was where the two of them had ended up after Danielle sold the apartment in Quito, learning too late that she was in fact more vulnerable as a whistleblower in the US, thanks to an arcane clause in an international trade agreement. Danielle had already whittled their belongings down to the essential and hard-to-part-with and signed a contract with a shipping company. She had started to scan real estate websites in Puget Sound and look for research positions at the university, to imagine camping with her daughter on the Olympic Peninsula and speaking English at the grocery store, despite Michaela's protests that she didn't want to move to Seattle because she didn't have any friends there and the mangoes would be terrible.

Yet even as Danielle became more invested in the dream, she was not crestfallen when it started to disintegrate. It had a certain appealing, glamorous quality, with all the edges smoothed and the grit washed away. In other words, unreal. She didn't know what to make of this bit of self-discovery, that a life in the country in which she was born and raised now seemed like a fantasy out of a magazine.

Past the end of the construction zone, they pulled onto a dirt road that clearly delineated the "outskirts"—a stretch of rolling brush-covered hills cut through by the occasional gravel road. Where the hills flattened into a valley hunkered a gigantic one-story house with a multi-car garage, Doric columns, and a tile roof. No rebar sticking out through the top in preparation for building another story when there was enough money. No skimping on incongruous flourishes to show off the owner's European-influenced tastes. It reminded her of some of the narco-mansions she'd seen from the bus traveling through Honduras when she was in her twenties.

"That belongs to the attorney for the city," Ricardo informed her. "This neighborhood is going to be very desirable soon."

At the road's terminus, Ricardo got out of the car and opened a map of the subdivision, showing the property extending far up the hill and the hundred-plus residential parcels that had been carved out of it.

"This all belongs to one landowner?"

"Yes, Jorge Santander. He lives in the US now and has a few big companies there. He's trying to liquidate his assets." He tilted his head and crossed his arms in a self-satisfied way, as if reassured by an immutable truth of how the world works. "You know."

She did know. She learned the story of land grabbing in the central Amazon ten years ago when she had first arrived in the country. Janeth Mamallacta, the only Kichwa woman the company ever hired, had ticked off the steps on her ring-laden fingers while they flew out to an oil field on the Peruvian border: Waorani territory had been invaded by Kichwa people on and off over a few hundred years, until eventually the Waorani retreated deeper into the eastern jungle. Then about a hundred years ago, Spanish descendants moved down from the Andes, taking tracts of rainforest from Kichwa people through juridical trickery, theft, and violence. Today old-money Ecuadorians and foreigners working for multinationals were scooping up parcels, driving prices up.

"So now there is a modern real estate market," Janeth said. "It would never occur to us to think about the rainforest as property. We've learned the hard way how the colonos handle these things." She pulled a pocket mirror out of her purse and fixed a stray black hair, then glanced at Danielle. "Here." Janeth offered her a sip of Coke. "You look a little funny."

Taking the bottle, Danielle gazed below at the carpet of trees broken up by clear cuts like a checkerboard for giants. She was concentrating hard not to vomit. She assumed it was air sickness, not morning sickness. At the time she thought Janeth's story had nothing to do with her: she was simply here to sock away money to pay off her student loans and then get a research job with the Parks Service back home.

Danielle scanned the lush slope and turned to Ricardo. "Which properties are still available?"

He pointed to a cluster on the drawing, his nails buffed to a shine. "We've got a larger corner property here that is just one block down from your friend Tito's plot."

"Tito's not my friend," she corrected him too quickly. "He's an acquaintance."

"Yes," he smiled. "Sorry."

Against her better judgment, she had turned to Tito when she decided that La Colina was the most practical if not least conspicuous place for her to go after leaving the capital. Now she was beset by the occasional pang of regret at inopportune moments, and all she could do was wait it out.

"Can I see it?" she asked after an awkward pause.

They walked a block uphill to an intersection of two wide paths that Ricardo claimed would eventually be paved streets. The property sloped gradually into a ravine, out of which grew paja toquilla and grasses that flourished after the diverse species of a native tropical forest had died off. She was not a botanist, but in the process of testing sites for drilling she had learned many things about the jungle.

Beyond the ravine, the Llanganates Mountains framed the horizon, just about to catch the setting sun. Ricardo chattered on about the proximity to the center of town, the planned green spaces, and something about him having started La Colina's first (and now defunct) recycling program when he was mayor. Danielle mostly tuned him out. She was picturing a two-story house with a view of these mountains, a balcony where she could sit with a cold beer every night and watch the clouds and the sun while Michaela did her homework or played with the neighbor kids. It was one of those views that could be a window on the world, or maybe a ledge. Watching the day end here would always remind her of what she knew lay on the other side of those mountains: more peaks that gave way to the Pacific Ocean of her adolescence, a link to a place and a past that stirred an unsettling ambivalence inside her, like a plucked guitar string.

"This is very interesting," she said, code for "Let's talk price." She opened her mouth before she thought about what was coming out of it, and at the various moments when she could have changed her mind, she didn't. Yes, the original plan had been to buy something small, unassuming, more difficult to seize than cash in the state-owned bank and easy enough to sell if she needed to in a hurry. Building would take a lot longer, and she'd probably have to put up with unscrupulous contractors who think they can swindle a foreign woman. So what, she thought. She had put up with worse. Her daughter was Ecuadorian, and Danielle had her moments. As far as "home" went, the situation was very clear: this was their last, best option.

*

A couple of weeks before Michaela started a new school and Danielle started her new teaching job, the two-story house with a pitched metal roof and brick walls was finished. A few other homes, all more elaborate than hers, had started going up. Danielle stood on the balcony after the last box was carried off the truck. She could see how the scraped earth to the south would be transformed into a large cluster of houses, as if they had sprouted spontaneously from the land. That was what made infrastructure around here so deceptive. Once it went in, it looked like it belonged as long as it continued being used. When people gave up on the roads, the buildings, and the oil platforms, the jungle reclaimed them bit by incomplete bit.

There was even a toast for it that some engineers who had family near the tailings ponds would assuage themselves with: "When we finish, it will all go back to normal." In those days, she believed that too. The first time she drank with the crew was when Antonio, having just been promoted to manager, invited her to join them at their favorite bar in Coca. She felt flattered, special, included. It became an almost weekly ritual until he died. After that she would drop in on occasion to be collegial, but by that point things were already changing. The more she read about people's strange, inexplicable cancers in the newspaper, the more farmers grew perplexed by unpredictable planting seasons, the harder it was for her to smile and clink beer bottles and reply, "Salud!"

Then from some other part of her, the question so sudden and belligerent she couldn't override it with the rational voice that usually governed her thoughts: How many decisions had she made in the last twelve years just because she wanted to fit in?

Shame flushed in her cheeks; she could feel the beginning of a panic attack at the edges, the fluttery sensation that something was closing in. Then tinny, distracting reggaeton music blared suddenly from inside the house.

"Mama," Michaela shouted, "help me unpack my room!"

*

On the first day of school, Danielle followed Michaela around the kitchen trying to braid her daughter's wavy black hair as Michaela made herself a roll with guava jam.

"Hold still for thirty seconds, please," Danielle said.

"Mama, promise me you won't embarrass me."

Danielle finished the braid and pinned it in a bun on the top of her daughter's head. "What kind of a thing is that to say? I'm not even going to be in your class."

She took a bite of the bread and mumbled, "But you might be there at recess."

"Don't talk with your mouth full," she said. "No, I won't. I'll be with the fourth graders."

Michaela chewed methodically and swallowed. "Mama," she replied finally. "Promise you won't get mad."

"I won't."

"If the kids know you're my mom, they'll be huge jerks. I mean it. It's bad enough that I'm the new girl anyway."

Danielle handed her daughter a napkin. In middle school, Danielle had been the graceless ginger kid who could barely play softball and liked to sing show tunes in the choir. All the popular girls had been horrendous to her, and that without a mother who stuck out like a sore thumb, almost literally. Michaela could pass as full Ecuadorian, at least for a little while, if Danielle kept a low profile.

She sighed. "Honey, you will make friends, you know."

"Please, Mama!" Michaela, unflappable during the all the chaos and uncertainty of being uprooted from Quito, now clenched her jaw in near terror.

"Yes, baby, OK." She grabbed Michaela in a bear hug, astounded that her preteen daughter still let her do this. She had the urge for both of them to ditch the first day of school and go swimming in the river, but that was out of the question. She now had a job that didn't wear on her conscience even if it barely covered the bills, and Michaela had to get on with the business of growing up.

"I'll walk with you to the tienda, and then I'll go in around the back of the school, and you can go in the front. Vale?"

"Vale." Michaela smiled.

Danielle tucked a stray curl behind Michaela's ear, noting her daughter's expression of relief. She stifled a wince. If only her little girl's face weren't such a heartbreakingly open book.

*

As soon as Danielle walked into the classroom, the regular teacher, Mario something, shook her hand, told the kids to behave, and slipped out the door to take a smoke. She'd been told she would be teaching science topics alongside the teacher, not instead of. Within the first ten minutes of the period, during which she was to teach nine-year-olds about greenhouse gases and deforestation, she exhausted herself corralling the kids into their desks and getting them to share crayons. When they started fighting over each other's drawings and wouldn't sit still while she explained how trees give off oxygen, she called into the hall for Mario, who was nowhere to be found. Desperate, she started shouting at the kids in English. Another teacher peered into the classroom when she heard the ruckus.

"Children!" the woman scolded. "In your seats now!" Tall and thick around the middle, she charged into the center of the room. She had the most elegantly sculpted eyebrows Danielle had ever seen.

"You will obey Miss O'Brian. Do you understand me?"

A few meek murmurs of consent from the kids.

"What? I didn't hear you."

"Yes, Mrs. Vargas."

She nodded curtly to the class and then whispered to Danielle. "You need to control them better, Ms. Daniela."

"Excuse me, who are you?"

She arched an eyebrow. "Gloria Vargas." She extended her hand. "Senior science teacher. Come see me after your classes, please."

She had only a few moments to feel put out before the bell went off and the kids streamed around her toward the door.

The rest of the day was equally frustrating. Only one teacher did not abandon the class when she arrived. That afternoon Danielle grudgingly showed up at Gloria's cramped office, which was furnished with three desks, one of which was occupied by a teenage girl sorting papers. She hunched over timidly and made the briefest of eye contact with Danielle.

"Good afternoon," Danielle announced to Gloria, who was flipping through a file folder.

She looked up and squared her shoulders. "Oh, hello, Ms. Daniela. Please sit." She gestured to the chair in front of the desk.

Danielle reluctantly complied.

"I realize you are a volunteer," Gloria began.

"No, I'm not a volunteer. I work for World Science Education."

"Yes, yes," she said. "But you don't seem to have much teaching experience."

"I am a *scientist*," she said.

"Congratulations. I am a science teacher. I am trying to give you some advice," she explained.

Danielle pursed her lips. She had resigned herself to condescending and patronizing engineers and mid-level managers in the oil industry, but at a small public school in the jungle? She was not getting paid enough for this.

"I have my own opinions about these international groups that come here and want to 'teach' us science," Gloria said. "But whether I agree with the politics of that, I know you are here because you want to help. And for that, I am grateful."

"Thank you."

"I want to help you be more helpful," she continued. "You must not come in here with romantic ideas of children's needs. That is not our culture, and children will take advantage of it. You must establish your authority, and once the students believe you, they will do what you say *and* they will learn."

She barely resisted the urge to explain to Gloria that she was not some naive American dabbling in international volunteerism as a way to work through a midlife crisis. She had not made the decision to take this job lightly. She knew it would be hard work for not much pay; she just hadn't expected it to be a pseudo-military exercise.

"You don't believe me, but I'm telling you. Your job will be much easier. The children will be like sponges." Gloria scrunched the fingers of her right hand together. "Trust me," she added.

Danielle, a little startled by Gloria's fist, kept her peace.

With an abruptly breezy air about her, Gloria returned to her file folder and pulled a piece of paper from it. "Did you used to work in the oil industry?"

Danielle blanched. How would she know that? She had listed her last occupation on her CV as "geological research advisor" with a sub-sub-contractor that had no obvious connection to Repsol.

"I'm sorry, Ms. Gloria. You'll need to excuse me," she blurted. "My daughter is waiting for me." She pulled her woven satchel over her shoulder, shook the woman's hand, and hurried out the door.

*

Frantically, Danielle waved down a taxi and clutched the backrest as the car bounced over the potholed streets to her neighborhood. The front door was unlocked, which worried her, even though they were not in the habit of locking it because there was never a need to. Her breathing was short as she climbed the stairs. She found Michaela and Tito playing cards on the deck outside.

"What's wrong, Daniela?" Tito asked.

"Mica, your grandfather and I need to talk inside for a minute."

"About what?"

"Honey, it's none of your business." Danielle forced herself to take a long, slow breath. It was important not to alarm her daughter.

Michaela rolled her eyes, and Tito, his long, gray-streaked hair pulled back in a ponytail, looked gravely at Danielle. "What is going on?"

She waited until he followed her into the sitting room and closed the door behind him.

"How does the senior science teacher at Our Sisters of the Immaculate Conception know that I used to work in the oil industry?" she demanded.

His broad, brown face widened into a half-blank, half-perplexed expression. "How would I know?"

"You didn't say anything?"

"No," he said simply.

"Are you *sure*?"

He crossed his arms. "Why would I do that? You think I want to endanger my granddaughter?"

She didn't necessarily trust him not to rat her out, but he knew how much he loved Michaela. "Tito." She sucked in a deep, noisy breath. "I didn't give anyone any information about what I used to do. How else would they know where I come from?"

"People talk, make up stories. You know this."

"This could turn into a very bad situation. It took just about everything I had to get here and make a normal life for Michaela." Her breath was coming in short and fast. *No, not now, Danielle, don't lose it*, she heard her own voice silently counseling her. "If I have to pick us up and run again…" She pressed her shaking hands to the crown of her head.

Displeased, Tito flattened his lips exactly the same way his son used to. She had long since stopped feeling anything for Antonio, but the flash of him on Tito's face gave her a start.

"Tranquila," he said.

No, she thought furiously. It was one of the few Ecuadorian habits she had not learned to abide, being told to calm down when there was no reason to calm down, and in fact there was reason to explode with anger or ball up and cry. But she *had* learned that there was no way to argue with that response.

"Repsol isn't paying you to turn me in?" she asked, managing to take a normal breath.

He gaped at her. "M'ija! First," he said, extending his thumb, "we haven't gotten one centavo from them since Antonio's accident. Second"—he stuck out his index finger—"You are family. I may not always like that fact, but I accept it. So, don't go accusing me of such a terrible thing."

He yanked open the door to the patio and rejoined his granddaughter at the plastic table where she had dealt him a new hand. He ate one of the chifles they were using as betting chips from her pile, and Michaela squealed at him to stop cheating. From inside, Danielle watched them in serious play, posturing, strategizing, and occasionally whooping as the sunlight faded behind them. Among the tops of the palm trees, the tanagers began their vociferous evening chatter and circular flights. There was no sign of danger or cause for concern. Everything looked peaceful, safe, as it should be. As she'd always hoped it would one day be.

*

The fourth graders, clad in their teal-blue-and-yellow uniforms and rubber boots, had staked out their positions along the stream that ran behind the school, which eventually wound its way along the edge of her backyard. Danielle called to Milton and Sandra, who were counting tadpoles on the opposite bank in the evanescent light: "Just about fifteen minutes, guys, then we've got to pack it up."

Viviana had spread out her jacket on a sandy bank so as not to dirty her skirt and stared dully at the other team of kids measuring water temperature.

Danielle called her name. When the girl kept staring into space, she repeated, "Viviana, you have to do something. Otherwise you can't be in the club."

"I don't have my boots." She was one of the weakest students in class, but she was Gloria Vargas's pet from last year. Gloria consented to let Danielle form the Explorers' Club only if Viviana got to join, "and only after school," she insisted. "I don't want students playing games all day."

"Do you want to take some photos?" Danielle reached in her bag and handed her the iPhone.

For the first time, Viviana's face showed a spark of life. "Cool."

"You slide this—" Danielle began to demonstrate, but Vivana had already figured it out.

Milton came leaping over the rocks in the stream, declaring that he'd counted a record number of tadpoles.

"Look at my notebook." He pushed it up to Danielle's face.

"Good!" She smiled, pulling back so she could read it. "So, what does that tell us?"

"If there are a lot of babies, they might not all die?"

"Maybe. We have to see if conditions are right for them to grow into adults."

Milton considered this as he picked his nose.

"I don't think they are going to live," Viviana announced.

Danielle looked over her shoulder. She'd almost forgotten Viviana was there. "The frogs? Why not?"

"Because. When I was little, they were so noisy you couldn't go to sleep at night. Now it's not like that. "

It was the very absence of nocturnal frog calls that had started this riparian field trip, and the article on the alarming rate of amphibian die-off from a *Scientific American* that she swiped from a doctor's office in Quito. On the first night in her new house in La Colina, she expected to be kept awake at night by the croaking toads, just like the first night she'd ever slept in the jungle, in a bamboo hut by the Napo River. She'd never heard anything so strangely deafening, both grating and soothing. Here there was almost nothing. She'd switched on the light and dug through boxes till she found the magazine, crouched in a corner by the closet, and read it again. Amphibians were an early-warning sign for other species. Eventually she went back to bed, loose-limbed and groggy but unable to quiet her anxious thoughts. Mentally she worked through the project for the fourth graders until she could coax herself back to sleep.

"So, your hypothesis," she suggested to Viviana, "is the frogs are dying when they are young?"

"Yes. It's only the old ones that make all that noise. Hello, hello," she began speaking into the phone. "Señora O'Brian, we should record the noises at night. Like as a test. This thing can do that, you know."

"That's a great idea." She'd completely forgotten about the voice recorder. "Do you want to be in charge of that?"

With a shrug, she handed the phone back to Danielle. "Sure." She shook out the jacket she'd been sitting on, meticulously but pointlessly brushed the sand off her shoes, and followed the other kids up the bank.

*

Along the dark path back to her house, Danielle counted it as a victory. Seven children eagerly learning about the natural world. She considered Viviana's interest in iPhone recordings as "eager" too, given the circumstances. The cool, close evening air felt delightful on her bare arms: she'd long since stopped being an attractive target for mosquitos. What a lucky turn her life had taken. She had found this easygoing, if ramshackle, rainforest town to make her home in. Her daughter was happy. Her bills were, mostly, paid. Palm-size butterflies pollinated the native tropical plants lining the edge of her patio; on cue, birds announced the sun's daily departure. She had stumbled upon something she didn't know she'd been looking for.

Silhouetted in the yellow porch light, two figures sat on the plastic chairs near the front door. Tito must have dropped in for dinner.

She heard Michaela's voice—"There she is!"—as Danielle approached the yard. At that moment, the woman stood and stepped into the glow, her long blue tunic falling the length of her legs, her straight black hair tucked behind her ears, and a choker of tiny red achiote seeds rimming her throat.

"Señora O'Brian."

Danielle froze with her hand on the gate. "Señora…"

"Irene Tanguila. You must remember me."

"Michaela, go inside," Danielle said.

She whined. "Why?"

"Now!" Danielle barked.

Michaela's face darkened. "OK, Mama, OK," she replied in a hushed, frightened tone and disappeared into the house.

Danielle's hands were trembling. Her lips were trembling. Her heart was probably trembling in whatever way it could inside the cage of her chest. How should she be? Aggressive? She tried it out silently: *What do you want, Irene!* Or maybe polite but curt, strong and in control: *How can I help you, Irene?*

"How did you find me?" she blurted.

"Ricardo."

That goddamn son of a bitch, Danielle fumed, not entirely sure how Irene, an indigenous leader from a remote village, would cross paths with a wealthy mestizo businessman who wasn't known to give Kichwa people the time of day, even one who was clearly a force to be reckoned with.

"Well, what do you want from me?" she asked angrily, still clutching the gate.

Irene stood unmoved, with just the faintest tightness in her lips. "Testify."

Danielle dropped her hand and the gate swung in a wide, creaky arc. "What?" She realized she had no idea why she was so terrified. Irene clearly wasn't going to attack her; she was not in any physical danger. For a few seconds, Irene's request seemed so absurd, so beyond the realm of possibility that she almost laughed. She was lost in a fog of unreality.

When Irene said nothing, simply stared at her with the gravity of death, Danielle snapped back to lucidity. "No," she replied. "Absolutely not." Her limbs worked again; she could control her mouth muscles. She strode past Irene to the front door.

"You saw what they did to the water. You did the soil tests," Irene declared. "You have to tell the judge."

"Irene, there are boxes and boxes of evidence," Danielle said. "There is plenty to convince the jury."

"They can distort it," Irene insisted. "But you are a scientist, and you were there. And you are a gringa. You know it's much harder for them to discredit you. "

"But Irene, Repsol wants to prosecute me!" This simply could not be happening. Irene didn't realize what she was asking of her. "They'll put me in jail for God knows how many years and take everything I own. I can't take that kind of risk. I have a daughter!"

"What about my daughters?" Irene cried. She clapped her hand to her chest and her face hardened. "No one has thought about my daughters!"

*

Dinner dishes washed and stacked, lights switched off throughout the house, Danielle curled up with Michaela in her twin bed, gazing over her daughter's shoulder as she silently read a book. Through the electric buzz of the cicadas, Danielle heard only the occasional bellow of a toad.

"Don't you want to read something else? You've already read this three times."

"I know," Michaela answered. "I like this story."

Danielle kissed her hair, breathing in the chemical floral odor of her shampoo, and wondered how Michaela, who'd been gregarious since she learned to smile, could possibly relate to 1950s New York and a loner like Holden Caulfield.

"Ten more minutes." Danielle announced.

"Fifteen," Michaela bargained.

Danielle gave her silent consent.

"Mama," Michaela asked, "who was that Irene woman?"

"Someone from…" Her heart was at it again, throbbing in her ears. "A woman I used to know from work."

"Did you fire her or something?"

"No, why?"

"She was nice at first, but she got all nervous when she saw you."

"She has a lot on her mind," Danielle explained. That seemed to satisfy Michaela, who slipped immediately back into her book. This eleven-year-old girl, who read at the level of a ninth grader, had no respiratory problems, no signs of skin cancer. She had not grown up near a poisoned watershed. Danielle stroked her daughter's perfect, soft, brown forearm, finding it hard to swallow and hard to breathe. What Irene's daughters did or didn't suffer, Danielle did not know.

She pushed herself off the bed and made every effort to walk casually to the doorway. "You're now down to twelve minutes. When I come back, lights off."

In the darkened kitchen, she stood in the circle of bone white light cast from the streetlamp outside and poured herself a glass of water. *Just relax*, she coached herself. *Breathe. Think this through.* Maybe her fear was getting the best of her. Maybe she could get a lawyer who would strike a deal for her. Maybe she wouldn't go to jail for very long. Who would take care of Michaela? Tito? Antonio's sister? Her parents in Tacoma? No, this was insane! She pressed her fingertips into her temples. She'd never get a light sentence here. Michaela was her flesh and blood. How could she give her up for someone else's children? It wouldn't make their suffering go away. She couldn't save all those kids now. The damage was done. The damage was done, she whispered. Why couldn't she just live with that?

"Mama," Michaela said as she padded into the kitchen.

As Danielle turned, she felt her daughter's arms encircle her middle and her head press against her ribs. "It's been twelve minutes," Michaela informed her.

"Yes, baby, it has. Time for bed," Danielle announced in a voice that she hardly recognized.

Michaela murmured: "It'll be OK in the morning, Mama."

"No matter what, there is always a new day, isn't there?" she said.

At that moment, steering her daughter toward the bedroom felt as terrifying as allowing her, in the glee of child's play, to run headlong toward the edge of a cliff.

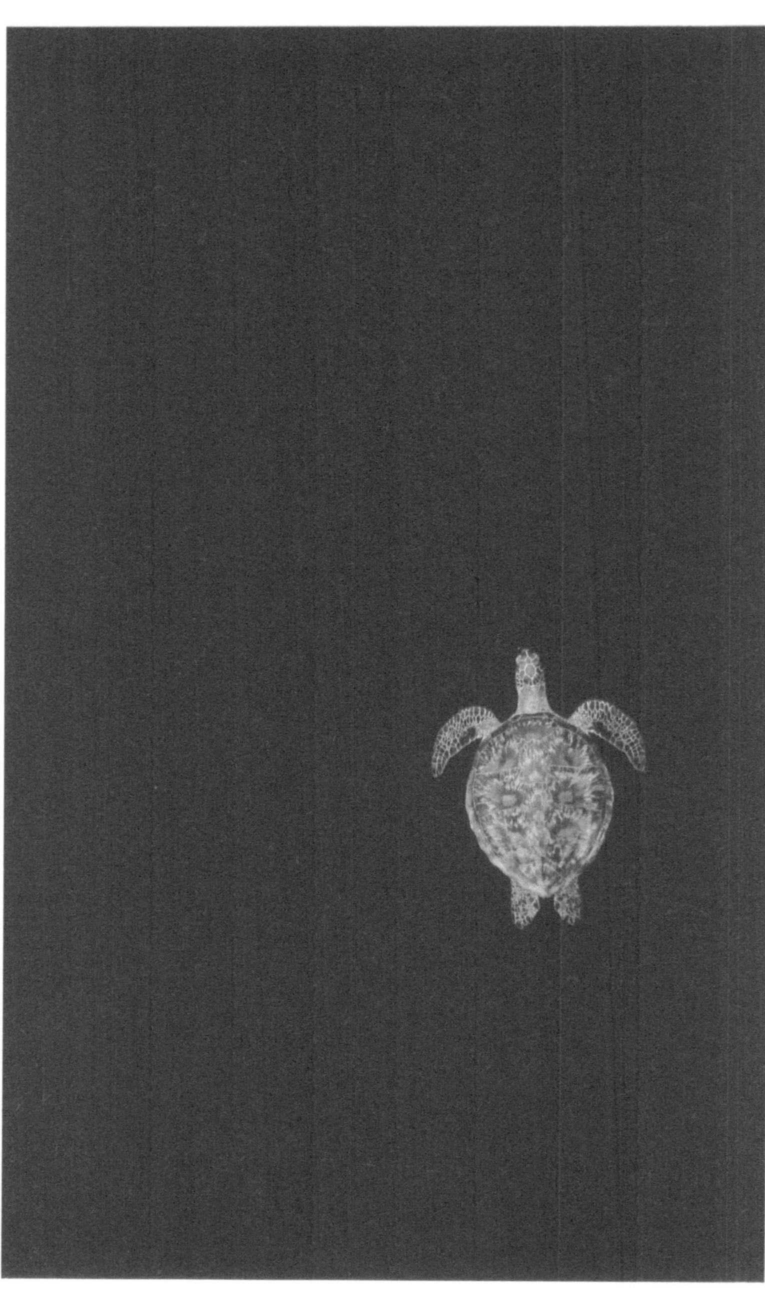

JOEANN HART

Reef of Plagues

These tourists are nothing but trouble, slapping and grinding through the water in their power cruisers, searching for a place to snorkel. Better luck milking a fish, we tell them, and they give us the rough side of their tongues. It was not so long ago we were adjusting their masks, leading them to where sapphire light once shone through branched cathedrals, the coral luminous as jewels. Our precious riches. Don't touch, we say, again and again; this is not a treasure hunt. The reef is still the source of our living for those of us who are left, those who survived the first few seasons of sinking tourism. Who wants to visit a Hades of bleached bones?

"Hey!" a bright-pink man shouts from a vessel that has snuck up on us. "Hey!"

We look at one another to see who's game. Our broad backs are to the sun, men and women alike, our bellies to the rubber boats as we scoop water samples into vials, scrape slime from lifeless coral, and take the reef's temperature as we would a dear child's. Out in deep water, buoys do all this and more, sending messages through the clear air to the office computers. But the sensors can only monitor, not mourn it as we do. Years now, the coral has been fading like a shadow on the water, but no help came until the tourists themselves became endangered. The scientists do not discuss what will happen if the reef dies altogether, but we can read the signs. We know our fate.

The pink man believes the problem is that we cannot hear him, so he inches closer, one eye keen on his depth finder. Electronics are not magic; it insults the gods to navigate a vessel like that in shallow water. Even we in our inflatable dinghies cannot always use our outboards and must pull with our oars. But that is not our job to tell him. Not anymore.

The man tests his luck and gets quite close. The cruiser begins panting in neutral; then suddenly he is on his deck waving at us. "Excuse me! Over here!"

We groan. We are sick of explaining the obvious to the oblivious. It is too damn hot. "What?" one of us answers. We know, of course, what he wants, but we pretend innocence. We lean back and drink deeply of our canteens as we look up at him.

"What happened to this place?" the man asks. He takes off his baseball cap and sunglasses and wipes his boneless face with his loud shirt. He is wide and top-heavy, like his black-hulled boat, which flies an American flag. His red hair is almost plucked clean, so with his sunburnt skin he looks like a tufted bloodworm. His two pastel children, slick with sunscreen—and we hope it is not the slop that poisons the reef—stare at us. A pale woman, the man's wife, we guess, looks down into her wineglass, searching. An old man, a crumpled version of the pink man, lies on a lounge chair with closed eyes and an open book.

Do we pretend to more innocence? We do.

"Happened? What do you mean, happened?" another one of us

asks. We no longer have to be nice to tourists, so we're not. Besides, the sick reef is their fault. That is what our bosses hint at. They say our coral is dying because the world burns too much oil, and it is sure as hell not us doing the burning. Every day, we must scrounge gas for our scooters to get us to the dock.

The man presses his great stomach against the rail, and as he leans forward to talk to us his skin flushes. Like the seaworm, he should not be out in the sun. "We've been going around in circles. Where's the coral? The fish? I told my kids it would be like swimming in a high-end aquarium."

We all look at one another as if we haven't a clue. One of us peers into the water, then sits bolt upright and shouts "Great Zeus, the reef is dead!" We all look horrified into the sea as if we don't know shit.

The man cannot tell if we are pulling his tender leg.

"I give up," the woman says. On stormy days we hang around the office, and our bosses show videos from cameras miles below the surface. We marvel at the strange greenish-white creatures at the very bottom of the sea. That is the color of this woman's skin. "I told you we should have gone to Atlantis instead," she says to the horizon.

"These kids need to experience real nature, not a water park," he tells her. "I don't want them to grow up sheltered from the world." He pauses as if considering. "Like you."

We shake our heads. You cannot speak to your woman like that or there will be a price to pay. He has a sickly smile on his face as she whispers something to him we cannot quite hear over the hissing of the surf, either "Fuck you" or "I'm warning you." She finishes her glass of wine, turns to the cabin, and disappears into the cavernous space. The children pay no mind to either of them. They have blue flippers on their feet and snorkeling masks in their little hands, ready to receive the world's blessings. We look past them, squinting into the strong sun to watch a pelican drop headlong like Icarus into the sea. We wait for him to rise in glory, a feasting bird, but he comes up with an empty beak. Even the charter boats must go far out to sea now while our people hold empty nets on the shore.

"What have you done to the coral?" the man asks, pointing at our equipment. "The last time I was here it was a tropical wonderland."

We? We stare at him blankly, and some of us go back to work. We have to get ourselves to Half Moon Bay where our bosses think they saw signs of black band disease in a healthy colony. They want us to suit up and dive with them for coral samples. Time is not on our side.

"I want to see the fishes, Daddy," says the little girl.

"I want to see a shipwreck," says the boy.

Ah, so would we, on both accounts. Rusted hulks used to sit where they landed on the reef, left as a warning to other mariners. We would collect some fine things from those boats. Our homes are made with so much salvage that the priests joke that we live in salvation. But now the tourist board, grown nervous and defensive, tows the vessels out to sea before we can get to them. They say tourists do not want to see that nature's power is greater than their own.

"You must have been here a long time ago," one of us says. "This part of the reef has been dead or dying for a good eight years."

"What do you mean dead?" the man asks. "Have you ever seen coral? It's just a rock. A colorful rock."

It is alive, or was, we tell him. Tiny animals, polyps. They grow a shell, creating hard and beautiful homes, and live on algae. We do not waste breath explaining symbiosis to this man, but tell him how the algae determines the color of coral, which grows in many shapes. We know them all by name. Elliptical Star, Boulder Brain, Corky

Seafinger, Mustard Hill, Yellow Pencil. We learned the language of sea life when we were guides; now we must learn the language of sea death. Not just bleaching, but disease. Yellow Band, White Band, Black Band. White Plague, White Pox. The reef is so sick it can no longer give birth to the tiny organisms from which spring the great chains of being. Now, clear jellyfish float like dead spirits through a labyrinth of thighbones and skulls. "Warmer water stresses the polyps, and they eject the algae," we say. "That is the bleaching that makes them look like skeletons. Sometimes they heal themselves, but lately, no. They die in a shroud of slime."

"Polyps?" the man says. "I know all about those. I had four polyps removed from my colon last year. Benign, totally benign. I had two removed a few years before that. If I can grow new polyps, so can this reef."

We wonder if he is now pulling our legs. There is no way of knowing. Their brains are as dense as conch meat. We pause at our labors and inhale the salty breath of the ocean.

"We wish we could help you," one of us finally says, although we do not wish that at all. "We have work to do. Parts of the reef on the other side of the island are still alive. Go there."

"I don't have time to motor all the way around the island," the man explains, as if we simply misunderstand his problem. "We're on a tight schedule. Today's the day for snorkeling."

Music comes blaring from the cabin. It is the woman's way of getting her man's attention, or it is her way of drowning him out. "ABBA!" we exclaim. "Cassandra." A song that is no "Dancing Queen" but sounds good to our ears. We hum the refrain and continue our work. The man goes to shout into the cabin, and we forget about him altogether when we find a sea turtle tangled in plastic filament. We pull him close with a grapple and cut the fishing gear away. But it is too late. Too late even to eat him and give his death meaning. It never ends. Last week we found a bloated manatee in a ghost net, his soft whiskered face nibbled away by the fishes.

The man returns. The music has stopped.

"Taking those water samples isn't going to help anything, if you don't mind me saying so." The man says this with such a smile, we can tell he's figured out how to fix our problem. "You should be spending your time building the coral back up. We visitors spend a lot of money here, you can afford to bring in new polyps. Get some biotech company to engineer ones that can tolerate warmer water." He grips the railing tight with satisfaction. We look at one another. Create a new species? We hadn't thought of that. Maybe that's because we are not gods.

Speaking of the divine. The cabin door opens and out comes not his wife but a semi-goddess at one with the elements. She walks on deck as if she'd rather fly but keeps her ravishing feet on earth as a courtesy to us lesser beings. Before she puts on her sunglasses, she pauses to stare at us with her wide-set eyes, gray as deep water.

"It's out of our hands," one of us says to the man. "We can't bring back the dead."

The children have abandoned their masks and flippers and are eating some sort of sticky ambrosia that the young woman, who must be their babysitter and not a goddess after all, is bestowing on them. She looks at us as if she would like to share the bounty, but we are too far away for her beneficence.

One of us starts rolling up some herb. We can't seem to let him alone.

"What are you doing?" he asks, rising to the bait. "You can't do that here."

We light up the spliff and hand it around, leaning from one raft to another. The man gathers his children before they can smell the sweet smoke and pushes them into the cabin. The babysitter looks at us with longing.

"It's just Mother Nature," we explain to the man, smiling.

"It's a drug," he says. "And I won't have it around my family. I think it might be time to leave this island."

Some of us, whose hands are not busy with work or weed, applaud. This makes the pink man purple. His throat is like a dark mast, and we wonder if he might burst. The babysitter steps toward him, and even though she says nothing, he takes a breath. Then another. "The hell with this pimple of Caribbean dirt," he says calmly, pulling his dignity around him. He turns away just as the wind shifts a bit. The boat adjusts, making him unsteady on his feet, and he trips on the lounge where the old man lies. The book slips to the deck. The old man does not wake, and we wonder if he is even alive. When the babysitter bends down for the book, the pink man, still trying to get his balance, bumps into her, knocking off her sunglasses. We feel the crack right through our hearts. "Sorry," he says to her then retreats up to the helm, muttering. She picks up her glasses and squints at him through the empty frame in a way that makes us shiver.

Rosy-gray cumuli appear on the water's horizon as the man puts his cruiser in gear. We are losing time, but we wait to see if our curs'd mariner can turn his boat around in such shallow waters. Sweat bleeds from his pores, but he does it. We have to give him credit. His stern faces us. *Odyssey*, Annapolis, Maryland.

"This man is very far from home," we say.

As the boat motors off, it leaves fingers of dark oil on the water. We watch him head out the wrong channel, but we find that our tongues lie heavy in our mouths. His depth finder will not tell him he is in trouble until it is too late, and soon enough, he doesn't have enough water to piss in. We hear the lifeless reef scrape his bottom and hold him tight. We go back to work. We are very busy collecting samples. By the time he bucks his vessel back and forth to free himself, there is a small puncture in his hull. Good luck with that, we say to ourselves. Good bloody luck. He leaves in a cloud of reeking fumes, and we hear him curse the heavens. He is a man of poor judgment but more creative with his words than we would have guessed.

"How far do you think he'll get?" we ask one another.

"Too far for us to help. Much too far."

We watch the babysitter, regal in her beauty, standing like a statue on the transom of the cruiser. As the man struggles to navigate towards open water, she unties her tunic from behind her neck and pulls it over her head. She stands before the reef like an Aphrodite in a silvery bathing suit, born on the half shell. She is slim legged and smooth as a smelt. A thin, gold belt embraces her waist like a wedding ring. She places her palms together and touches the tips of her fingers to her rosy lips, then raises her arms and dives like a marlin to windward, displacing a perfect arc of water that captures the sunlight. Drops splash on the old man, and he sits up, blinking. Her body moves swiftly through the turquoise temple of water, gliding just beneath the surface. Her hair floats, then submerges, as she goes deeper, dissolving into the sea like salt. The old man stands with difficulty and raises a palsied hand. The wind stirs the water so that she is no longer visible, but we know she is there because small ecstatic fish leap at her approach. Love water, we hear them sing. Love the water! Our hearts are high with excitement. Daughter of the mighty sea, she's come to save us, or she's come to destroy us. Either way, we hold our breath and wait to see her rise.

SHAUN LEVIN

A Sea of People

Sometimes when the tide is out you can see a couple of men on the shore building statues in the sand. For the second day running, M has come down to the river where the breeze cools the air and takes the edge off the heat that has settled over London. Today, one of the sculptures is a mermaid. The other is shaped like a sofa, and the men recline on the sand-sofa and chat to passersby who stop at the embankment railings to throw coins at a small crater as if into a wishing well. Thanks. Waving. Moving on. M gives nothing. He's in awe of anyone with skill so ingrained they can build furniture out of sand on the banks of a river in the hours it takes for the water to rise again. But the thought of throwing, missing, saying the wrong words, being too shrill, being thanked, having to smile. His lower back is tight. The weight of the world. Sharp and unbending. Now that he's fully accustomed to the grey drizzle of England, the intense heat is disorienting, three days of it, flinging him back to places he's lived. Deserts. Heat itself is home, temperature—memory.

A friend says: Take the day off. A few days. It's not like you're writing anything anyway. Recently back from a week in Barcelona,

M had been caught off guard by the heat in London. He'd expected to return from Catalonia to the erratic cool of England. Extreme summer is the exception, still a novelty. It throws the city off course. On the Tube down to the river, Finsbury Park to Green Park, the Jubilee Line to Waterloo, there are signs advising passengers to carry water, to hydrate: correct behavior in high temperatures.

People need to be taught. He fights it. At this rate, London could become home. Twenty years in the city and he's still happiest doing tourist things, meandering, mingling in the crowds, walking along the river. Here, alone, away from his street, his flat in North London, hunched over a desk as if the arc of his body could protect his inner organs, his heart, but this is the posture that brings on the pain, a rigid curving of the spine. Here by the river he begins to fuse with the city. It's a kind of disappearance, a participation in the phrase *a sea of people*.

There are parts of London he associates with sex. For a long time Shoreditch was one of them, there in East London, far from where he is now. A couple of times a month he'd go to the bathhouse off Great Eastern Road, sometimes after teaching a class near Liverpool Street Station, or if he was having dinner with a friend at Spitalfields Market, or if he'd been to an exhibition at the Whitechapel Gallery. In the absence of a man to return to, going to the bathhouse was a way to end the evening. Whenever he is in a part of London close to a bathhouse, there is always the option of sex. For most people, the option arises in the confines of their home. For him, the presence of certain buildings around London offers the opportunity for coupling: Vauxhall, Shoreditch, Covent Garden, Oxford Street, and here beneath the railway arches of Waterloo East, just a short walk from the river.

*

On the masseur's table at Pleasuredrome, the gay bathhouse on Alaska Street, M is flat on his stomach. The room vibrates with each train that passes overhead, carrying people in and out of London: to Sevenoaks, Gravesend, Folkestone. M likes this masseur's technique, his touch, the way he starts at the calves and moves upwards. Lately, when he wants to be touched deeply, the hands he wants are the masseur's, Piotr, a Russian in London, working quietly or, when he does speak, making inane jokes. "How have you been?" M says. "Shit," Piotr says. He wards off questions as if they were lewd advances. M knows that Piotr, known as Pete, left Moscow in his early twenties, maybe earlier, and moved to—where was it?—Chicago? First Chicago, then Spain, no, Ireland. Dublin. His English is fluent, though he still has an accent. It's comical: the expectation is a pairing with bad grammar, limited vocabulary, but the Russian makes no mistakes, even if he speaks rarely.

Before the massage, M had hooked up with a German in the dry sauna, a young man who was the kind of lean M likes. Even when he himself was young and lean, young and lean had appealed to him, though he'd never have used those words to describe himself. It had taken him years to pluck up the courage to come to a place like this. Even now, ten years later, he feels a sense of liberation and triumph, a feeling confined to these rooms, to this space, as if this is where his true self comes to life. Usually he's here for the sex, but today it's the massage. The back pain has persisted since Barcelona. His buttocks are tense, soothed by the heat of the wooden slats.

*

"What's your name?" he'd said to the German in the dry sauna in a gap between kisses.

The name was pronounced Mischail. He'd moved to Berlin five years ago from Wuppertal, was here in London for the weekend, spending the night in the sauna—he pronounced the word *sour-nah*—until a room in a friend's house became available.

They kept talking, exchanging the bits of information that strangers pass between themselves. Thirty years ago, M's lover had taken him to see Pina Bausch in Tel Aviv.

The German was surprised to find an enthusiast of modern dance in a place like this. He told M he *loves loves loves* Pina Bausch, that he and his best friend used to go and watch rehearsals in the Wuppertal theatre after school.

"I haven't seen any modern dance for years," M said.

"What did you do in Tel Aviv?" the German said.

"Good question," M said.

The memory of that lover is weightless. Soon after they split up, the lover moved to San Francisco and still lives there with a man he met while hitchhiking in Nicaragua. M went to visit him once, and they'd driven up—or was it down?—Highway One and stayed overnight in a log cabin on a campsite. All this floated languidly through M's mind as he relished the German on the ledge beside him.

This is where we are in history, M thinks. Friends are moving back to where they came from, or away: Sicily, Israel, Greece. Europe is reshuffling its people—you go here, you here, some outward to former colonies, Angola, Brazil. The Portuguese are doing it. Others have been coming from over there to cities like this. Him, for example. Last month there'd been a van driving round London carrying a sign: *Are you here illegally? Go home or face arrest. Text this number to hand yourself in: key in* H *and* O *and* M *and* E. It shattered the illusion that London belonged to no one, a liminal space where the English didn't matter, language didn't matter, being lost didn't matter. M has nowhere else to go. Home is not an option. Wherever he went he'd be lost all over again.

"Lost," his friend had asked, "or alone?" The friend who'd left London and returned to Greece, on Skype, the one he'd been in Barcelona with, waving from his living room in Athens.

"What's the difference?" M had said.

It became clear in Barcelona that getting lost was not his thing, not in such heat, not again, not in a foreign tongue, a foreign city, even one he liked, but the heat and the language. He needed London for the familiarity of its vocabulary, the safety of this island life, the melancholy weather to match his temperament. The relief of English after years in the desert, like diving into cool water, knowing how to swim. But now, after twenty years, he is restless. Is it really language he is longing for? He cannot bring himself to use the phrase *mother tongue*. A couple of days before they'd left Barcelona—M for London, his friend back to Athens—they climbed to the top of Tibidabo, and as on every trip to every city since leaving home, M asked himself as they walked: *Could I live here? Is this where I could be?* But the language imposed exclusion, a feeling of inadequacy; he'd felt so thwarted that he'd wanted to crawl back to the hotel and ask for things in English, this language that was his, lived in for half a lifetime, love affairs conducted in it: room service, an extra pillow, a taxi, anything to reduce to a minimum the delay between wish and fulfilment.

The one escape is sex, a realm without language where the tongue is vocabulary.

Men he meets in places like this, pressing up against each other, almost in slow motion, in sync, the way lovers do after months apart, reacquainting themselves with the body, the person they've loved more than anything. The one true one. Kissing gently, the way he and the German had been doing. Tentative, tender. Fingertips on ribs, along chests. Tenderness is a question mark. Our lives filled with questions regarding desire and its limits: to touch and be touched. By whom? Where?

Youth is bold, and the German leaned over to take M into his mouth just as other men entered. Two older men. Why not, men are fucking in public, nakedness on show, a lean chap exposing himself, so why not join in? One of the older men touched, a finger straight to it.

Ouch. The German was not averse to touch—he'd offered himself to M—but the old man neither stroked nor waited for an invitation, did not kiss his neck. Straight to it. The German removed the hand, and the old man settled back, happy to have touched such buttocks, and watched as the young man surrendered to the other.

*

This was how M had filled the time before his massage appointment. "Go deeper," he says to the masseur, "harder." The Russian laughs. "You need a knife to go deeper," he says. He too, M thinks, is showing hints of psychopathic rage? London does this to us. How angry are you on a scale of one to ten? On the way up from the river, this had happened. Some women! Zero spatial awareness. In the middle of the pavement, standing there with her friend and her friend's husband. Blocking. M's anger had spilled out onto the street. He'd nudged her. "Excuse *me,*" the woman had said. Some men!—him—looking for a fight.

*

Earlier, before the German, an Englishman had followed him into a cabin, pushed him, provoked him to be the overpowering one. He wanted to be pinned to the wall. But then.

"Not so hard," the guy said.

"That wasn't hard."

"Stop."

"I'll show you hard," M said.

"I'm not into this," the Englishman said.

"Are you not?" M said, thinking the guy was teasing.

The Englishman slapped his face. M slapped back.

"I'm really not," the guy said. "So, fuck off." Grabbed his towel and left.

M stayed in the cubicle, locked the door, lowered himself onto the mattress, sat there. One option would be to find the man, tell him to think twice before slapping someone. Be careful who you slap, he'd say. Or he'd smile: That wasn't a good start, was it? Let's try again. But he knew that an olive branch would not be an appreciated gesture.

*

Fear is the aphrodisiac, the life force, lying under the masseur's touch, letting go into this ultimate state of abandon, thumbs pressing into both sides of his spine, C1, C2. Snap. Kill me. The room vibrates. A train in or out of Waterloo. The jacuzzi rumbles. When M first started coming to this place, the massage room had been a steam room. Positioned between two flights of stairs that go up to the cruising area and private cabins, the massage room is now at the heart of the bathhouse. Both flights of stairs lead to the same place, yet each flight descends into a very different part of the sauna. At the foot of one flight is the bar with its high chrome tables and barstools, where two overweight men had been drinking tea, a young man sipping from a bottle of Heineken. Just wait there, the man at reception had told M, the masseur will come and get you. But he'd used his waiting time to make out with the German. Near the other flight of stairs is the dry sauna, big enough for two or three people: that's where he'd said goodbye to the German. The jacuzzi hums and bubbles. There are always a few men sitting in it, pressed against the edges of the whirlpool. Opposite, other men lie on a padded raised banquette, some asleep, beached. He'd never allow himself to fall asleep like that in public. It would be as good as admitting that he had, for a while, settled in and made this place home.

*

In the dream he turns up at a party unannounced to see an ex-lover. He wants to surprise him, and the guy *is* surprised, looks uncomfortable, then disappears into the crowded room, called away by friends or swallowed up by guests. M ends up standing next to a North African guy who's chatting in Russian, refusing to converse in any other language. M speaks to him in Hebrew, so the guy responds in Dutch, and M throws back some Afrikaans, triumphant in being able to understand some of what he's saying. The guy says something in a language M does not recognise. They laugh. They're enjoying the game, as if they could continue playing forever, ping-ponging snippets of language back and forth.

M tells the North African in French that he was born in Israel… "No, I mean I was born in South Africa, *then* I lived in Israel for quelques années before escaping to London." The guy was born in Tunisia, then lived in France, then spent a few months on Kibbutz Tzorah. "I grew up just a few minutes from there," M tells him, even though he didn't. It's a lie, but it's the right thing to say to keep the conversation going. Weird that the Tunisian, a Muslim, would stay on a kibbutz, but M doesn't ask, plays it cool. The guy says, "While I was there, I got, like, two hundred tattoos." M can't see any, even though the guy is wearing shorts and a T-shirt, one of those ripped and faded Ramones T-shirts that an ex-lover of his used to wear, a Sicilian who went back to Catania.

*

The inside of his mouth is dry, and there's spittle on his lips. M turns his head just a fraction to wipe it off. His eyes are pressed shut. The touch is firm, the masseur's hands in constant motion along the oiled contours of his body, avoiding nothing, teasing, *is he teasing, the way he brushes against my arse-crack and balls?*

"Remember last time," M says, "what we spoke about?" He hadn't planned to say this, but he says it anyway, the thing he'd said as a joke when he was here a few weeks ago.

"I think you fell asleep," the Russian says.

"Was I snoring?" M says.

"I thought you'd stopped breathing."

The Russian is massaging his inner thighs, his glutes, working his way across his back towards his head. When he is at the top of the table, his middle level with M's gaze, he waits for M to turn over, then says: "So, tell me, what did we speak about?"

"Sex," M says.

"How much did we say?"

"Fifty."

"Good. Very good."

"And we said you'd be naked," M says.

"No problem," the Russian says and pulls down his shorts.

M has been compensating others for taking care for him, cleaning his flat, making food, running errands, helping with paperwork, doing for him what he'd happily share the burden of if he'd had a lover. But there is no lover. Now, on his back, exposed like a piece of meat, no, like *a work of art*: the table is the canvas and he—layers of impasto. In Barcelona he'd gone to the Antoni Tàpies gallery alone. If his friend had been with him and not shopping at El Corte Inglés, they'd have been amused by the desk bolted to the wall, the canvas placed on a straight-backed chair, discussed the difference between the contents of a gallery and the contents of a book. M would have said: If on a wall is art, then between two covers is a book. Anything. That which is mounted is art. Put a table on a wall, a box in a frame, hang a sack from the ceiling, turn your painting to the wall, nail planks to a frame to make a cross. Whatever. It's art. But what to put in this book? The weight of the world.

"That's nice," M says.

The Russian's grip is firm. Thoughts about him for a long time, months, the fantasy of waking up to these hands pressed into his flesh. M has become a man who goes for a massage and gets a happy ending. He is the client. This is what happens, fifty pounds and he's entitled to touch the Russian: torso, buttocks, his tiny balls, and soft penis. Unsure how much is included in the fee, yet emboldened by the transaction, M rests his hand on the crack between the masseur's butt cheeks. Conflicted. Alone. He cannot let go—he won't. M will not give, holding back, keeping what he can to himself. This is how he stays whole. To relinquish would be to reenter the world with nothing. He declines the offer of a hand job and thanks the masseur in Russian, spasiba, words picked up from lovers along the way, like idi syuda, idi domoy, like shto ty khochesh, kotory chas. He fetches the cash from his locker to pay for the groping that went on there.

The guy behind the bar could be Spanish or Brazilian, hands on the counter, watching. M walks past him on his way to the showers, catches his eye. Isn't he…? He's seen him before, somewhere. Not here. Recently. Somewhere else. The bartender looks without hunger, which doesn't mean there isn't any: handsome men are cautious in these places.

*

Esteban has been in the city for six months, got the job because his flatmate is one of the cleaners.

How much longer he can stick it out in this cave, he doesn't know, not to see sunlight all week, no mobile reception to check comments on the photographs he uploaded yesterday. Tripod set up near Waterloo Bridge as the sky turned from orange to pink to purple. And then, just as he was leaving, the man with the notebook on the bench, the same guy walking past the bar now, the broad back, the towel across his buttocks, the slow, purposeful steps.

This flicker of recognition boosts M on his way along the corridor, makes him smile as he stands under the water in the cavernous shower room, flirting with a Thai man who's just arrived and implores M to stay. His eagerness only adds to M's sense of elation and makes his exit back out into the world, back out into the evening that is still warm, only more delicious. That is what one wants from a city, gestures of yearning. The city feels wide open before him. London has spilled out of its terraced houses, its bedsits, its hotel rooms. Here by the river again, crowds drink and converse the way they've been doing for centuries at the end of long days on balmy nights like this. The tide has returned, sandcastles have been washed away. The thick, humid air reminds us foreigners of home and summers, and for these past few days, and this evening in particular, the damp of the city is forgotten, its grey forgotten, the struggle that is the mainstay of our existence—that too is forgotten. Give in to the heat and make this city home. The last London heatwave was two or three years after M first arrived in the city (*more than fifteen years ago!*) still obsessed with its greenness, such a contrast to places he'd come from, places with so little of it. Deserts. During that hot summer, he'd made regular visits to the overgrown cemetery on Church Street in Stoke Newington, sat among the fern bushes and plane trees, sketched and wrote, grafted himself onto the city through transcription.

*

Water reassures him now. The man on the bench next to him reads a book. A man at the railings talks on his phone. A mother and a pram. A woman and a mauve handbag. A jogger in a pale-yellow T-shirt. This sea of people. A pigeon on the paving stone. Three pigeons in a row, hello! A kid says: "Let's play so they're not allowed to touch the ground," and they shoo the birds upwards to stop them from landing. A girl in a pink pajama suit plays with her mother's crutches. And then these two fucking idiots plonk themselves down on the bench beside M—*where did the man and his book go?*—and he, the one alone, his defiance is in his grumbling. A solitary man rages. That's his power, to hate. The way the English plonk themselves down on benches without even a may-we, as if the bench were land. Plonk. But the one alone needs to breathe. *Such rage.* M tells himself, *You're only angry because there's no potential for love here.* His friend's voice in his head, *This can only mean one thing: You need to get laid. Raging*, his friend says, *is a toxic form of relating.*

Funny, M thinks, catching himself smiling. *I should have let the Russian finish me off, should have gone looking for the German.*

"It *was* you," Esteban says, there with his camera and tripod.

"It was," M says. "And still is," pleased not to have missed a beat. "Was it fun in there?"

"Mildly," M says. "Was it fun behind the bar?"

"Not really," Esteban says.

He looks bashful, says to M: "Do you want to get some ice cream?" and points to a bus parked further along the embankment, a bright pink double-decker converted into a frozen yoghurt stand, a glorified ice cream van. Young men and women hand out pink vouchers to redeem for free samples of frozen yoghurt in shot-size cups, an amount easily gulped whole into the mouth.

M and Esteban are, for these moments, tourists in the city, standing at the railing, sampling different flavors: peanut butter, raspberry, blueberry. They watch the barges, the lights, the clock above the Savoy approaching midnight, the tide rising, a seagull on the surface abandoning itself to the river's current. Esteban points his camera at M, tells him to smile. Around them the entire city is awake, intent on participating in this heatwave, or uneased by it, tossing and turning with memories and longing.

M smiles for the camera.

"Careful," Esteban says, pointing to the water that's leaking over the edge of the wall, just a trickle, making a puddle at their feet.

They move away from the railing, but the water follows them, creeping along the embankment. The kids have lost interest in the pigeons and are taking off their shoes to skip in the expanding puddles that slowly cover the paving, half an inch, an inch, people laughing, relieved to be cooling their feet, looking at each other, *does anyone know what's going on*, phones out to take pictures, an event for tweeting and retweeting, every moment a potential once-in-a lifetime, definitely this one. The water flows across the walkway into the skateboarders' pit behind them. The young men move to higher ground, hold onto their boards, jump between raised sections of concrete as if across stepping-stones. Everyone's moving to higher ground, the woman with the crutches is balancing on a bench with her daughter.

"Vamonos?" Estaban says.

"Not yet," M says, the water now at their ankles, their shoes in their hands.

It's cold and fresh, and it keeps rising.

"I'm going in!" one of the skateboarders shouts, throws down his board, takes off his shirt, his pale body reflected in the water, then dives in.

People laugh and cheer. The young girl in pink shouts, "Mummy, can I swim?" and the mother looks over at M and Esteban, and they shrug and smile, *what can you do?* and the little girl stretches her arms out above her, hands clasped together like she'd seen on TV during a recent swimming contest, and launches herself into the cool water. The river covers everything, submerging chairs and café tables outside the National Theatre, people streaming out like balloons being released, like in a clip M had seen where millions of shade balls are released into an LA reservoir to stop the water from evaporating. *We are the balloons*, he thinks. *We will cover this water!* He and Esteban lift with the water as it rises toward the bridge.

Barges and clipper boats help those who don't want to swim, and it's cool and fresh, and the serious swimmers take it seriously. At last! A race along the Thames. *Race you to Canary Wharf*, *race you down to Battersea*. Buses stop on the bridge, and passengers join those standing at the edge looking down, unsure whether to rescue the swimmers coming toward them, floating away from them, or to dive in and join them. Someone in the water shouts toward a couple standing on the ledge: "Do it! Jump!" And so, roaring with delight, they do.

The river is a vast outdoor swimming pool, and everyone is swimming, paddling, breaststroke, freestyle from one bank to the other. *This is how you cross a river.* They laugh, and M thinks that, yes, we're definitely not drowning here, none of us, all of us lifted above these streets, moving between buildings, peering through windows as we swim like we're flying, all finding a way to stay afloat, holding onto buoys, hitching a ride, laughing, egging each other on, heading for dry land but also avoiding it, letting go into the cool constant pull of the current, all of us here in the city, calling out to each other, waving. All of us waving.

KRISTIN THIEL

Morse Code of the Yellow Rail

Daria fully expected to die by volcano. Not by lahar, as, say, if the twenty-six glaciers on Mt. Rainier melted under that volcano's heat and helped to create a mudflow so big and thick and violent that it buried everything in its path. Not even by ash clogging the air and trapping greenhouse gases. Even though the United States was second in the world for number of volcanos, Daria didn't fear volcanos in that way. No, what she'd learned from her mother—indirectly—was that volcanos offered foolproof suicide. When the climate got bad enough, Daria would just walk right up and jump. If the fall didn't kill her, the sulfur dioxide fumes would choke her. If that didn't get her, the 1,800-plus-degree lava would, though of course Daria never spoke this plan aloud. It seemed perfectly reasonable to Daria, given the circumstances, but her parents would never understand.

*

While Claire cooked dinner, Daria was on her weekly video chat with Clara, her grandmother, the one person who reliably calmed her. For the past year and a half Daria had been moody, swinging wildly from neutral to furious, devasted, or terrified, and barely passing her freshman classes. Sometimes when she took her emotional plunge, Claire and Mateo were left bereft among the flying tephra, helpless to do anything but watch their only child fall. Sometimes she swept them up along with her into the caldera.

Now Daria was telling Clara how she'd learned that urban birds sing louder than their rural counterparts because they have to be heard above honking cars, roaring trucks, and shrieking construction tools. Clara laughed—"I *know*!"—and told her about the pandemoniums of parrots that live in the treetops above Los Angeles. "It can sound like Jurassic Park, they're so loud!" Clara said.

"Talking bird" was a common thing between the two. Clara, who used to work as an ornithologist at Audubon de México before moving to LA, liked to talk about the yellow rail, brown with golden licks of flame, tiny white vertical dashes along the feathers, buff-colored eggs speckled reddish brown at one end.

"When they're dating," Clara said, "they show they care by grooming each other."

Claire smirked at her mother-in-law's quaint choice of the word *dating*. Clara managed to be such a scientist and woman of the world and so cloistered in some distant yesteryear at the same time. If Claire or Mateo had described birds as "dating," Daria would have rolled her eyes with exasperation and disdain. Yet Claire watched Daria's expression grow both transfixed and dreamy as she listened to Abuelita talk about the sweet little yellow rail of her younger days.

"Have you seen one recently, or heard one, or anything?" Daria asked. Claire detected the anxiety in Daria's voice. Her grandmother hadn't lived in Mexico for decades, but she occasionally visited Daria's great-aunts there.

Clara made a sound somewhere between a tsk and a sigh. "Oh no, they're thought to now be extinct."

Daria suddenly slapped the laptop shut.

"Daria!" Claire said.

Her daughter was staring at the closed case. "I'm sorry!" Suddenly Daria was reopening the computer and hitting the mousepad to wake it. Of course the call had already disconnected.

"What in the world?" Claire asked, joining her.

"I just…I just… I freaked out and slammed the computer shut." Daria looked like a helpless little kid on the brink of tears. "I didn't mean to hang up on her."

Claire ran her fingers through Daria's exhausted curls. "It's almost time for dinner anyway. Send her a text. She'll understand."

As Daria reached for her mother's cell phone, she went surly again, muttering, "I told you I have eco-anxiety."

Returning to chopping the salad veggies, Claire pressed her lips shut. She and Mateo knew all about eco-anxiety, or eco-grief, even without the links to articles and Medium posts that Daria sent them. She'd like to go to Daria's counselor for herself and be told, soothingly, as she imagined Dr.-Wixon-But-Call-Me-Anastasia had told Daria, "Yes, dear child of Mother Earth, this grieving, this tension you feel about Her pain could be an issue." Wouldn't it be nice if that were it. Yet somehow that response seemed as comforting—meaning, as meaningless—as Mateo's response to their daughter, which seemed to be an undulating combination of "the world's climate is always changing"/"anything we as individuals do won't be enough to matter"/"might as well enjoy life while we can!"

"When you're done texting Abuelita, would you go get the mail?" Claire finally said.

She listened to the sigh, the stomps, the door. Then Daria threw the bundle on the counter beside her mother and flounced toward her room. "Wash up!" Claire yelled.

*

Claire was staring at a glossy mailer in her hand when Mateo arrived home and strolled into the kitchen.

"Let's send Daria to camp," she said.

"Hmm?" he asked, kissing her.

Her childhood summer camp had announced it was honing its mission focusing on goodness (godhet, in Swedish) into environmental stewardship. She thrust the mailer at him.

"We don't have camps here?"

Claire dropped her hands to her sides. "Of course, but I don't know which ones do this. I went to this one, I know it's good, and now they're focused on the environment. It's like a sign!"

Mateo just looked at her.

"Daria! Dinner!" Claire yelled. "Why are you looking at me like that?" she asked her husband as she handed him a stack of plates.

"Does Daria want to go to a summer camp on the environment?"

"For chrissake," Claire said. "The environment is all she talks about."

"Well, I know, but…"

"Daria," Claire said to the form representing her daughter that slouched to her place at the table, "what would you think about camp this summer?" She took the flyer from Mateo and set it in front of Daria.

"We just found out about this, Daria," Mateo said. "We'll need to read up on it some more—"

"I spent so many incredible summers at Camp Godhet," Claire interrupted.

"Camp Godhet," Mateo said, sounding like he was tasting the word without putting his lips too closely around it.

"Camp Godhet," Claire pronounced.

"Good Head!" Mateo joked.

They both caught Daria's slight smirk.

"G-O-D-H-E-T, Matty," Claire said, both happy he'd gotten Daria to crack and frustrated that he wasn't being serious for her.

Mateo laughed. "I'm not sure spelling this word helps, Claire."

"Godhet," Claire said, as though it were the easiest word in the world to say.

"God's Hot!" Mateo flung his arms wide and winked lasciviously toward the ceiling.

Daria's face flickered with amusement—on and then off again, so fast—but they noticed.

"So, what do you say?" Claire asked Daria. She turned the mailer toward herself and read aloud: "'Counselor-led activities around understanding and moving through eco-grief to smart, savvy solutions.'" Claire pushed it back. "OK, marketing-speak aside… sounds good, right?"

"I think so," Mateo said, serious and gentle now.

Daria sighed loudly, but Claire noticed her daughter's eyes kept drifting to the flyer all through dinner.

*

The night Daria flew to Minnesota—after the workday, after take-out, after Claire had gotten Daria's text that she was not only in her mother's home state but at her mother's summer camp, after Mateo had kissed Claire good night and retired to their bedroom with the crime novel that had been distracting him—she had padded into her home office, dreading being alone with her thoughts but also certain she couldn't sleep.

She'd changed into the *Subduction leads to orogeny* T-shirt Mateo had given her for their anniversary years before. It was showing its age, but she still loved it. Daria, however, had been vocal in her hatred of it. "It's not just that it's gross, Mom," she'd said. "It's not cute to joke about what you do for a living." At first she thought it was just her daughter taking things too seriously, like any typical teenager. But as Daria became more distraught, Claire began to wonder if her daughter was reading Jan Litchfield's papers by flashlight under her covers. Solar radiation management reduces rainfall…BAD. It won't stop ocean acidification—not that it's supposed to, Claire thought—but also, apparently BAD.

Basalt, her pet chinchilla, was in his cage in her office, waiting for her to fill his bath pan with dust that mimicked the volcanic ash his kind had bathed in since the dawn of their time. Stooping over his cage, she blamed herself for her daughter's current difficulties. Mateo didn't bring climate change and the environment into the home, but Claire did. Did rising sea levels stimulate volcanic activity? Do glaciers—which are melting at an unprecedented rate—weaken eruptions? These were questions Claire couldn't ignore and, she now understood, had erroneously contributed to too many family-dinner conversations.

Claire watched Basalt flop, flip, right himself, pause except for a nose twitch, and then flop, flip, stand, pause all over again, repeatedly. He looked like a delicious ball of dough flouring himself. He'd seen her through her dissertation in geology and her pregnancy, and he'd always been a perfect brain resetter, amusing and calming at the same time.

What we know about volcanos is also helping us think outside the box—really outside the box—to do something positive about climate change, she told the image of Daria that she carried now in her head as she watched Basalt's acrobatics pick up speed. *Did you never listen to my stories about the work I'm doing?*

*

"Gratitude."

Daria looked up.

Counselor Molly, as she'd introduced herself at breakfast that morning, was standing under the oak addressing the ten teenagers sitting on blankets personalized with the Camp Godhet logo: human hands morphing to become tree branches.

"Gratitude is step one in our eco-therapy."

A couple of the kids audibly groaned; a couple fell back on their blankets. Daria rolled her eyes and slapped at a mosquito.

"I am grateful that our systematic destruction of the environment will eventually lead to the extinction of mosquitos," she called.

A few snickers.

"Nah, they'll just adapt," the girl nearest Daria said. "People suck. We kill all the beautiful things and make the annoying stuff more annoying."

"OK, OK," Molly said, smiling along with the laughter. "Seriously, folks, you're here to learn some tools to cope with this very real form of anxiety, and this is where we begin. I know it sounds counterintuitive—when the world is burning, what is there to be grateful for? But there is lots, I promise you. Here's the big thing I'm thankful for." Molly sat cross-legged on her own blanket. "When

I was your age, I was a camper here. And all I thought about was passing the swimming test, would I have my first kiss here, and how gross most of the meals were. And"—she slapped her arm—"the mosquitos." Daria squinted at Molly, behind whom the sun was shining. How old was she? Her mom's age? Kind of old for a camp counselor. Daria suspected she was actually a psychologist. Daria shifted and looked around. The boy Mac—they were supposed to use first names only to keep from looking each other up on the phones that they didn't have regular access to anyway anymore, but Daria had to wonder if his name was just an abbreviation of his last name—was raising his hand.

Molly held up her finger to indicate he should wait till she'd finished. "But you're lucky," she continued in a rush, noticing most of the kids losing focus on her. "You see what too few people understand, even with all the evidence before them. You're special. You're at camp to ask the hard questions and learn the tools to deal with the answers, and I'm grateful for that." Her last words were said as one long word as suddenly the sun bore down with all its steamy might, and the mosquitos who would not rest grew surlier, and people shifted from kneeling to sitting to sprawling to kneeling again.

"Yes?" Molly said tiredly, pointing at Mac.

Everyone swiveled to face the boy with the mop of dark hair. Daria thought how it was funny that there was a Daria and a Mac at this camp. Once they found out she was a quarter Mexican, most people thought her name came from her father's family, but really she'd been named by both her '90s-TV-obsessed parents, for Daria Morgendorffer. And now here was a Mac, whose cartoon form had been the only guy who ever showed up repeatedly for Daria.

"I didn't get to say at, um, breakfast, so I wanted to say here that I'm totally a camper, but I'm also a reporter. The town here hasn't had a paper since, like, I don't even know, so the high school paper operates year-round. I'm reporting on the change in mission at the camp. I just wanted to be, um, transparent, and, um, you can trust me that nothing you say will go in my articles unless we agree in advance you're being interviewed."

"Thank you," Molly said. "Yes, that's right. We accepted Mac knowing he'd also be gathering information for his articles while here," and then she proceeded as Mac sank back onto his blanket to offer no new details at all, a problem Daria had noticed a lot of adults had. They were basically all mansplainers to teenagers, even the women. Daria snapped two dandelion heads from their stalks and rolled them between her fingers, staining her fingers yellow.

"OK." Molly slapped her palms on her thighs. "I want you to think about the good things. Pair up. Having a community, remembering you're not alone"—Molly emphasized each of those words—"is one of the things you should be doing."

Daria turned to the girl nearest her.

"I'm Srabanti," the girl said, joining Daria on her blanket.

"Daria," she said. "Listen, I'm not interested in talking about rainbows and puppy dog tails."

Srabanti smirked. "Believe me—I am not either."

"Where are you from originally?" Daria asked, noticing but unable to place her accent.

"Bangladesh. Where are you from originally?"

"Portland. Oregon."

The girls slapped mosquitos.

"Where do you live now?" Daria asked.

"New York. But it wouldn't be so bad to live here. Even blood-suckers are still better than crazy flooding."

Daria held Srabanti's gaze before she said, "But you're not

a 'climate refugee.'" She made air quotes with her index and middle fingers.

"No way!" Srabanti held up her hands.

"How come?" a voice said. They looked up to see Mac backlit by the sun. "How come you don't seem to like that, 'climate refugee'?" He hooked his fingers in the air too, not mocking them.

"I mean, seriously? Like we're all just helpless, faceless masses?" Srabanti said. "You can't just label everyone from another country as a refugee and assume that helps them—and doesn't hurt people who really are refugees!"

Daria shielded her eyes, caught a whiff of what even one day in the Minnesota sun could do without deodorant. She tucked her knees up, her free arm wrapped around them, hoping that sitting like a turtle hiding in its shell would keep people from smelling her stench.

"How are things going here?" Molly asked, her body blocking some of the sun. "Have you found even one thing about this situation you can be grateful for?"

Daria chewed on the inside of her check, glancing at Srabanti and then Mac, realizing she was almost having fun. When neither of them spoke, she told Molly, "Give us another few minutes."

*

Roger Lamar wanted Mateo to pull off the nearly impossible: planning from square one an eightieth birthday party with a huge guest list within the month. After the meeting in Mateo's office, barely ten minutes into which Lamar blurted his demands and rushed out to a car waiting to take him to the airport, Mateo was left to drink the entire press of coffee he'd made as well as eat two, then three of the beautiful, delicately wrapped pastries. Fuming, he dumped the rest in their fluttering papers in the garbage and went out for a run in Forest Park.

Bobby McFerrin's whistling ring tone replaced the Florence + The Machine track pumping through his earbuds, and he stopped.

"Daria?" he answered the phone, catching his breath.

"Hi," his daughter's voice said. There was definitely no exclamation point at the end of her greeting, but she sounded more upbeat than she had been recently.

"Amor! I didn't think you would get to call so soon."

"I won a 'reward' for something I said in class today."

"What class?" Mateo imagined his daughter in a cornfield or shooting arrows at hay bales or swimming in lakes, not sitting in a classroom. "What'd you say?"

"Oh…"

He pictured her shoulders collapsing in on themselves. He'd asked too many questions. She felt cornered and prodded.

"What's that sound?" he asked.

"What sound?"

"That—" It was a clicking; she was worrying something between her fingers. He let it go. "I'm so glad to hear your voice!"

Silence.

"I was just out running."

"Oh. OK. I'll let you go."

"No, no!" Wanting to keep her on the line as long as she was willing to be there, Mateo found himself complaining about his meeting with Lamar, the family friend who dismissed all of Mateo's professional advice and insisted Mateo would get a lot of business from the tacky, clichéd party he wanted to throw. "And on top of that, he actually called fruit vendors *unclassy*." And of course, Mateo thought, what Lamar really meant by that was *trashy*.

More silence.

"I don't think fruit vendors are unclassy, Dad," Daria said, and now he could imagine her meeting his gaze, those tired, but sparking, eyes. "But huge parties with a bunch of wasted food and single-use plastic that ends up in the landfill might be."

It was Mateo's turn to be silent. And then, in a tone he didn't often use, with her or with anyone, he said, "I'm going to go." He wondered why she'd chosen to call him for her "reward." He added, "I love you," but did not wait to hear her reply, if there even was one.

He ran hard, keeping thoughts from his brain with each grinding step up the root-and-rock-strewn path of one of the country's largest urban woods. He ended up in front of the education center and wildlife sanctuary, wanting to see Vera. The peregrine falcon had been found as a chick and raised by a family until they realized they could no longer care for such a powerful bird of prey. By the time they handed Vera over, the bird was too used to the domestic life to be released back into the wild, and he would spend the rest of his years delighting school groups. Vera was biologically a male, but the Audubon staff decided there was no reason he couldn't keep his name. Daria hated Vera, or rather loved Vera but hated that everyone thought it was cute how "he" had a "girl's name." Another example of environmental manipulation for marketing. Such logic escaped her father—this was not the organization's first bird named uniquely in that way, and as an event planner who refused to coordinate gender-reveal parties, he saw the organization's choice as being open-minded—but he'd long ago decided not to argue with his daughter about such things.

Waiting to get into Vera's enclosure, Mateo thought about the falcon's journey from the Rocky Mountains, how the bird found refuge in Oregon, how many species find refuge in other places.

How many people do, how many Angelinos, like Lamar's and Mateo's own families, came from other places. By the time one of the volunteers informed Mateo that Vera was in a regularly scheduled checkup and may not be visiting for the rest of the day, he was already feeling better about Lamar. When he got back to the office, he put on another pot of coffee and began to plan.

*

Daria's absence, and its ensuing silence, did not sit well with Claire. In Mateo's old life, he'd been the one cooking dinner by the time she got home, but now as an event planner, he kept more erratic hours, and she'd become Daria's greeter and first-line caretaker. Now when she came home after work, she was alone but for her thoughts and Basalt, and both seemed extra agitated lately.

For the umpteenth time, Claire checked her "Manual for Parents and Guardians." When she'd first heard about Camp Godhet's changed mission, she truly had been excited. Parenting felt more dangerous these days than when Claire had been a kid, like if she missed one sign or took this step instead of that, she was putting her child or another at grave risk. Now that the house was quiet and Claire had been lulled into imagining her daughter getting better—someone else taking care of her, better than she could—she realized she hated that her daughter was at a summer camp learning not how to swim but how to manage her feelings about disappearing coastlines, wondering not if she'd be kissed by one of the other campers but if all life was doomed, why kiss at all? Claire remembered that Daria once said that not having babies was one of the best things Daria could do for the planet. Did her daughter think she shouldn't have been born?

There was already a coffee splotch on the page about phone

calls. Claire read again: *Unless there is a medical emergency in your immediate family, please do not call your child while they are at Camp Godhet. They do not have access to their phone, and our staff is too few and too busy to deliver messages. Your child will have opportunity to call you as a reward or on special "phone holidays"*... Claire dropped the booklet with a sudden thought. Daria would probably call Clara first. She stabbed out a too-long text to her mother-in-law, hit send, and looked up to see that Basalt had upended his food bowl and was sitting on top of it, still dusty, unkempt, from a recent bath. They stared at each other for a long, strange moment, as if at an impasse.

*

By the time Mateo came home, Claire was feeling remorseful.

"I'm so sorry," she said by way of greeting.

"For what?"

"I texted your mom, and that was not my place."

"Texted her about what?" he didn't seem concerned, not even after Claire explained that she'd sort of out-of-the-blue reminded his mother to lay off the doom-and-gloom with Daria. He poured them both some wine. "I'm sure you phrased it just fine—you're hardly a mean person. Besides..." He had other things on his mind. He told her about the meeting with Lamar. "And," he said, bouncing to the next topic, "Daria called me today!"

"Oh!" Claire said, leaning on her forearms. "Well, how is she?"

"You know Daria. The same, maybe a little more upbeat, I suppose," he said cryptically. "Long story short, this idea came a little bit from Daria and, hey, a little bit from my mom, but I think I know what I'm going to propose to Lamar: the wild parrots of LA."

"Oh, Daria is going to hate that!" Claire said.

"Why?" Mateo looked crushed. Claire laughed. "You know,

I don't know why, but I'm sure there will be some reason. I mean… they're not native to LA, right?"

"Noooo…*but* now they're the parrots that are thriving—their cousins still in Mexico are endangered. *And* they're changing the area for the better because people are planting trees they like to eat from, and they're talking about what other nonnative species the city can"—Mateo waved his hands—"rehabilitate or whatever."

"You've done your research."

"Yes, I have!" Mateo puffed out his chest to make his wife laugh. "I've got party favors of seed packets—some all-purpose stuff good for parrots to penguins, my supplier assures me."

Claire smiled at him.

"To cut down on waste," he added, clinking his wineglass against hers.

*

"Pain."

Today, Molly met with her campers inside. Outside, thunder roared, and lightning painted the dark day with eerie colors. Looking through the floor-to-ceiling windows of the Godhet common room, Daria thought the outside looked like someone had used on it an Instagram filter designed by an alien who didn't know what Earth daytime looked like *exactly*. Daria had experienced thunderstorms rarely in Portland. She braided the fringe on the rug while Molly talked.

"Today, we are honoring our pain for the world. What do I mean by that?"

Rain tapped a maniac's Morse code against the panes of glass. Daria looked over at Srabanti, wondering how she was feeling. The girl sipped tea, looking calm in a nest of pillows on the couch. She didn't seem freaked out listening to the deluge. At first Daria felt jealous that Srabanti could be so relaxed, but then guilt began to swell in her. Heavy flooding was caused in part by deforestation, and that was caused in part because of agriculture, specifically in much of the world, palm oil plantations. Palm oil was in everything: shampoo, Halloween candy, sandwich bread. In only fifteen years, Daria herself had consumed so much of the stuff just in her school lunches. She found grit under the rug's fringe and began crushing the larger pieces between her fingers. *One piece, two, three…* She could hear Molly again.

"When I say the word *pain*—pain regarding the environment, our role in it, your role in it, our fears about how climate change might affect us and our loved ones—is there a person in your life who comes to mind?"

Her mother—the image flashed in Daria's brain like the lightening outside. Molly was moving around the room now, dipping her hand into a box she'd pulled from behind her chair. She was handing out their personal packs, which contained, among other regulated items, the campers' phones.

"I want you to call that person," Molly was saying. "If you can't reach them right now, you can write them a letter. But the phone's better because neither of you can escape the topic. You have to at least sit together in uncomfortable uncertainty."

It was the middle of the workday on the West Coast. Daria figured she wouldn't get her mother, which was the primary reason to choose her, so Daria wouldn't have to talk with anyone. She could then pretend to write a letter. She clicked her mom's contact.

*

Today, the air was particularly thick with ash blowing over from a fire in the Columbia River Gorge, and the county health department advised against going outside, so Claire was working from home. Claire tried to focus, but everything, not just the air, was unsettled. Basalt was pacing his cage but was uninterested in being scritched. Claire was pacing from her office into the kitchen and back again, neither eating nor working, just obsessively checking for emails she had no reason to expect.

Her phone buzzed. Claire pounced without looking at the caller ID.

"This is Dr. Guy-Donés."

"Hey, Mom."

"Daria!" Claire said, stifling a sigh and sinking onto the carpeted floor of her office. *Focus*, she told herself. She stuck her fingers through Basalt's cage, wiggled them, trying to catch his attention. She wiggled harder. Why was he ignoring her?

"Sorry to call you when you're at work." Daria did not sound happy.

"Oh, it's OK. I'm actually—Ow!" Basalt had bitten her!

"Mom? Are you OK?" Daria asked.

Claire grabbed the cage with her uninjured hand and gave it a good rattle. *Damn you! What is wrong with you!* she thought at Basalt. She cradled her phone in her neck and held her bloody finger upright.

"Yes, Daria, sorry." she said. "Tell me how you are."

Daria snorted. "Today's topic is pain. Kinda ironic."

Claire was in the bathroom, quietly running the tap. "That is kind of ironic, or at least a weird coincidence."

"So..." Daria said after an awkward pause, "I don't even know what I'm supposed to say, really..."

More silence.

If Daria didn't know, Claire didn't know either. She watched the water flowing red off her finger. "Are you enjoying the lake? Do they give you time to swim?"

"It's all full of lily pads. Some kids tried to go in once, but it was just like swimming through weeds. It's gross."

Despite herself, Claire laughed a little. The lake had been full of lily pads when she was a camper too, but they hadn't complained. Lily pads were a natural feature of lakes.

She found antiseptic, bandages. "Do you guys still have to do final projects?"

"I don't know."

"Mine was on volcanos." Claire pushed forward. Silence between her and Daria was more painful than talking. Was that the pain Daria was talking about? "Isn't that funny? I researched volcanos in Minnesota. I guess that was the magic of that place—my brain was just open to possibilities."

"Did you think you'd be doing what you're doing now?"

Claire paused in the middle of cleaning her wound. She hadn't been expecting such a thoughtful question. "No. No. I couldn't have. This branch of science didn't even exist then."

"Does it bother you that people protest your work?"

Claire wrapped the bandage too tightly. No, the silences weren't painful; the talking was. "It does, Daria. Especially because some of them are my colleagues. Sort of." Litchfield and others she knew from grad school would never claim to be her colleagues. She got into semiregular email fights with her, Litchfield's all-caps emails insinuating Claire's foolishness, Claire's screaming back: TIME IS RUNNING OUT. People like Litchfield were out for a Sunday drive in the country while Claire was speeding down the autobahn toward a solution.

"I don't understand."

"We…are all climate scientists. But I work in solar geoengineering. My colleagues are researching putting mirrors in space and making the ocean's surface more like a mirror, thinning or brightening clouds, making crops and buildings shinier—let's make everything more reflective to bounce more sunlight back away from Earth. That's what solar radiation management is all about."

"What about polluting the air with sulfur dioxide?" Daria asked.

"It's not 'polluting the air with sulfur dioxide,' honey," Claire said, trying to be patient. "It's stratospheric aerosol injection, much like what volcanos produce, which does have a cooling effect. And by the way, the work I'm doing isn't a new idea. A guy in Russia first dreamed it up in the early 1980s. We just weren't ready to hear it till recently, and we didn't have the technology. But now, it could cost way less than any other idea.

"Are you still there?"

Finally, Daria said, "But if that can change that much, couldn't it also cause other changes, but bad ones? I mean, if we change the effects of the sun, we change rainfall, and that could affect, like, farmers."

That was what the naysayers were always going on about. "A scientist from the University of Cambridge once said the work we do is like talking about the pill or condoms to teenagers. It doesn't mean you're encouraging casual sex. You're just trying to do some good."

"Gawwd, Mom," Daria said.

"What?"

"Like I want to hear you talking about sex."

"I'm not talking about… Gawwd yourself, Daria. Do you want to talk about what I do or not? I'm trying to answer your questions that I don't even really know where they're coming from or what you're getting at and—"

"So, who exactly would be in charge of this?" Daria interrupted. "The president of the United States? What about the prime minister of Bangladesh? Millions of people there are affected by climate changes, you know."

Claire's mouth twisted. "Hmm. I'm not sure about Bangladesh, specifically..." Her finger was throbbing. She tried to keep perspective: her fifteen-year-old daughter was just trying to understand. "I get your question. Who is this 'we' we keep talking about? What are the ethical issues around geoengineering, like which country's government gets to alter the whole world's atmosphere and when? That's why we've got the United Nations or the World Meteorological Organization, lots of other global agencies—"

Daria was not swayed. As she launched again into concern about the giant changes Claire's science was proposing, all by human hand and without Mother Nature, Claire grew impatient. Why had Daria called? Just to argue? She went over to Basalt's cage and made faces at him while her daughter droned on. She was so mad at that little beast.

Finally, Claire interrupted her: "The way we humans live, that's a big part of why our climate is changing too much and too fast, right? Well...why not intervene on the large scale but to reverse the damage?"

*

"Today," Molly announced, "we're going to learn how ritual can help us see a problem with fresh eyes. This is part of our third step of processing our eco-grief. New perspectives can help lead us to healing—and maybe to solutions."

Daria listened as Molly explained an article she'd read on mourning glaciers. We consider glaciers as things, yet they grow—a healthy glacier expands more each winter than it melts each summer—and crawl on their toes, two very animate terms glaciologists use. In the rings of dust—from pollen, man-made pollution, fires, and more—that whorl their surface, they hold memories. Should we not mourn a dying or dead one as one would a human or other animal?

No one answered Molly's question. When she sighed, Daria said, "We thought you were asking rhetorically."

"You kids are too smart," Molly said, which Daria thought was ridiculous. She'd hardly made a great leap in logic.

Still, she liked where Molly was going with this. Molly didn't seem particularly suited to being a camp counselor, but at least she clearly had good taste in articles.

"Anyway," Molly explained, "it described a ceremony for a dead glacier in Iceland. The people commissioned a memorial plaque. What was interesting was the words on this plaque would have to connect with people of today and, hopefully, assuming it was still standing, with people a couple hundred years from now, when our Earth may be very different. What could they tell people about our feelings now that would still be very relevant to people in the future?"

This time, Molly didn't wait for an answer. "Today," she said, "we're going to do the same. The oak we've been sitting under all summer has just been diagnosed with oak wilt. It will die, though probably not for a couple of years. And since we have no other oaks on the property to become infected, we'll let it stand for as long as we can. It's not only part of our logo but our camp's heart. Now, a couple of years is nowhere near a couple of centuries, of course, but it's still a significant amount of time, especially for teenagers. What should you, today, say to the teens who are here tomorrow?"

When no one moved to take the paper and markers Molly was holding out, she said, "Reward phone calls tonight if you do this."

*

Her grandmother's face encircled by long gray curls came up on her phone screen.

"Corazon!" She blew Daria a kiss. "How's camp going?"

The sound of Abuelita's voice always calmed Daria, from the time she was a little kid. Her mother called her grandmother the "Daria whisperer." When she came to visit when Daria was a baby, Abuelita supposedly taught her to recognize the birds by their songs, but Daria didn't remember most of them.

She would have called her grandmother with her first phone privilege, but she didn't want to hurt her parents' feelings. "It's OK, Abuelita. They are teaching us how to cope."

"Baby, I want to tell you something. Your mom told me not to be too doom-and-gloomy."

Daria rolled her eyes. "Figures."

"M'ija, she's right. Do you remember when we were talking about the yellow rail, how it had gone extinct in my lifetime?"

"Yes," she said quietly. This sounded a lot like it was going to depress her more.

"Well, I did some more research after we talked. Do you know… the yellow rail is likely gone from Mexico, but it's not gone from this world. Not by a long shot."

Daria's eyes grew wide, and her grandmother gazed back, kind and excited.

"They're in Louisiana. The rice farmers there even invite birders to come and try to catch glimpses of the birds when the farmers flush them out before the rice harvest."

Daria hadn't realized she'd been holding her breath until she exhaled in one long, strong push. "Really?" she said, feeling her eyes dampen, but for the first time in a long time, they were good tears.

"Yes, really! And Daria." Now Clara looked a little embarrassed. "I didn't realize that the yellow tail has always been difficult for humans to spot. They rarely come out during the day. They may change breeding grounds from year to year. The Audubon Society even calls them one of the most secretive birds in North America."

"So, do you think there are still some in Mexico?"

"Oh." Clara twisted her lips a little. "Experts think they are extinct in Mexico, but they are one of those species that can be hidden in plain sight. You know that clicking pattern I taught you? Sometimes you can get the males to call back if you do that with the right type of rock."

*

At the end of the summer, it was time for the final project, an exercise Camp Godhet had kept from Claire's days, though now campers had to focus on the fourth and final step of the eco-grief process: going forward, showing up, making meaningful efforts. One of Molly's big examples of the importance of this came "from our neighbors to the east," she said, holding up her right hand, palm side out to the group. "That friendly mitten, Wisconsin." She paused while the local kids explained to the kids from other places that Wisconsin, with its jutting-out easternmost Door County, was said to resemble a mitten.

"These are maps from the Wisconsin Department of Natural Resources." She held up two maps of Wisconsin, one with a light smattering of red dots near its northern border and one heavily speckled with dots all over the state. "They attribute the passage of the Clean Water Act and the banning of DDT to"—she slapped a mosquito on her leg that was so juicy that campers in the front row grimaced when the blood splattered—"DDT, not DEET." Molly laughed awkwardly. "Anyway, because we made those real, big, systemic changes, look how many more bald eagle nests Wisconsin has now, compared with in 1974."

Mac slid next to Daria. "I just uploaded a bunch of stuff to the folder." His whisper wasn't so whispery, and Molly shot him a weary look.

"We're going to break into our groups soon," Daria whispered back. "Let's talk about it then." Daria was a little embarrassed that she'd so obviously chosen Mac as her project partner, but she told herself it was because he was good at research. That wasn't embarrassing—that was smart. With sideways glances, she noticed how the sunlight made his eyes glow deep amber.

As soon as Molly started talking again, Mac whispered again but this time lower, his mouth against his bent knee. "I found. So. Much. Stuff. I mean, Louisiana is being literally swallowed by the Gulf, and the government's a total joke, but there's so much stuff about what the people are doing. Like ordinary people. I kinda went down a rabbit hole on reforestation, but maybe that'll lead us back to stuff on the yellow rail too."

"OK!" Molly yelled. That shut Mac up. She sighed. "Start working already."

"Did you send your mom our questions?" Mac asked Daria, seeming completely oblivious to Molly's annoyance.

Daria tapped together the two smooth lakeshore stones in her pocket. Two-three, two-three, two-three… "No." She was still pissed at her mom. Her dad too. The environment wasn't a party theme. She grinned at Mac. "But you know we can find answers on our own. I've got all of Mom's papers, and I've been reading the other people she cites. One guy talks about Gaia-engineering. I don't know exactly what it is, but something about earth not being a marble but a living being."

"A goddess!" Mac's eyes glimmered.

Daria agreed that all this sounded cool, but she wasn't sure she wouldn't get caught in the same trap as her mother, twisting at sci-fi straws, or her father, throwing literal straws into a landfill. Two-three, two-three, two-three… She imagined a yellow rail hearing the muffled code and being drawn from Louisiana, over the miles of interstate and field and copse and river, to her, in Minnesota, maybe even all the way back to Oregon. Abuelita hadn't really explained what the sound meant, just how to imitate it. Was she calling to a yellow rail, or luring it?

ETAN NECHIN

Nature Morte

Things do not change; we change.
—*Henry David Thoreau,* Walden

My car broke down, just like that. I bought it two years ago. It was heavy blue, with upholstery that struggled to stay in one piece. It had room for seven but was meant for one. I would sail down wide roads, surrounded by mammoth semitrailers, making my vessel drift on clouds of diesel fumes. And now it was dead. No warning signals, no clinks or clanks. Merely the death of a machine.

It was midsummer, and the road danced in the heat, bending and steaming, pushing to reach an oasis to cool its tar-made skin. I touched my car. The hood was broiling, the last fever before the mechanical rigor mortis set in.

I had been waiting for an hour or so when I decided to take shade at the top of the hill and wait for evening before trying to get some help. I walked down the narrow highway shoulder. Zooming trucks were playing a game of catch with one another, and local radio stations blared from their open windows as they sped by.

I walked along the shoulder until it diverged with a dirt road. It was a nice dirt road, white and broad, dry with lime, so that when you walked on it, small dust clouds formed around your feet. I walked up it with the sun following me, grabbing me by the neck. At first, the hot breeze scoured the brush, making it seem dry and sparse, but as I ascended the path, the vegetation became denser, moist with fuel and soot, creating a viscous trail as I moved deep into the flora.

I waded through prickly, tarry bushes and arrived at a clearing, an arid interval. Everywhere lay mementos from people's visits: soda cans, plastic bags with smiley faces printed on them, some rope, rusty pegs, a half a pair of sunglasses, even a faded chrome wheel. I collected all the souvenirs and put them in a neat pile so that whoever wanted to leave something for the path would feel welcome. The metal objects gleamed in the sun. I was rolling a rusty wheel onto the pile when a man and a dog appeared at the clearing.

"Hello," I waved.

His dog ran up and down the path when it spotted a beer can. He sniffed it, took it in his mouth, and brought it to me.

"That's a very smart dog," I said to his owner. "And beautiful."

"Yeah, he's special, all right. He used to be a bomb-sniffing dog in the army."

Just then I noticed the dog's legs. His front left paw was completely gone. Instead, he had a tennis ball attached at the ankle.

"Wow, he is brave." I took the beer can that the dog had brought me and put it on the top of the pile. "That is an excellent idea. To put a tennis ball instead of a paw, I mean."

"Yes, it is," he said. "My wife got the idea after noticing that her mother had tennis balls attached to her walker so when she rolled it around, it wouldn't squeak."

I nodded at this couple's cleverness. "What brings you here?"

"Fishing. I've been looking for the spot for two hours now. It's strange. I swear I went fishing here two years ago and there was a pond."

He spat out a gob of tobacco. It ran down the path, creating the world's smallest, dirtiest mudslide.

"Hell, it's the strangest thing. I swear..." The man let out a small sigh. The dog lowered his head. Perhaps it felt shame because it couldn't find the pond for his master.

"Oh, well, I'll head back home. My wife will probably be waiting for me."

"That's a shame," I said. "Your wife would have probably loved to have some fresh fish for dinner."

"Yes, she would. Well, I guess it's boiled chicken again."

He waved at me, and I petted his dog. They both headed down the road until all that was left was the sound of the afternoon wind agitating the vegetation. As I continued walking, my nose was consumed by the scents emanating from the plants, trees, and soil, citrus mixed with clay, verdant gusts infused with sulfuric fumes.

I was walking down a wide clearing in the path when I began to hear a peculiar din, starting and stopping, mulching through the shrubs. I crept toward it. I thought I would come across a new species. If I found one, I could name it after anything I wanted. Maybe a great scientist. Or maybe after a constellation that was named after a great scientist.

I turned the corner, but what I saw was not an animal. It an old man wearing large, protective orange earphones, carefully guiding a rusty lawnmower on the edge of the trail. I hastened my step and waved to him.

"Hey!" I yelled. The man did not hear me.

I ran in front of the lawnmower, but he was looking down in

a deep mowing meditation. Clearly, he was one who had mastered the art of cutting grass. I tapped on his shoulder. He turned off the machine, and it came hiccupping to a halt.

"Good day!"

"What?"

I signaled to his earphones. He took them off reluctantly. "Good day! What are you doing?"

"I'm mowing the path!"

His voice boomed like a car backfiring, a bit too loud for the intimate setting we were in. He went to turn the mower back on, but I continued the conversation to his apparent chagrin.

"Why are you mowing the path?"

The old man looked at me, mystified, as if he were talking to a mindless urchin. "I'm clearing the path for the football field."

Not that I wanted to agitate him even more or confirm his suspicions regarding my intellect, but I had to satisfy my curiosity.

"There is no football field here, though."

The old man flashed his piercing blue eyes.

"With what the world is coming to today, there will be a football field here in no time." He turned with a dismissive huff, bent down, and pulled the cord. The machine came alive, coughing and grumbling. He put on his orange headphones and continued walking, steering his metal creature down another path.

I continued walking for a while, trying to find the just-right shady, quiet, scenic spot, but all the rocks looked like black rubber, all the plants seemed to be covered in tar. I looked up at the cowering treetops. The refractive rays offered no warmth, or maybe it was only dusk.

It was too late to go back now, I thought. I should make camp for the night and regroup when it was light. The darker it grew, the more the animals and plants came alive. The insects seemed to be affected by this the most. They became audible, leaping from flower to flower in a frenzy, like a line for dinner in an old folks' home. The ants were carrying their last loads of the day, trying to finish their day's chores before going back home to watch the eight o'clock news, or whatever worker ants do in their spare time. The flowers and grass stretched their limbs and opened their pores to feed on the rich night dew.

The path spiraled, leading me with increasing speed downward. I was trotting so fast, I was walking on air. I was flying over the path until it ceased to be a path. I flew and fell into a pit. I stood up and looked around. The hole was shoulder high, so I jumped out. I looked around and realized that it was not a pit at all. It was a pond.

The pond was bone dry, a graveyard of rocks. I wanted to yell to the man and his dog that I had found it. But I realized that the man was probably sitting on his porch petting his dog with an uneasy satisfaction, the kind that can only come from a boiled chicken and potato dinner. I walked over to the pond and stared deep into it. There was no reflection.

I wondered what had happened to it. I treaded down into the basin. It was cool and dry, and I could almost hear kids splashing while their parents lay at the water's edge, getting a tan. I lay down in the center of the pond, clearing the area. The evening had set, and the stars were flickering to the tempo of the crickets. Their color was that of electrical sparks.

In the morning, I woke up famished. I knew that I was too weak to head back, so I went scavenging for food. I walked lethargically, picking berries that grew silver on gray vines. By the time I got back to the pond, I had decided to take a nap. It was a deep, dark, sweet sleep, like a cup of coffee from a sidewalk café that tastes better because someone else made it for you.

When I woke up, it was afternoon again. I decided to stay another night at the pond and try and figure out why it was dry. So, I waited. I ate the berries I had. They were sweet and tart in my mouth, the taste of lollipops and gasoline.

Then my mind turned to my old car. It must be lonely and cold by now, stiff with oil clots. It was probably saying, *What's the point of me being a car if I can't move? Without motion, I am merely a nicely designed hunk of metal or just a place for people to make out.*

Maybe it could hitch a ride with a lonely traveler. It could hold up a sign saying, *WEST*, or, *Great mix tapes. Great conversation.*

"Did the water get too polluted? Were you drained out into small plastic water bottles? Did too many kids pee in you?" I asked the pond why it didn't want to have water in it anymore.

But the pond remained still, unwilling to divulge any of its secrets. So, I stayed for a while. Days passed by, snailing along lethargically, undulating audibly, on the earth's dried grooves.

*

After a couple of days, or a couple of weeks, or a couple of months, I started to feel comfortable in my new surroundings. Before this, it had been a while since I had spent time in nature. It was a thing that was out there, outside the city, outside my car window. It was flat and imagined as the nature documentaries I would watch on my TV in my apartment in the city.

Soon, the ground around the pond became wet and cold. The plants wilted, bowed their heads, heavy with death, ready to disintegrate into the ground, only to be reincarnated once more. The insects, long dead, had left behind the next generation, clustered in underground caves or exterior uteri hosted in old trees, the animals nestled underground in subterranean high-rises, sheltered from the elements, the stiffening, stifling cold, the deep winter that crept in under doorways and up streams. The rain poured down, but not a drop fell into the pond. It was as if summer—wicked, stifling summer—had never gone. I would spend my days there, looking at the heavy clouds transporting water and soot, acid rain, residues of industry from distant cities. The foliage burned red in my eyes. Or maybe it was just the realization that soon everything would fade into itself.

Then the snow began to cover the ground, fixing into place all that couldn't hide, creating a frozen relief image of what was once flourishing, mating, and dying. I sat in dead winter and remembered summer, when beech trees would sway in the heat to cool themselves off, the sycamore clapping its branches with delight as sparrows and bats tickled it, picking fruit and meaty leaves. From my warm, dry bubble, I captured every rock, every weed, every insect that dropped to its death and added them to the vast canvas of my mind. I would talk to the pond about its importance to the food chain, to the bugs and foxes and leeches that depended on it for hydration, to the chrysanthemums and the olive trees and the daffodils.

I would even get upset, pace back and forth on the pond floor, and shout, "You call yourself a pond? What kind of pond doesn't have water in it? I'll tell you what you are: you are a hole in the ground, a ditch! Why do I even care about you?"

But that was a momentary lapse. I cared about it, I guess, because nobody else did. It just stood there, chained to the ground. Maybe it was dead. Perhaps I should take a shovel and bury it, making it level with the land. But then I would have created another hopeless pit.

Then spring came. I was lying on the ground, and my head was tilted back so I could see what was directly above me. I stretched my limbs and sat up. And I noticed a white sprout piercing through the tired, gray ground. It was instantaneous, as if the shoot were trying to win a race with other plants, a doomed race to reach the sun. If it weren't for winter, I'm sure we would have Penny Drifters and Sad Sundays growing up to the sky.

I sat up, stroking the ground, trying to awaken the pond to see how beautiful the day was. A droopy-eyed hare stumbled over to the pond to see whether there was any water in it. "Not yet," I shrugged. "You should go downstream, to the brook. Maybe you'll have luck there." The hare hopped off and left me to my thoughts. I didn't remember whether I had hibernated. How long had I been asleep?

Then my mind turned to the highway and how different it would be in spring, all clean and sparkling and new, the tar crystals twinkling in the sun, the open road stretching for miles, carrying families on spring vacation, trucks with loads of food, oil, live chickens and chemicals, and motorcyclists tearing along, trying to defy loneliness. The roads must have expanded over the winter, leading to new towns, new petrochemical plants, and manmade lakes.

Here I was, stuck to a pond that wouldn't respond, that wouldn't offer a reflection to the world. Maybe it had seen something it shouldn't have and drained away to forget. Maybe it had seen too much and evaporated into the clouds, waiting to be reincarnated as a small wave at the edge of a vast ocean. But maybe the pond is a reflection of the world; the pond would become the world, the earth would dry up, I would be able to drive across the arid ocean floor, through whale boneyard and shipwreck rest stops.

I surveyed the area around me, trees and trees and trees, like bones, calcified, calcifying, bent and broken, under a sky of dust and soot, encircled by a choking chain of tar. Nature, wilderness, has nothing wild in it, I thought. It is we who are wild, we who are untamed.

I grabbed a loose branch that was standing erect, shooting up into the sky, threatening me with its stillness. I climbed as high as I could. I wanted to get a bird's-eye view. Maybe I could spot my car or a water station. Perhaps I could get help, light a flare or create smoke signals. Maybe a busload of school kids would come with pink and blue buckets filled with fresh water and revive my pond.

I smiled faintly, and just then, I heard a snap. I fell slowly, in profound silence, in between everywhere I was before, descending like a drop of water that will never reach the ground, suspended by the absence of air.

Contributor Bios

Tomas Baiza was born and raised in San José, California, and now lives in Boise, Idaho. He is a Pushcart-nominated author whose work has appeared in *Parhelion*, *Writers in the Attic*, *Obelus*, *In Parentheses*, *Meniscus*, *[PANK]*, *101 Proof Horror*, *The Meadow*, *Peatsmoke*, *The Good Life Review*, and elsewhere.

J. D. Evans lives in Washington, DC. He teaches at NYU's DC campus and George Mason University. He is working on a collection of too-long short stories; "The Rain Diary" is the first third of one. Some of his writing can be found at *The Point Magazine* and *Typishly*.

Mary Fifield has published fiction in *Midway Journal*, *The Write Launch*, and others. Her collection, *Last of the Species and Other Stories*, was a finalist for the Black Lawrence Press Hudson Prize. She lives in Oregon and is writing a darkly comic, cautiously hopeful novel about the climate crisis. (www.earthinhere.com)

Bishop Garrison is a national security professional and army veteran with nearly twenty years of experience. He's written non-fiction on a variety of issues and challenges facing the United States and the world. He writes science fiction focused on character-driven situations in both the near and the distant future.

JoeAnn Hart is the author of *Stamford '76: A True Story of Murder, Corruption, Race, and Feminism in the 1970s*, a memoir; the novel *Float*, a dark comedy about plastics in the ocean; and *Addled*, a social satire. Her work also includes short fiction, essays, and drama. (www.joeannhart.com)

Anthony S. James was born in Wales and graduated in English and philosophy at Swansea University. After he traveled Europe, Turkey, North Africa, and Russia and lived in Spain, he published three books on contemporary culture, including *Orwell's Faded Lion: The Moral Atmosphere of Britain 1945–2015.*

Stefan Kiesbye is the author of six books of fiction, including the novel *Your House Is on Fire, Your Children All Gone*. Born on the Baltic Coast, he lives with his wife, Sanaz, in the North San Francisco Bay Area, California, and teaches creative writing at Sonoma State University.

Jack Kirne is based in Melbourne, Australia. His work has appeared in publications including *Necessary Fiction*, the *Meanjin* blog, *Subbed In*, and the anthologies *Growing Up Queer in Australia* and *New Australian Fiction*. He coproduces the podcast *Spooky Speaks!* with his partner, Aaron Billings. (www.jackkirne.com)

Carlos Labbé was born in Santiago, Chile. He is the author of two short story collections and nine novels; *Navidad & Matanza*, *Loquela*, and *Spiritual Choreographies* have been translated into English. He has published essays, poems, screenplays, and music albums. He has been part of the collective Sangría since 2008.

Shaun Levin is the author of *Seven Sweet Things*, *A Year of Two Summers*, and *Snapshots of The Boy*, amongst other works. He is a South African writer based in Madrid, after living for many years in London and Tel Aviv. (www.shaunlevin.com)

Jessica Meeker was born and raised in the heart of Montana where she came to love and learn from her wild surroundings to create fiction. She graduated from Rocky Mountain College in Billings, Montana, with a degree in environmental science and creative writing. "Glacier Bear" is her first publication.

Jennifer Morales is a queer Latinx poet, fiction writer, and performance artist based in rural Wisconsin. Her short story collection, *Meet Me Halfway: Milwaukee Stories*, was Wisconsin Center for the Book's 2016 "Book of the Year." She's president of the Driftless Writing Center in Viroqua, Wisconsin. (www.moraleswrites.com)

Etan Nechin is a Brooklyn-based Israeli writer and editor of *The Bare Life Review*, a journal of immigrant and refugee literature. His writing has appeared in *Zyzzyva*, *The Washington Post*, *Boston Review*, *World Literature Today*, *The Independent*, *Jacobin*, *Jewish Currents*, and more.

Vivian Faith Prescott lives at her fish camp in Wrangell, Alaska. She's authored seven poetry books and a collection of linked stories, *The Dead Go to Seattle* (Boreal Books/Red Hen Press). She writes the column Planet Alaska for the *Juneau Empire*, and she's a member of the Pacific Sámi Searvi.

Kristin Thiel, a Midwesterner till she twirled her finger over the map and the forests and rivers of the Pacific Northwest welcomed her with open branches, started writing before she knew how to spell, dictating stories to her mom. She now makes her living writing and editing. (www.kristinthiel.com)

Jan Underwood is the author of an academic satire, *Utterly Heartless*, and a forthcoming novel called *Fault Lines*. She has also written two short story collections: *Day Shift Werewolf* and *The Bell Lap*. She lives in Portland, Oregon, and teaches at Portland Community College. (www.funnylittlenovels.com)

Will Vanderhyden is a freelance translator. He has translated the work of Carlos Labbé, Rodrigo Fresán, and Fernanda García Lao, among others. He has received fellowships from the NEA and the Lannan Foundation. His translation of *The Invented Part* by Rodrigo Fresán won the 2018 Best Translated Book Award.

Tara M. Williams earned her MFA and EdD at Fresno State University in California. She has published in *Southwest Review*, *Entropy's Black Cackle*, and *Apparition Literary Magazine*, among others. She divides her time between Portland, Oregon, and Arizona, where she teaches English, literature, and creative writing. (www.tarawilliamswriter.com)

www.ingramcontent.com/pod-product-compliance
Lightning Source LLC
Chambersburg PA
CBHW020331030826
48979CB00021B/596

* 9 7 8 1 6 2 5 5 7 1 4 4 1 *